HOPEFUL HERO

BAYTOWN HEROES

MARYANN JORDAN

Cover by: Graphics by Stacy

ISBN ebook: 978-1-956588-48-4

ISBN print: 978-1-956588-49-1

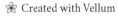 Created with Vellum

Heavenly. The day was heavenly.

Joanne tilted her head back, settling her gaze on the crystalline expanse of clear sky stretched above the Chesapeake Bay. A few stray clouds were scattered across the vast blue, creating the perfect fall day. Closing her eyes, she allowed the warmth to chase away the nip in the air as the boat cut a path through the water's surface.

Secured in a neat ponytail and encircled by a scarf, her long, golden hair was shielded from the wind's attempts to create a mass of tangles. The temperature hovered in the seventies, perfect weather for an outing, but she was grateful for the light jacket that not only kept her comfortable but also protected her from the occasional water spray. Of course, she also wore a life jacket, hardly fashionable but infinitely needed while on the water.

Despite wearing sunglasses, she used her hand as a visor, peering out over the diamond sparkles of the water. Ensconced on the thick-cushioned seat of the twenty-eight-foot boat, she drew in the salty air with each breath.

Black pelicans soared in low arcs as they skimmed the surf. Gulls screeched overhead, periodically plunging beak first into the water's surface, emerging with an oyster. She'd hoped to see dolphins, considering numerous sightings had been reported, but seabirds were all she'd observed so far.

The new item she'd purchased for the trip was nestled at her feet. It resembled an old-fashioned wicker picnic basket but was a cooler filled with sandwiches, fruit, cheese, and a bottle of wine from a local vineyard. It was a beautiful fall day on the Chesapeake Bay with all the elements of a memorable experience.

A little slice of heaven.

Well, it would be if it wasn't a slice of hell. Dating hell. Or, more specifically, the particular torment of a blind date gone awry.

Without warning, the boat careened sideways. Her hands flew out to grip the arms of her seat, and her face twisted into a grimace. This wasn't the first time she'd grimaced that morning, and given the current state of her blind date, it wouldn't be the last.

"Look at this! Isn't this great? I'm going to get us close to the shore!"

Her gaze shot to the area near Fisherman's Island, and she realized they were precariously close to the shoreline, and the tide was low.

"This area is protected, William!" she shouted over

2

the roar of the powerful double motors at the back of the boat. "You're not supposed to be here."

"No, it's fine! I do this all the time!"

She sincerely doubted his reply, considering he'd spent the first part of their date telling her about *recently* getting his boating license and buying his vessel. Hardly enough time to *do this all the time.*

She'd also already heard about his financial ventures, financial portfolio, family ties to a now-long-deceased state senator, and the importance of proper clothing and footwear necessary for being on a boat. He looked like a model but not the *GQ* variety, although she felt that was the image he was going for.

He turned the wheel sharply again, causing her to lurch in the other direction. Despite having a strong constitution, she wondered if her breakfast might make an impromptu reemergence. A chuckle-snort slipped out at the idea that such an act would undoubtedly mess up his pristine boat. Or maybe if she aimed in his direction, his expensive docker shoes wouldn't withstand the blow of her stomach contents.

When she lifted her face to the sun again, her chest depressed with a heavy sigh. Another miserable blind date. *Why do I do this to myself?* She knew the answer, but another lurch in the opposite direction jolted all thoughts from her mind other than hoping they didn't wreck. Another snort-chuckle threatened to erupt as the theme song to *Gilligan's Island* came to mind. Yeah, they were shipwrecked for a couple of years after setting out on a three-hour tour. As a child, she'd been fascinated with the idea that Gilligan, the Skipper, and the Professor wore the same clothes in every episode. Yet, somehow, Mr. and Mrs. Howell, Ginger, and Mary-Anne seemed to have an inexhaustible supply of outfits.

Another lurch. At least she wouldn't be stuck with William on the bay near the Eastern Shore if they wrecked. *I'd be able to get home. That is if I live through it!*

She looked toward the wheel or, more specifically, the man standing at the wheel. Tall, lean muscles honed at the nearby Dunes Resort gym. His dark hair was neatly trimmed, slightly longer on top, and due to the fact that it didn't move much, she was sure he'd slicked it down with some kind of hair product. Weird. He'd been more attractive on the dock than now out on the open water, where if his hair was natural, the windblown look would have been sexy. Now, he just looked silly.

She slipped her phone from her pocket to check the time, hoping they could stop soon to eat. *The faster we eat, the faster the date will be over.*

"Hey, get a picture of me at the helm!"

Her attention jolted upward to witness William striking an ostentatious pose, his gaze smugly fixed on her instead of the water. An instant later, a jarring thud echoed beneath them, followed by a harsh grating noise that vibrated through the boat's hull and into the soles of her feet. The sudden jolt sent her careening from the padded seat onto the unforgiving hardness of the deck. The boat had collided with something and come to a grinding halt.

"Dammit!" she spat out. With her teeth clenched in frustration, she wrestled herself upright from the deck.

Bursts of pain streaked through her body, a not-so-gentle reminder of her less-than-graceful landing.

"Oh shit!" he sputtered in response, his hands struggling as they gripped the wheel.

"Just stop!"

Scowling, he powered down the motors, then stood with his hands on his hips, staring out over the water. "Damn, the shoreline was too close."

Blinking in disbelief, she couldn't help the heavy dose of sarcasm that tinged her voice. "The shoreline didn't suddenly decide to move to a different location. You ran into it!" She felt ridiculous stating the glaringly obvious, but it appeared that he had no idea that his ire at the sandbar was misplaced.

He pulled out a metal ladder and attached it to the side of the deck rail. Climbing down over the side, he disappeared from sight. She hurried to peer down, seeing him standing in thigh-high water. He waded around, and she called out, "What are you doing?"

"Inspecting the boat." After a moment, he grinned as he waved up toward her. "We look good!" he called out with glee.

It didn't escape her notice that he hadn't inquired about her.

With her hands on her hips, she shook her head before shifting her gaze to see they were indeed stuck on a sandbar. She had no way of knowing whether the bottom of the boat was intact and felt sure that he didn't either, despite his assurances. "You need to call for help."

"No, no," he retorted, shaking his head while waving his hand. "It's all good."

"It's all good? How do you figure it's all good when we're stuck on a sandbar?"

"We just have to wait for the tide to come back in. Once the water rises, we'll be able to get out of here."

"That won't be for hours."

He turned his expensive sunglasses back toward her and smiled. "That'll give us more time to get to know each other."

She closed her eyes slowly in a deliberate act of surrender. This was it. *This was the last blind date I accept —no more.* Yet she'd said those words before, and her well-meaning, albeit overly persistent, mother had always managed to find another *catch* for her to go out with. She turned and slumped back onto the seat, her chin now resting on her chest in resignation. The prospect of languishing under the unrelenting sun, making forced conversation with a man who no longer held any appeal to her, all while anxiously waiting to see if their grounded boat would become sea-worthy again, was not her idea of a delightful afternoon.

She watched with growing despair for the next hour as William climbed in and out of the vessel. Each time he splashed through the surf around the boat, he returned with the same empty promise that they would be on the move shortly. His attempts to fill the silence with more self-absorbed narratives lasted all of ten minutes before her responses dwindled to disinterested grunts.

He'd finally resorted to giving her five-minute

updates, continually assuring her that "It'll be soon." With the tilt of the boat on the sandbar, she doubted that his definition of soon was anywhere close to hers.

The sun that had offered such gentle warmth earlier was now broiling, and with no shade, she glanced around before realizing her phone was lying on the deck when she'd been tossed. Snatching it up, she noticed purple bruises on her knees. Ignoring the pain, she dialed 911.

"North Heron County. What is your emergency?"

"The boat I'm on has hit a sandbar, and we're stuck in the water."

"No!" William cried out, waving his hands over his head as though she wasn't right there, staring at him. "We don't need any help!"

Ignoring him, she gave the closest direction she could, receiving assurances that the Virginia Marine Police and Coast Guard would be notified. Leaving her name and contact information, she disconnected as William climbed back onto the deck. He stood over her with his hands on his wet, no-longer-neatly pressed khaki shorts.

"Why did you do that, Joanne?"

She stared up at him and shook her head. "Because I have no desire to sit here while we wait to watch the tide come in, hoping it will loosen the boat from the sandbar."

He started to grumble about the hassle and being able to handle everything himself, but she shifted her body and stared back out at the water. She tried to close her eyes and pretend she was simply enjoying the bay, but her date's constant stomping around on the deck made that endeavor impossible. At least the sound of approaching watercraft caused her chest to expand in relief.

Shading her eyes again, she kept her gaze on the approaching long, gray boat until she finally recognized one of the men standing next to the wheelhouse. Her cheeks pinkened, and her shoulders shook in mirth when he came into closer view with a grin on his face. Jose Martinez. *I should have known. The way my day was going... I should have known he would be here.* At least she was being met by a friendly face. She had a feeling he would tell his wife, and she'd have to live through the retelling of this date all over again.

The marine police vessel approached, and Jose called out. "Is everyone accounted for?"

William blustered, "Of course. There were only the two of us."

"Is anyone injured?"

"No! This is totally unnecessary!"

She watched in interest as their vessel came close without hitting the sandbar and then anchored. Before she had a chance to speak, William continued to try to take charge of the situation. "I didn't call for assistance. My date did. She doesn't understand how the tide would soon allow us to be on our way."

Her brows lifted at his insinuation of her lack of intelligence but was saved by having to defend herself when Jose called out, "Good morning, Joanne."

Chuckling in astonishment, she lifted her hand to wave. "Hello, Jose. How are you?"

"I'd say I'm better than you are right now."

"That wouldn't be difficult," she muttered.

William's continued sputtering protests faded into the background as her attention shifted to the man standing next to Jose. The officer had brown hair, slightly longer than William's but with the casual air of someone who'd just dragged his hand through the strands to push them away from his face. His uniform was the standard navy blue, identical to the other officers, yet it looked anything but ordinary on him. His biceps strained the short sleeves, offering a tantalizing showcase of strength. She blew out a long breath. She was a sucker for muscular biceps.

He released a small inflatable rescue raft onto the water and deftly climbed inside. He shifted over, making room for Jose. In less than a minute, they were at the side of the boat where she sat. Like the other officers, he wore reflector sunglasses, and she was disappointed that she couldn't see his eyes. Giving a mental shake at her mind's wandering path, she grimaced. *I'm lusting after one man when on a date with another? God, what's wrong with me?*

Just then, William whined again. "As I said, I had everything under control. She's the one who called."

Shooting him a glare, she no longer felt guilty about lusting after someone else. *This date needs to end!*

The officer's sunglasses-covered gaze moved from her to settle on William. "Seems like your passenger knew exactly what to do."

Pressing her lips together, she fought the urge to throw her fist into the air and shout, "Told you so!"

Jose laughed as he climbed aboard their boat and walked over to her as the other officer moved to William.

Jose looked down at the cooler's contents, now spilling over the deck. Lifting a brow, he asked, "Date?"

She sighed.

He prodded. "Blind date?"

"Oh, shut up," she grumbled.

"Again?"

"Look, not all of us have found our happily ever after like you." She sighed again, then smiled. "And how are Melanie and Suzette?"

His smile morphed from friendly to a man obviously enthralled with his life. "Melanie is fabulous, and Suzette is growing like a weed, more adorable every day."

"I'm sure she is." Joanne nodded her agreement with a smile. "I'll come by and visit soon."

"You do that. They'd love to see you."

After she'd given her brief description of what happened, her gaze drifted to the officer attempting to gather William's account of the situation as he deflected his lack of maritime skill.

"Looks like this will take a while. You want to head back to the harbor with us?" Jose asked.

"God, yes!" She looked down at the cooler but decided William could use the food if he had to stay until his boat came unstuck from the sandbar. Bending, she grabbed her tote bag, swung it over her shoulder, and followed Jose as they walked toward the side of the boat tethered to the raft.

"I'll get in first and then assist you," Jose instructed.

"You're leaving?" William asked, his eyes bugging as though the idea was preposterous. His hand shot out to wrap around her wrist.

Before she could answer, the officer standing next to William stepped closer. At this distance, she could now read his name badge. Officer Townsend. Her gaze moved up to his face, but his eyes were still hidden behind the glasses. "Take your hand off the lady," he ordered.

His voice was low... calm and steady. But completely in charge. The officer could flex his muscles with just his tone. Her breath caught in her throat, staring into his eyes.

William dropped her wrist as though burned, and his face blushed bright red as he groused. "What about our date, Joanne?"

"I think under the circumstances, it's best if I return to the harbor. I hope you get things taken care of quickly."

Her polite words dripped of sarcasm, something that appeared lost on William, but the officer's lips quirked upward slightly.

"Come on, Joanne. Let's get you back," Jose said as he steadied the raft.

"Here, ma'am, I'll help you over." Officer Townsend waved his hand toward the ladder. "I'll make sure to steady you as you climb down. I'll hand your tote bag to you once you're there."

With a graceful nod, she passed the tote bag over to him. True to his word, he firmly grasped the top of the metal ladder as she swung her legs over and gripped the top rung. Focusing on him, she blurted, "I can't swim."

He reached out for her as he said, "Good thing you're prepared."

Realizing he was talking about her life vest, she nodded, offering a little smile. At the touch of their hands, a gasp escaped at the unexpected sensation that sent a shiver down her spine. Her hand tingled, reminiscent of an encounter with a mild electric shock. She wondered if the feeling was genuine or imagined, but when her gaze darted to his face, his gaze was locked on their hands.

Unable to think of anything significant to say, she continued to stare at him, still wishing she could see his eyes as she climbed down. It didn't miss her notice that he also remained focused on her. Jose steadied the raft as she settled onto the seat.

"Here's your bag, ma'am."

Looking up, she caught it easily as Officer Townsend dropped it to her. "Thank you!" She wanted to say more, but with others present, she simply smiled.

His lips barely quirked upward as he responded, "My pleasure, ma'am."

"Help yourself to any of the food in the cooler," she managed to offer. His lips twitched, and she added, "There's no reason for it to go to waste."

She sat in the raft, unable to take her eyes off Officer Townsend even as Jose guided the raft safely to the VMP vessel.

Suddenly, William appeared next to Officer Townsend at the railing. "Joanne! I'll call you!"

Jose made a choking sound, but she kept her gaze on Officer Townsend. His face was turned her way, and she shivered despite the warmth of the day. Ignoring William, she simply offered a slight nod to the officer before he dipped his chin and turned away.

As soon as Jose assisted her onto the VMP vessel, he ushered her into the wheelhouse and introduced her to Jared, another officer. He hurried out to pull the raft on board, leaving her to stare out at William's lopsided boat, her gaze locked onto the officer now in the water as he moved around the hull.

They pulled up the anchor, and she whirled around to Jared. "What about Officer Townsend? Are you going to leave him?"

If he thought it was odd that she didn't mention William, Jared didn't let on in his response. "He'll stay with the owner and the boat until our larger vessel arrives to tow him into the harbor."

"Oh…" she mumbled, strangely disappointed. Sighing, she turned as she sat in the wheelhouse and stared out the window as the beached boat faded away in the distance.

"You want to talk about it?"

Jose's softly asked question drew her attention to him as he neared. Tall, lean, handsome, with warm dark eyes. And nice. So incredibly nice. A little sigh escaped at the memory of their first meeting. Their mothers had set them up on a blind date, not knowing he was involved with someone. He'd handled the situation with grace when it could have been a monumental blowup of epic proportions. For that matter, so had Melanie, his now wife. And it was at that moment she'd tried to convince her mother to stop the blind-date madness.

But Joanne hadn't stuck to her guns, and now she had another disastrous partial-date notch in her belt—a belt she'd love to toss into the deepest part of the Chesapeake.

Her shoulders slumped as she shook her head. "No. It's all too humiliating."

Jose reached out and squeezed her shoulder. "Joanne, you're a wonderful woman, and you'll find someone."

He turned back to his duties as she sucked in a deep breath, relaxing for the first time in hours. Her mind rolled to Officer Townsend, and for just a second, she considered asking Jose to introduce them. A grimace passed across her face, and she sighed. It wouldn't be long before the officer heard about her lousy date record. *And I'll be the last person he'd want to be introduced to.*

As the wind whipped his hair, Bryce Townsend watched the VMP boat disappear into the distance, unable to take his mind off the beautiful woman it now carried. He would much prefer to be on the retreating boat, having a chance to be introduced to her.

Turning back to the blustery man standing in front of him, he placed his hands on his hips. "Mr. Hurd," Bryce finally said, cutting through the man's flow of excuses. "The waters can be unpredictable. But it is your responsibility as a boat operator to take the necessary precautions. This includes understanding the water-ways, the weather, and how to handle your vessel."

His Navy training had made the transition to working for the Virginia Marine Police easy. His back-ground as a mechanic served him well when someone was having marine vessel difficulties on the water. But right now, staring at the horizon, he wished he was not the one left behind.

Bryce was fortunate to work with some of the best

people he'd ever met, considering them friends and not just coworkers. Now, he was envious of his fellow officer, Jose, who was not only with the beautiful woman they'd just met but obviously knew her.

"I tried to tell her that we could just wait," the man complained. "I guess she just wasn't very used to being out on the water."

Bryce sucked in a deep breath and kept his voice calm. "It's probably good that she returned to the harbor to get out of the sun. The other police vessel will be here soon to see if we can tow you back into the water. But before you continue using it, you'll need to take the vessel back to the harbor to have it checked out."

"Checked out? I'm sure it's fine!"

"Any boat that's been grounded needs to be evaluated. The vessel's license will be pulled until proof has been provided that it's cleared to return to the water."

"You've got to be kidding me! And who's going to pay for that?"

"It's all part of owning and operating a marine vessel," Bryce said. He found that most people responded well to a softer, albeit commanding tone, but if this guy kept pushing his buttons, he had no problem forcing his authority.

William turned to the side, his jaw tight and lips pressed together. "She should've never called this in! I told her I had everything under control."

"Well, your date appeared—"

"Girlfriend. Joanne's my girlfriend."

Brows lifted, Bryce simply stared. Joanne. While he

had no reason to question William's statement of his relationship, he had to admit that her actions didn't scream girlfriend when they arrived.

"Have you and Joanne been dating long?" The question slipped out, surprising himself. Even though Bryce wanted to know more about her, he wasn't about to infringe on anyone else's relationship.

"No. Uh... not long. First time on the water, though."

Nodding, he listened as the dispatcher alerted him to the Coast Guard's ETA. William kept up a continuous running dialog about his boating skills, making Bryce understand why the woman was so quick to leave. Finally, the larger CG vessel pulled alongside them, and he climbed aboard their boat to give them a status report.

"Jeff, good to see you."

The barrel-chested CG Captain chuckled, the sound rumbling from his chest as he looked over at William, still muttering on his deck. "What the hell is that guy wearing? Looks like he stepped out of some yachting magazine."

Bryce's shoulders shook with mirth as he nodded. "Right down to his shoes."

"Was he out here alone?"

"Nah. Had a woman with him he was trying to impress."

Jeff shifted his gaze around and then turned back to Bryce. "Where is she?"

Now laughing, he kept his voice low. "She couldn't wait to get out of here. Went back with our guys to the harbor."

"Smart girl. Well, let's get him hooked up."

A small Coast Guard station resided on the Baytown Harbor close to the Virginia Marine Police station. Considering some of their similar missions, the two services often answered the same callouts. A couple of the VMP officers had served in the CG, loved the area, and didn't re-enlist when their tour was over. Bryce always enjoyed when the two services had a chance to work together and had occasionally used his boat mechanical expertise to assist. On this callout, the CG's larger boat would be able to tow William's boat off the sandbar.

The tide had begun to come in, making their job easier as they attached William's boat to the CG vessel. It didn't take much to tow him into deeper water and ensure his boat would stay afloat. Once William started his motors, he dutifully headed back to the harbor while Bryce stayed on the CG vessel as they followed him.

"I heard you were retiring soon. Are you staying in the area?"

"Yeah." Jeff nodded, looking out over the bay. "Been all over the world, but I decided that Baytown and the Chesapeake Bay was where I wanted to plant my final roots. I've just bought a little place on an inlet with a small dock in the back. My own little slice of heaven."

"Sounds good. I'm glad you're staying local."

Both men were active in the American Legion, and Jeff had instituted a youth water safety class that had also morphed into a youth beginning kayak class. Bryce had volunteered a few times, finding the captain's energy hard to beat.

As they neared the harbor, he wondered if Joanne would still be there, waiting on William. Approaching, he observed the VMP vessel that she'd returned on docked at their station, but no sign of her.

Glancing over at the other boat following, he spied William searching up and down the dock. Stifling a grin, he walked over and pulled out the clipboard with his initial report. After gaining William's signature that he understood he had to have the hull of his boat inspected, Bryce waved at Jeff and his Coast Guard crew docked nearby at their station.

All finished with William, he headed inside, surreptitiously looking to see if Joanne waited in the comfort of the station. Not seeing her at all, he found Jose in the workroom.

"You get the intrepid sailor taken care of?" Jose's smirk told of his thoughts on William.

"I thought the man was never gonna shut up," Bryce replied. He waited a moment to see if Jose would say anything else, but when he didn't, he opted for what he hoped was a casual expression. "What about the girlfriend?"

"Joanne?" Jose scoffed and shook his head. "Believe me, she's not his girlfriend."

"Seems like that would be news to William."

Jose's chin jerked back slightly. "Are you fucking serious? He called her his girlfriend?"

Bryce nodded, waiting to see what else Jose revealed.

"It was their first date. And a blind date at that."

Now it was Bryce's turn to jerk slightly, and he tilted his head to the side. "They'd never met before today?"

"Nope. It was another one of Joanne's disastrous blind dates. Hell, if she'd seen the way he was dressed beforehand, she would have never agreed."

Rubbing his chin, he asked, "She's had a string of blind dates?"

Jose threw his head back and laughed. "The poor woman has a history of nothing but shitty blind dates. Me included."

Caught off guard, he was about to ask more when Jose kept talking.

"Do you remember when Melanie and I first got together, and you all knew about the situation with our daughter Suzette before I even told my family? We showed up at my parents' house, and my mom had invited a woman to be introduced to me. Both our mothers set us up."

"Oh shit," Bryce muttered.

"You can say that again. It was uncomfortable, embarrassing, and honestly, if either Melanie or Joanne had not been the classy, sweet ladies they are, it could've been a real shit show. Joanne understood the situation and left, but I still felt really bad."

Bryce thought Jose's description of classy and gracious seemed to fit Joanne even though he'd only been in her presence for a moment.

"As it turns out, Melanie and I have run into Joanne a couple of times since then, and the two women have struck up a friendship. Joanne's grandparents were local, and her mom moved back a few years ago. Joanne recently came here to live."

"So, what's with all the blind dates?"

Jose shrugged. "It seems her mom is a lot like my mom. She doesn't want to see her child alone, equating that with loneliness. So she networks with all the other women she knows, finding one man after another to introduce to Joanne."

"Didn't look to me that she'd have a problem getting a date on her own."

"Absolutely! I know she's talked to her mom, and I think it's calmed down. But today was obviously another blind date gone wrong."

It was on the tip of his tongue to ask for an intro-duction, but Jose stopped him in his tracks when he said, "I once thought I might try to invite her around to meet some people, but I think the last thing she'd want me to do is try to hook her up with anyone. Hell, I know just from all my mother's efforts that's the last thing I'd want to happen."

Bryce snapped his mouth shut and nodded. Joanne was a beauty and, from what Jose had said, a really sweet woman. But if she had that much bad luck on first dates… *what chance do I have?*

"Staff meeting!"

All other thoughts slid into the background at the sound of his chief's call. Bryce followed the other offi-cers into the conference room. Callan Ward had served in the Coast Guard before joining the VMP. Like him, Joseph Newman and Andy Bergstrom had served in the Navy. Ryan Coates had served as the VMP's station captain since Bryce was there. The silver-haired, friendly boss made the change from military service to the Virginia Marine Police. Ryan was a patient leader, bringing out the best in each officer.

Ryan looked down at the tablet in front of him and lifted his gaze to Bryce. "Any problems getting back?"

Shaking his head, he replied, "No, sir. The man was a blowhard who overestimated his boat-handling skills. It seems he was more interested in showing off to his date than paying attention to the sandbars. He'll have to get his hull inspected, but my guess is that it'll be fine."

"Glad you had the CG pull him off. No sense in waiting until the evening to see if he could have gotten off the bar himself."

Since Bryce and Andy were the mechanics with the most experience, Ryan used them on many callouts. But he had both teach the others much of what they knew so they weren't just used as mechanics.

It had been a slow week for the VMP, much appreciated by all. When the summer crowds descended upon Baytown, they expected multiple callouts each day, and the possibility of water accidents increased significantly. But now that fall was here, they had a chance to catch up on some of the more mundane duties.

As the meeting concluded, Bryce reflected on the day Ryan interviewed him for a position with the Baytown station of the VMP. "Every day on this job will be different," Ryan had promised.

That variety and uniqueness drew Bryce to the job and made getting up every morning to come to work that much easier—that, and the other officers he considered to be friends. Bryce had heard of Baytown growing up in Maryland, but when he served with Andy in the Navy, he had accepted the invitation to check out the area. Once there, he'd fallen in love with the small town and rural county surrounding it.

Now, walking out to the parking lot, he smiled at the sight of Jose's wife greeting him and their daughter, smiling as she clapped her hands. Their relationship had begun unusually, but Bryce knew that families came in all shapes and sizes. Sometimes unusual was exactly what was right.

Several others were met by their wives, and he swallowed a sigh. He had no problem admitting that he wanted the same. His childhood had been unconventional, and he hoped for someone to share his life, raise children, and grow old with.

It wasn't for lack of female attention but finding the special someone had eluded him so far. As he climbed into his SUV, the image of Joanne moved through his mind again. But if she had such poor luck on dates, maybe an introduction would be the last thing he should pursue.

3

"No more, Mom. I just can't do it." Joanne cleared her throat. Deepening her voice slightly, she tried again. "No. Not another date. No more." *That sounds too harsh.* "Mom. Please. I don't want you to fix me up again." *That's too whiny.* Looking into the mirror, she sighed heavily but had no more time to practice before she heard the knock on her door.

"Yoo-hoo!"

"Coming, Mom." She darted from her bedroom and into the kitchen of her small cottage, seeing her mother's smiling face through the glass at the back door.

Her mother was short, topping at only five feet, two inches, and had brown hair streaked liberally with silver. The hair framing her face was almost white, and the whole effect was beautiful, a style that came naturally to her mom. Joanne knew many women would pay to have a salon copy the colors. Her brown eyes, ringed by silver-framed glasses, peered through the glass. As soon as they landed on Joanne, her mom's smile widened, brightening her already pretty face.

Joanne had gotten her dad's blond hair, his blue eyes, and his leaner frame, but it was obvious to everyone that she had her mother's smile.

"Come on in, Mom. I've got the coffee on."

"I was so surprised when you called. You're back from your date awfully early." Her mother's smile wavered as she pulled Joanne in for a hug. She leaned back, and her sharp eyes roved over Joanne's face. "Oh... it wasn't good?"

Leading her mom to the small two-seater table in the kitchen, she said, "Have a seat while I pour, and I'll tell you all about it."

Once she settled at the table, she stared at her coffee cup for a moment, then lifted her eyes, finding her mother's smile had drooped. Heaving a sigh, she said, "He wasn't as experienced a boater as he let on. We got stuck on a sandbar in an area he shouldn't have been in anyway. I had to call the Virginia Marine Police to get me back to the harbor—"

"Oh, my goodness! His mother said he had his boating license and a brand new boat." Her eyes narrowed. "Imagine that! Lying to get a date for her son! I'll give her a piece of my mind the next time I see her!"

Her mother's indignant outburst had Joanne chuckling, and she leaned over to pat her hand. "Mom, seriously, it's okay. I got back safely, but it wasn't just that. He was a boring braggart, and we had nothing in common."

Her mother's lips were still pinched, but Joanne

pressed on. "I just don't want any more blind dates. I'll find someone when the time is right." The face of the handsome officer who'd come to her rescue flashed through her mind. Taking a sip of coffee to recenter her thoughts, she continued, "I know you love me, and I know you want me to have what you and Dad had. But please don't set up any more dates. I really need a break from the blind dating scene."

Tears welled in her mother's eyes, tugging at Joanne's heart. "Oh, sweetheart, I am sorry. I know after the debacle with Jose, I said I wouldn't do this anymore." Her shoulders slumped.

Joanne left her seat to kneel next to her mother, pulling her into her arms. "Mom, don't take it personally. The fact that you care so much just means I have a wonderful mother who loves me and wants me to be happy."

"I do, Joanne. I want you happy."

Holding on, she leaned back enough to stare into her mother's beautiful brown eyes full of emotion. "I am. Whether or not I have a man in my life doesn't determine if I'm happy. If I meet someone and it happens, then it happens. If it doesn't, then I'm satisfied with my life. I'd rather be alone than go on dates when I haven't had a chance to talk to someone first. To see if there's a spark. To see if there are commonalities. For now... no more blind dates. Just let me see how life unfolds."

Her mother's smile peeked out as she patted Joanne's cheek. "You really are the most wonderful woman, Joanne. Your father would be so proud of you."

Now, it was Joanne's turn to swipe under her eyes to

brush away the moisture. With a long, heartfelt hug, she separated and returned to her seat to enjoy the coffee and share a few laughs from her disastrous date.

The screen door of Bryce's house clattered behind him, leading straight into the kitchen. The familiar chaos ensued as four felines immediately met him with meows while swirling about his legs in a dance of affection. "Hey, guys," he greeted, bending to rub their velvety-soft heads.

He'd never envisioned or intended to become a cat parent, but fate intervened when a buddy who operated the local animal shelter called. Bryce had spent some of his days off volunteering, so when someone brought in a litter of four kittens, orphaned shortly after their birth, his buddy needed help. Bryce brought them home to foster, feeding them around the clock with eyedroppers and a kitten bottle.

The sight of them now, hearty and healthy, was a tribute to his dedication. He hadn't wanted to give them away, desiring to keep them together. In truth, he'd fallen in love with the tiny kittens. Having watched them thrive, he couldn't imagine parting with them. Their meows intensified when he popped open their cat food cans. He grinned as their heads disappeared into their food dishes, and the kitchen was suddenly silent.

Opening the refrigerator door, he eagerly pulled out the leftover casserole. A number of women in town dropped off casseroles at the VMP station, but with more and more of his fellow officers no longer single men, he and a few others were the ones who took the generosity home.

Heating it in the microwave, his mouth watered as the scent of baked ziti wafted past when he sat at the table. With a beer and a slice of thick fresh bread bought at one of the town's bakeries, he was ready to dive into his own meal while the cats sat around licking their paws and preening as they rubbed their ears and whiskers.

He cleaned his plate, much like the cats had, and after rinsing the dishes, he headed into the living room, settling on his sofa. It was the one extravagance he'd indulged in when he bought the house. The L-shaped sofa was big and deep, with plush cushions that rivaled his bed for comfort. Before his fingers could reach the TV remote, his phone rang. The ringtone was as distinctive as the person on the other end of the line, and he grinned as he accepted the call. "Hey, Debbie."

"I haven't talked to you all week, so I thought I should call to see how you were."

His aunt Debbie called each week, and considering she was the one who raised him, they were very close. "I'm fine. In fact, I was going to call you this weekend to see if you'd like to come visit soon."

Her gentle laughter met his ears. "Actually, I'm going to take you up on that."

His feet landed on the floor as he leaned forward, a smile spreading across his face. "You're kidding!"

"Nope, I figure it's time I came to visit you since you used your vacation to come see me."

"Debbie, you know it's never a waste of time when I come there."

"I know, I know. But you have a lot better things to do with your time off than to come here and check on me. I thought I would take you up on your offer and visit you."

"When can you come?"

"That depends on you and your schedule. I'm retired, so I can travel whenever I want."

He quickly ran through his schedule and grimaced at having the next weekend on-call at the station. "Anytime after next weekend would be good. You decide and call or text to let me know what works for you."

"Sounds lovely. I'll plan for when we can have the whole weekend together if you can put up with me."

Laughing, he shook his head. "You know you're my favorite person, Debbie. I think I can easily deal with you for a weekend or longer if you want to stay."

"Goodness, no. The last thing I want to do is cramp your bachelor style."

Now, he snorted. "I hardly have a style. The most I've got going on are my cats running around like crazy."

"Well, I can't wait to play with them and spend time with my favorite nephew."

Even though he was her only nephew, he never corrected her. It was a nostalgic catchphrase from his childhood. Saying goodbye, he tossed his phone to the coffee table before planting his feet next to it.

He flipped on the TV, searching through channels that held no appeal until he finally found a game that held a modicum of interest. But his thoughts stayed on Debbie as the teams battled up and down the field. Her husband, Bernie, had died years ago, leaving a void in Bryce's and Debbie's lives. She sold their home and business, finding the stress too much to deal with. Bryce suspected she'd held on to them at first just to have a part of Bernie still with her. She moved into a rented townhouse, but he could tell when he visited that it never really felt like home to her. At the time, he was still in the Navy, but since landing in Baytown, he hoped to convince her to move there. But Debbie was stubborn and needed to proceed at her own speed.

He drained the last dregs of his beer, then lifted the bottle in a silent, reverent salute to Uncle Bernie. Filled with gratitude, Bryce could only imagine what would have become of him if it hadn't been for his aunt and uncle. The grim specter of foster care. Being thrust into the system of shifting homes. His youth could have been total shit. And even if he'd landed with a good foster family, the odds of staying in one stable home until he was eighteen years old were almost nil.

But those thoughts never lasted long, considering that wasn't what happened to him. Instead, the fates truly showered him with blessings when Debbie and Bernie courageously stepped up from day one, giving him a childhood full of love and good memories.

He turned his attention to the TV, now discovering the game was finished. He had no idea who won, but in truth, it didn't matter. He was ready to call it a day, so he pushed to a stand, walked around to check the doors, ensured the cats had water and clean litter, and headed to his bedroom. The day's dirt and worry were washed off in the shower before he slid under the covers, the mattress giving just the right amount of support underneath his tired body.

His faithful companions soon joined him—three sleeping at the foot of his bed and the little princess beside his pillow.

With an arm thrown over his head, he fixated on the ceiling fan as it rotated slowly. Ever since meeting Joanne today, her image had hovered just under the surface of his mind. Now, she floated back to the forefront.

Blond hair, the color of ripe wheat, gleaming under the sunlight, held back with a colorful scarf that swirled with a riot of colors. Pragmatic yet captivating. He wondered what it would be like to loosen the scarf's knot and let the tresses flow over his fingers and discover if they were as silky as he imagined. Her blue eyes had held his gaze, sparking a glimmer of shared attraction. He sighed. But she was on a date, and if she was as nice as Jose indicated, she would have never acted on an attraction with him.

He wondered about her relationship history. Was she a serial dater—always looking, never satisfied? Or maybe she hoped for someone with money or prestige? He valued Jose's judgment but had to acknowledge that since Jose's eyes were only for Melanie and their daughter, perhaps his friend was overgenerous in his estimation of Joanne. *So why was she with a wanker like William?*

A snort slipped out, the sudden sound disturbing Princess, who opened her eyes and glared at him before laying her head back down. *I'm one to talk after my last dating disaster.* Despite knowing after their first date that Allison wasn't the one, she'd turned out to be hard to get rid of. He'd resorted to rudeness and then ghosted her to get her to leave him alone. *Yeah, I haven't won any dating awards lately.*

Slowly shaking his head, he acknowledged the tingle he'd felt when his hand touched Joanne's. He'd never felt that physical reaction to a simple connection before. And if her expression was anything to go by, he was sure Joanne had also felt it.

Rolling over, he shifted his gaze from the spinning fan to the window, revealing a sky embroidered with stars. Several minutes passed as he pondered serendipity. Still believing in fate, he chuckled. *If I see her again, I'll get to know more about her. If not... we truly were just two ships passing. But I can hope...*

4

Joanne's low heels clicked along the tiled hallway of the Eastern Shore Community College before turning into the Student Services offices. She liked to arrive at work early and was surprised to spy Cheryl, the secretary, already at her desk. "Good morning! What's got you here so early?"

Cheryl grimaced and said, "I was lying in bed this morning when I woke up and suddenly realized this was your day to go to Tangier. I do not know how it slipped my mind when we talked about it yesterday! Menopause is turning my brain into Swiss cheese… there are so many holes up there, I can't keep anything straight."

Joanne snickered at the imagery. "You certainly didn't need to come in early for that."

"I just know that whenever you're gone, the office never runs as smoothly, so I wanted to assure that James had everything he needed."

Unable to hide her eye roll, she leaned closer and

said, "You are the true backbone to this office... not James."

Cheryl waved her off but grinned. Joanne walked to her office, stepping around the reception desk, and past the large area for students to work if needed. Flipping on the light, she was thankful for the small window, needing natural light like a plant starved for the sun. She draped her blue sweater over the back of her chair and sat down, firing up her laptop. The Student Services department held four small offices, a conference room, and a larger room with numerous tables and laptops for students to use. Cheryl's desk was in the open room as well.

Richard, their career counselor, occupied one office. The man of substantial stature with a booming voice and equally infectious smile always seemed to be in a perpetual good mood, a trait she greatly admired. The students loved him, often seeking him out for career and job information. He worked closely with their workplace mentors, a group of part-time assistants.

Lisa was their registrar, and she often filled in for Cheryl when needed. A bouncy, bubbly former student, she tried to keep up with the college faculty gossip.

Another office held James, a seasoned veteran of financial aid, assisting students in navigating the intricate pathways available to obtain their degrees and certificates at the community college and those who wanted to transfer on to a university. He had been hired before Joanne, and while always very professional, Joanne had to deflect his interest in her that lay outside the college. He was not a flirt and sometimes hard to read, but she had let it be known early on that she would not consider dating anyone she worked with. He'd given no outward indication that her words stung but had been more tight-lipped after that conversation.

In her role, she coordinated the department, including the other career coaches and mentors, and worked individually with students looking to further their education at the university level. One of her favorite added duties was to travel to Tangier Island twice a month to work with a few high school students for educational and career counseling. While James certainly didn't want that duty, he always seemed to manage to have a crisis to deal with on the days she traveled, making him grumble as though somehow it was her fault.

As her coworkers arrived, she finished her to-do list and placed her laptop in her briefcase. She smiled hello and goodbye to her department at the same time, and James's shoulders slumped. "Tangier day today?"

"Last week was too stormy for me to make the trip," she gently reminded. "Today it is. I did have it on the calendar."

"Yes, yes," he muttered as he nodded.

Catching the others' smiles hidden behind their hands, she waved and headed back out to her car. It didn't take long to drive to the small harbor at the county's northern end, where she would catch the ferry to the island. Parking in the gravel lot, she waved to one of the fishermen she often saw.

"I'll have some crabs for you when you return!" he called.

"Thanks, Mr. McAfee!" Hurrying along the wooden dock, she approached the ferry, grinning at the man behind the wheel. The ferry was a thirty-six-foot-long fiberglass boat and could hold twenty-five people. She only traveled during the school year and had never seen it filled.

Saul Winters ran the ferry, and even though others made the trip over and back, she liked his easy banter and how he always stuck to his schedule, making it easy for her to plan her trips. He greeted her with a smile as he leaned over to offer her a hand. She clambered aboard and settled onto the bench seat, nodding politely at the man who boarded after her and sat nearby. She had seen him on the ferry a few weeks ago but had never sat close enough to have a conversation. Two couples came aboard and sat on the other side of the boat.

Saul looked at his watch and called for the dock master to toss the rope to him. He started the engine and pulled away from the dock. "Alright, ladies and gentlemen, we'll get started. It'll take about an hour to arrive at Tangier, and once there, make sure to keep an eye on the time. I'll do a run back at three thirty. If you miss that, you'll have to make other arrangements or find a place to spend the night. There are no hotels, and I can't guarantee that the few bed-and-breakfasts will have any available rooms."

Lifting her gaze, she made eye contact with the man sitting near her. He smiled and inclined his head toward Saul.

"I wonder how often he's had to leave someone behind on the island when they missed the boat?"

Chuckling, she said, "I can't imagine. But the island is so small that I find it hard to imagine that anyone would lose track of time and forget."

"I've seen you on the ferry before. Do you visit it often?"

She nodded. "I visit twice a month. I remember seeing you a couple of weeks ago."

"Yes. I've gone over a few times myself."

"Business?" she inquired.

"Salesman." He held her gaze and asked, "You?"

"I go to the school to work with the high schoolers."

He twisted slightly to face her more fully. "Oh, are you a teacher?"

"No. I work for the Eastern Shore Community College as a career counselor, and while the school on the island is self-sufficient, I come over every other week to meet with the teens to assist them in planning their post-high school education, career training, or connecting them with a workplace mentor."

"Wow, I'm impressed," he said, his smile wide. "I'm Brian, by the way."

"I'm Joanne. Nice to meet you."

"I hope that didn't seem too forward," Brian said. "I just thought if we were going to see each other occasionally on the ferry, it might be nice to have a name to go with the face."

Smiling in return, she nodded. He looked away as Saul pointed out a flock of pelicans flying nearby, and she noticed the two couples on the other side of the boat snapping pictures. She took a moment to stare at Brian's profile surreptitiously. His brown hair had just a tinge of gray at the temples. His coat made it hard to tell his size, but he appeared fit. Her gaze dropped to his hand, noticing the absence of a wedding ring and no white indentation that would give evidence that he'd taken one off.

They continued chatting as the boat took them farther out into the bay, and she was struck by how much more pleasant the conversation was today than when she was out with William. There was no spark with Brian, and she had no interest in him other than as a fellow passenger, but she wished she could have that ease in conversation with someone she was dating.

"I can't believe I didn't realize that the island had its own school," he said, shaking his head.

"It is amazing, isn't it? I visited my grandparents who lived on the Eastern Shore but never really thought about the kids on the island until I was an adult."

"I wonder if they find it really constricting. You know, desperate to get off the island and see the world."

Laughing, she replied, "I'm sure they do, yet some will join the family fishing business there. But then, what you described pretty much fits any teenager wanting to escape home."

"You're right about that," he said, nodding his head slowly. "My teenage years are long behind me, but I remember wanting to forge my own path away from my parents."

Just then, the boat shook slightly, and her attention swung to Saul, whose brow furrowed as he stood at the ferry's controls. The engine sputtered several more times and then continued its normal rhythm.

Brian turned his brow-raised face back to her. "Whew. I have to tell you that getting stuck out here isn't what I want to do, even if the company is delightful."

Her shoulders shook as she chuckled. "I agree. Both with not wanting to get stuck and with the company."

Soon, they approached Tangier Island's harbor, and once docked, they stood to disembark. Brian offered his hand, and she accepted his assistance. There was no tingle. Not that she expected one, but it was a stark difference from the touch she'd felt with Officer Townsend.

Brian waved goodbye and walked briskly down the road. She headed in the opposite direction toward the school. Breathing deeply, she was always excited to be back with the kids. The long, one-story building came into sight, and she was always awed at the facility. The students and staff live on the small island, and the school serves kindergarten through twelfth grade in one building. They have a teacher who also serves as a counselor, but they were thrilled to have Joanne come twice monthly to offer her special services to the ninth through twelfth-grade students.

Once inside, she checked in with the office and headed to the high school room. Greeting the teacher, she smiled at the twenty-six students working on their laptops, each taking different classes needed for graduation. Making her way around the room, she spoke to each one, then settled at a small desk in the corner and opened her laptop.

Calling each one up individually, they discussed their futures. For the ninth graders, she gained an understanding of what they hoped their post-high school plans were. Offering information on various careers, she logged them into her computer program that would send them information based on their needs. For the sophomores, she reviewed their plans from last year and tweaked them as they matured.

Her juniors varied from those who wanted to start work after high school, join the military, move to another area to go to college, and those who wanted to stay on the island. By now, she was able to offer them more specific information on their career and educational options.

Finally, she talked with the seniors, planning for standardized testing, college applications, military recruiter information, and job opportunities for those wanting employment.

There were seven seniors this year, and she'd met each last year when she started her job. Rob was Navy-bound, and she typed in a request for him and his parents to meet with the Navy recruiter in Norfolk. Hank couldn't wait to get off Tangier Island and was applying to the Norfolk Shipyards apprentice program.

"I know my parents wish I'd stick around, but I want to become a welder for the shipyards."

She smiled as his eyes lit up when he talked about the opportunities he'd have, excitement moving through her, just listening to him.

Ted was laid-back and easygoing but also ambitious, wanting to focus on his family's fishing business. "I've got a ready-made job waiting for me, and considering I've been working the fishing business with my dad since I was old enough to go out, I know I can start making money."

"I think that's wonderful, Ted. Do you plan on staying on the island?"

The tips of his ears pinkened, and he rubbed his chin. "I met a girl. She goes to Baytown high school, and we're getting kind of serious. I know we're not ready to get married, but I'd like to be on the shore and not on the island."

Laughing, she nodded. "Oh, the things we do for love."

Ted's ears reddened even more, and she put him out of his misery as they moved on to other topics. She met with the girls next, eagerly listening to their plans. Carol and Cynthia would continue living on the island with their families while they commuted to the community college. Giving them lots of information, she assured them she couldn't wait to work with them when they came into her office next year.

Nicole was working on her application for Old Dominion University. "I want to major in education, but not here. I don't want to move back to the island."

Smiling, she patted the young girl's hand. "We all have to follow our own path. I'm excited for where yours might take you."

Sherrita was the last senior she spoke with, and she was in the process of putting in applications to culinary schools. "There's one in Maryland that I'd really like to go to," Sherrita confessed. "It will be a stretch financially, but I've got a cousin who lives outside of Baltimore, and she's already said I could share her apartment."

By the time Joanne had finished with her seniors, she packed up her laptop and glanced to see that she had enough time to stop at one of the restaurants on the island for lunch. With goodbyes said to everyone, she hurried out of the school and down the street toward the harbor.

5

She had just plopped down in a booth when she heard her name called. Twisting around, she spied Brian. He walked over and asked, "I've never eaten on the island before, but I saw you enter and thought I'd take a chance on lunch. Are you meeting someone?"

"No, I'm alone." She hesitated for a second, then waved at the booth across from her. "Would you like to join me?"

He agreed and slid onto the padded bench. There wasn't a spark with Brian, and she didn't consider their lunch to be a date, but excitement moved through her at the possibility of having a pleasant meal that carried no expectations other than it wouldn't end in disaster. But sitting across from him, Joanne nibbled on her shrimp salad as he divided his time between being a charming lunch partner and glancing at his phone. It was hard not to be insulted that he couldn't separate from his electronic device, but she also had to admit that this was a workday for him.

He glanced up and had the grace to blush. "I'm sorry, Joanne. My manners are horrible right now, and this is not how I meant for our lunch to go."

She circled her fork in the air as she chewed and swallowed. "It's fine, Brian. I realize this was an impromptu meal in the middle of our workday."

His smile appeared sincere, and the tension she'd felt eased from her shoulders.

"How were the students today?"

"Wonderful, as always. It's fun to help them determine what they want to do with their lives after high school."

"Tell me about your work at the community college."

"Well, I work in the—"

The vibrating next to his plate indicated his phone was ringing, and while she wished he would silence it, she wasn't surprised to see him snatch it up.

"Hello? Yeah. Yeah. Got it."

He disconnected, and she expected to see chagrin, but a grimace crossed his face instead. Standing, he pulled out his wallet and tossed several bills onto the table. "I'm so sorry, Joanne, but I've got to go."

"Oh... okay. I hope everything is all right."

No response came as he was already walking away. Her gaze followed him through the window as he hurried down the lane. Glancing around, she offered a tight-lipped smile to the server, who stopped by the table and asked, "Are you finished?"

"Yes, I think I am," she replied, knowing the server had no way of knowing she meant her answer in more than just the meal. She looked at the money on the table before picking it up, seeing he had left two hundred-dollar bills. Refusing to have him pay for her meal and not wanting to force the restaurant to make change, she pulled out her credit card. Leaving a hefty tip, she shoved the two hundred dollars into her pocket. *I'll give it to him on the ferry going back.*

With a wave to the server, she left the restaurant and made her way to the dock where the ferry waited. Looking around, she spied the two couples from earlier arriving at the same time. Saul heartily greeted them, and another couple joined them. Brian never appeared, and she glanced at her phone to check the time, knowing Saul always kept to his schedule.

He walked over and asked, "Do you know if the other man traveling with us this morning was coming?" He looked down at his clipboard. "Brian Atwell?"

Shaking her head, she replied, "I have no idea. I assumed so, but perhaps he made other arrangements." Saul was not the only ferry that traveled the bay between the mainland and the island. The thought that he deliberately missed this journey due to her caused her lunch to sit uneasily in her stomach. She reached her hand into her pocket and felt the crisp bills he'd left, and she was determined to give them back the next time she saw him. With him having continued business on the island, she felt sure she would run into him again.

Soon, Saul maneuvered away from the harbor, and she instinctively glanced back toward the dock, half hoping and half dreading to see Brian race toward them. But as the dock receded into the distance with no sign of him, she twisted around in her weather-beaten seat. Offering a slight smile toward the others, she pulled out her e-reader, having no desire to converse with anyone during the journey.

After twenty minutes, with the island far behind them and the shoreline still not visible, the boat jolted to the side, and her gaze snapped toward Saul. His complexion had transformed into an alarming shade of red, and his right hand clutched at his chest while his left hand gripped the controls loosely, causing the boat to veer. His face contorted in pain, and he swayed violently to the side.

"Saul!" she screamed, leaping to her feet. Rushing to him, she looked over her shoulder at the others. "Help!"

One of the men managed to pry Saul's fingers from the control bar, and another assisted Saul to the boat's deck. The others talked over each other as they tried to figure out how to help.

"Do any of you have medical knowledge?" she asked.

"I'm a pediatric nurse," one of the women said, dropping to Saul's side. "We've got to get him to a hospital."

Another woman began crying hysterically, and the man with her appeared in shock. The first man grabbed the wheel but shouted, "I don't know how to drive the boat."

Leaning over Saul, she worked with the nurse to loosen his shirt. "Toss that seat cushion to me," she ordered, grabbing it as one of the men handed it to her. Placing it under his head, she talked softly to him. She felt panic rising but steadied her breathing.

The boat lurched, and she looked at the man

standing at the controls. "I've got to slow it down," he said, his face in panic.

"Shut it down," she cried.

The engine finally stopped, and the ferry slowed, then began rocking back and forth to the side with the low swells of the bay. The hysterical woman continued her screams, and Joanne shouted, "Shut up!"

Twisting around, she dug into her purse and, for the second time in a week, called 911.

She talked to the dispatcher but had no idea where they were. "All I know is that we had been traveling about thirty minutes from Tangier, so that would make us about halfway to the harbor."

Gratefully, the dispatcher reminded her that the boat's GPS signal would let the police know where to find them, then told her that help was on the way and for them to stay on the line.

Saul groaned her name, and she thrust her phone into the hands of one of the men kneeling nearby. "Talk to them," she ordered before leaning down to whisper comfort to Saul again. The nurse looked at her, and the two women shared expressions of concern and resolve.

"Oh God, is he going to die?" the hysterical woman cried. "We're stuck out here!"

"Shut up!" Joanne barked again, pressing her lips tightly together. Looking at the woman's companion, she growled, "Keep her quiet. She's not helping!" She was startled when the man handed her phone back to her.

"They said help was on the way."

Nodding, she assured, "I know. The Coast Guard and Marine Police are nearby. They'll be here soon."

Leaning toward the nurse, she whispered, "How is he?"

"I don't know," the nurse admitted. "But he's still alive, so at this point, I'm going to take that as a win." The hysterical woman cried out again, and the nurse rolled her eyes. "I swear, if I had a sedative, I'd knock her out."

Nodding, Joanna agreed. "I'm ready to toss her overboard if she doesn't shut up."

Finally, the woman's husband managed to get her to stop screaming. Each second ticked by slowly, but eventually, the sound of motors over the water rang out, and Joanne stood from her kneeling position to see several boats approaching at rapid speed.

"A helicopter is coming!" one of the men called out.

Everyone swung their gazes to where he pointed upward and could see a helicopter in the distance. Looking at the nurse, she said, "They can airlift him to a hospital."

"That would be the best thing. The faster he can get to an ER, the better his chances are."

As the others focused on the hum of the approaching helicopter, Joanne's attention gravitated back to Saul. She was hurled back in time to when her father suffered a heart attack, and she sucked in a ragged breath to try to still her racing heart.

Holding his hand firmly, she bent close to talk to him over the impending cacophony of sounds. "Help is here, Saul. You've got to hang on. You know Martha will have a fit if you're late to dinner, and what about seeing your grandson Jimmy playing in the game Friday night." He gripped her hand a little tighter, and she was encouraged, letting out a relieved rush of air.

The ferry lurched to the side, and she looked up quickly to see several uniformed men and women leaning close as they secured a network of ropes between the vessels. Soon, the rocking of the ferry settled.

She scanned the sea of uniforms, searching for Jose among the law enforcers, but another face seized her attention. Her gaze landed on the face that had filled her mind for the past several days—Officer Townsend. His eyes were veiled with reflector sunglasses again, but she watched as he scoured the gathered group before his gaze landed and held on her.

A sharp intake of breath and a wave of dizziness hit. Shaking her head at the ridiculous notion that he was staring at her, she broke the visual contact and focused on Saul once again.

She tried to separate the voices all coming at once. The shrill cries of the hysterical woman being shushed by her husband. The man still standing at the controls of the ferry was talking to one of the other officers. Another officer knelt next to the nurse, and they began a conversation liberally sprinkled with medical jargon. The others murmured softly.

She was aware of a presence just before she felt a tingle on the back of her neck. Shooting a glance sideways, she spied Officer Townsend as he lowered himself next to her.

"Joanne, right? Jose's friend?" he asked, his voice slicing through the pandemonium.

"Yes, that's me." A faint smile briefly curved her trembling lips. "I'm sure you didn't expect to see me again so soon."

"No, ma'am, I didn't. But I assure you that it's not unpleasant to meet you again. I just wish the circumstances were different."

Her head bobbed in agreement, Saul's hand still firmly in hers. Blowing out another breath, she suddenly realized her chin quivered. "I'm scared," she confessed in a whisper.

"We're going to do the best we can for Saul."

Her gaze jerked back to his face. "Do you know him?"

"Saul is well known around these parts as the best ferryman. I take it you know him, as well."

Swallowing, she tried to dislodge the lump in her throat and nodded. "What's going to happen?"

The roar of the helicopter muffled his response. His hand patted her shoulder as he stood. She watched in awe as a basket was lowered from the helicopter, just like she'd seen on TV. The basket swayed in the rotor downwash, making it difficult to maneuver, and fear of Saul being transported in that manner caused her to look back at his face, trying to smile encouragingly. Officer Townsend and two other officers reached up to grab the basket when it approached.

The Coast Guard and Marine Police worked in tandem, transferring Saul to the rescue basket, where he was then lifted off the boat and into the air. The basket swayed, and her heart was in her throat as she watched it ascend, unable to keep the terror from rising in her throat that something might go wrong. When the basket finally disappeared into the Coast Guard helicopter, she felt weak with relief. Dropping back to her knees, she tried to catch her breath.

"Hey, are you okay?"

She turned her head, and her eyes met a pair of gray eyes staring deeply into hers. With the offending sunglasses gone, her gaze roved without hindrance over his features. Up close, his dark brown hair was touched with lighter sun streaks. His stubble-covered jaw was firm, and his lips were full. He was wearing a jacket, hiding his arms, but she'd already seen the evidence of his muscular form.

"Joanne? Are you okay?"

"What's your name, Officer Townsend?"

He blinked, his brow lowering as he stared back at her. Feeling foolish, she cleared her throat. "It's just that if we're going to keep meeting like this, I feel like I should know your name since you know mine."

His astonished expression morphed into a small grin as his lips curved upward. "It's Bryce. Bryce Townsend. And please don't take this the wrong way, but I really hope that we don't meet this way again."

Now it was her time to blink, her body jerking slightly, and she could feel heat slashing across her face. *Oh God, he doesn't want to see me again.* She wished she could think of something witty to say, but instead, she just stared in embarrassment.

She dropped her gaze from his face down to his

chest, hating that his rebuff stung so sharply. He stooped slightly, capturing and holding her attention. "Joanne, it's not that I don't want to see you again. I'd just rather see you when it's not an emergency."

The air rushed from her lungs as a relieved smile curved her lips.

6

When Jared steered the VMP vessel close to the ferry, Bryce felt a surge of adrenaline, bracing for whatever might greet them. The dispatcher had radioed that the ferry driver, Saul, was still alive and that a nurse was on board, providing whatever aid she could. He heard the distant hum of the Coast Guard helicopter dispatched from their Norfolk station on its way to transport Saul as quickly as possible to the hospital.

As the two VMP vessels came alongside the bobbing-in-the-waves ferry, he worked with other officers to tether to the ferry's side, providing stabilization. Climbing aboard, he scanned the passengers, seeing wide-eyed faces etched with fear and relief as he approached the stricken man. A distraught woman was wailing, a man was holding white-knuckled onto the wheel even though the engine was off, and another woman who had been kneeling next to Saul jumped up to identify herself as a nurse.

But the sight of the other woman still kneeling as

she held Saul's hand caused his feet to stutter and his chest to tighten as he made his way over. *Joanne.* He couldn't imagine the odds of him meeting her again so soon, but it seemed the fates' particular sense of humor had once again dealt him an unexpected hand and smiled down on him. Dropping his gaze from her pale face to Saul, he rushed over, urgency taking precedence.

Callan, Joseph, and Andy had boarded the ferry as well, leaving Jared and Marty in the wheelhouse of the two VMP boats. With a calm, authoritative voice, Joseph settled the other passengers while Andy took over the wheel, checking to ensure the engine had been turned off properly. Callan coordinated with the CG officers in the helicopter, who lowered the empty basket and, once Saul was carefully strapped in, raised it into their waiting arms.

With Saul now in the care of the CG crew and safely on his way to the hospital, Bryce and his fellow officers began the plan to get the ferry back to the harbor. Callan and Joseph would return to their vessels to ensure that both VMP boats had two officers on board. Andy and Bryce would steer the ferry back to the shore.

Once underway, he turned to Joanne. When she'd asked his name and then explained that she should know it if they were going to keep meeting this way, all he could think of was that he wanted to meet her in a less stressful situation.

But then her face fell, and he realized what he'd said made it sound like he didn't want to see her again. *Fuck!*

He'd often watched in amazement, mixed with envy, as Jared, Joseph, and even Andy had managed to flirt so smoothly when they were single. Whether at a bar, a casual meal, or even at the ballpark, witty comments, innuendos, and out-and-out propositions fell effortlessly from their lips. On the other hand, Bryce always felt tongue-tied, and his attempts at witty conversation were often entangled in awkwardness instead of impressing. *I'm more likely to say something that comes out all wrong!*

Seeing the expression of dejection on Joanne's face, he'd stumbled over his words, rushing to assure her that it wasn't that he didn't want to see her, but he'd prefer it not to be an emergency. Finally, a smile graced her lips, and a spark of amusement returned to her eyes. He breathed a little easier at the look of delight on her face. Now, he had the chance to spend some time with her, even if the situation wasn't ideal. He had taken the wheel, restarted the boat, and they continued the trip back to the shore.

Several other passengers called out to Joanne and the nurse, thanking them for their quick thinking. He observed Joanne brush off their appreciation, deflecting the praise toward the nurse.

After a few minutes, when everyone had settled back down, he turned the wheel over to Andy and moved to stand close to Joanne. "How did you know Saul?"

"I take the ferry a couple of times a month to the island. Even though there's more than one ferry company that makes the trip, I enjoyed Saul's company the first time I came over. Since then, I've just stuck with him."

"He's a good man," Bryce acknowledged. "He always

takes care of his passengers." He looked at her and smiled. "And you took good care of him."

"Oh no," she rushed, her eyes widening. "I was terrified. It was Louise, the nurse, who did everything for him."

"Don't sell yourself short," he admonished. "Comfort, care… just holding his hand was a big deal to him."

A gentle smile graced her beautiful face. She tucked a flyaway strand of hair behind her ear, only for it to escape immediately, dancing in the breeze again. He was captivated by the halo caused by the light blonde tresses and wondered if they were as soft as they appeared.

Despite his longing for a more private location, there were others around, making it impossible for them to have any real conversation. And before he knew it, they were pulling into the harbor where Saul's ferry normally docked. Their arrival disrupted the everyday rhythm of the harbor as they were greeted by numerous fishermen and others in the little community nearby, all having heard about the emergency by listening to the radios.

As soon as the ferry was secured to the dock, Joanne left the ferry with the other passengers, but her face was pensive. As he and Adam secured Saul's ferry, he noticed she hung back slightly.

He started toward her when his name was called. "Bryce! We've got another callout!"

He turned to see Callan radioing from the VMP vessel that traveled with them to transport him and Andy back to Baytown.

He instinctively sought out Joanne one last time, finding her standing at the edge of the dock near the parking lot. He jerked off his sunglasses, and the moment seemed to hang in the air as their eyes met. She lifted her hand in a little wave before walking to her car. Heaving a sigh heavy with unsaid words and missed opportunities, he jogged to the VMP boat and jumped aboard. As he stood on the deck, he cast a final glance toward Joanne's vehicle leaving the parking lot.

Their callout was an easy stop to check on the fishing licenses of several vacationers who a local fisherman had reported. By the time they made it to the VMP station in the Baytown Harbor and had restocked the vessels for the next callout, Ryan walked onto the dock to congratulate the crews. Bryce grinned as his boss reported that Saul's wife had made it to the Virginia Beach hospital. Saul had had a heart attack but was currently stable. Backslaps and congratulations ensued.

"Who wants to head to the pub?" Callan asked, looking around at the others. "I'm meeting Sophia there."

"Sure," Joseph agreed. "I'll call Shiloh to see if she wants to come."

Bryce nodded his agreement, thinking a cold beer and pub burger would be a better dinner than anything he could cook.

It was a scene that had become familiar—the officers filing through the doors of Finn's pub. Aiden and Brogan MacFarlane were behind the bar, calling out greetings as they entered. Bryce was still getting to know many Baytown locals, but the charismatic MacFarlane brothers were well-known to everyone. As co-owners of the lively pub and active members of the American Legion, he spent time in their company, almost always coming away with a smile.

Engrossed in his meal, he glanced up as Jose and Melanie walked inside. Jose had one arm around Melanie, and Suzette snuggled up against his chest, securely held by his other arm. Bryce felt a tightening in his chest at seeing their domestication. That was the future he wanted someday. While some men swore long and loud that they loved their freedom and bachelorhood, Bryce wanted a family. The fervent desire was why he'd sometimes gone out on a date when his gut had already told him that the person wasn't right. It was always that hope that he'd find his other half.

With smiles, Jose and Melanie walked over, and he remembered that Jose had mentioned Joanne becoming friends with Melanie. He greeted them warmly as they walked by his seat at the bar.

Melanie turned, her words cutting through the noisy pub chatter. "We're getting a booth. Come join us."

Eager for the opportunity, he offered a chin lift to the server and grabbed his half-finished plate and beer. Trailing the couple to one of the booths, he slid in, set his meal down, and reached his hands out. Jose shifted Suzette into his arms while her parents busied themselves with the baby seat. Looking down at Suzette's cherubic face, he smiled. Bugging his eyes and puffing his cheeks, he elicited a gummy grin. "I can't believe how big she's getting." His voice carried a touch of awe.

"They grow fast. You blink, and they're in the next size of clothes, doing things you never expected." Melanie lifted Suzette from Bryce's arms and settled her in her carrier.

"I was telling Melanie about the rescue you guys got called out on today," Jose said. "I was stuck checking fishing licenses on the lower part of the shore and knew I couldn't get out there in time. But those are the kind of rescues you really remember."

Melanie turned her wide-eyed gaze toward Bryce. "I can't imagine what that must've been like to see the ferry pilot lifted by a helicopter! And the other people on the ferry! How frightening for them. That was certainly something they weren't expecting when they got on the boat this morning!"

"Funny, you should mention that," Bryce began. "You'll never guess who was on the ferry." Seeing he had their rapt attention, he continued. "Your friend, Joanne." Having gained both Jose's and Melanie's attention, he suddenly felt self-conscious.

"Joanne?" Melanie gasped, her mouth dropping open.

Jose jerked slightly, his brow lowering. "What the hell was she doing on the ferry in the middle of the workweek?"

Melanie swung her head to her husband. "She goes out to the island to talk to the kids at the high school there. I totally forgot she mentioned that one time." Shaking her head, she added, "What a nightmare! She must have been so scared!"

"More than likely, she wouldn't believe she had two

incidents in the same week out on the water!" Jose said, shaking his head as he wiggled his fingers in front of Suzette, talking while distracting his daughter.

"Is she okay?" Melanie asked.

"She handled herself like a pro," Bryce replied, once again, gaining the full attention of Jose and Melanie. He looked down at his plate and realized he'd eaten most of his pub burger but had no appetite for the rest. He hesitated, wanting to ask more about her, but hated that he was exposing his thoughts.

"Do you know what Joanne needs?" Melanie asked, her question drawing his curiosity.

Having no idea, Bryce waited anxiously.

"She needs someone like you."

Melanie's pronouncement startled Bryce, and his gaze jumped to see Jose nodding his agreement and staring intently at him.

"Me? What makes you say that?" He hoped his voice sounded as casual as he was attempting, but the way Jose kept staring, he wondered if his interest was tattooed front and center on his face.

"Because she's sweet, nice, smart. Because she's caring and such a good person," Melanie enthused.

"And because she's too nice to push back when set up on a bunch of blind dates, she ends up having a lot of miserable times," Jose added. Still staring at his friend, he grinned. "I wouldn't dream of fixing two friends up, but if you have any interest, Bryce, I'd say go for it."

Melanie's head bobbed up and down so hard, it was comical. Saved from a response when their food was served, he entertained Suzette while they ate, then said his goodbyes before heading home.

Deciding that the fates had cast the die, he wasn't about to refuse. Now, it was time for the fates to have a little push.

7

_____

Joanne briskly pushed her cart through the grocery store, her mind on the mundane mission of gathering a few necessary items. Several days had passed since the intense ferry trip, and the residual stress had eventually caught up to her. She'd found out that Saul was still in intensive care but was expected to recover fully. The story had sparked a flurry of inquiries among her co-workers, fueled by the report from the *Shore Press*. She understood their curiosity, but there were scant details she could add to the story.

"Joanne!"

Hearing her name through the hum of background noise, she twisted around, seeing Melanie walking toward her, her cart half filled in front of her. Smiling widely, Joanne waved as the other woman walked over. After warm embraces, she asked, "Where's Suzette?"

"I ran here after work, so Jose's mom still has her." Melanie grinned with the look of a young mother whose idea of a good time was to grocery shop while someone else watched her baby.

Joanne hadn't encountered Jose's mother since their first ill-fated meeting. She'd arrived at Mary's home for a dinner set up by their mothers. Joanne had been excited about the date, hopeful that perhaps the blind date would shatter her streak of romantic misfortunes. After all, she'd been assured that Jose was interested in meeting her. However, when he arrived at his mother's house with a baby in his arms and holding hands with another woman, Joanne's heart plunged as her face flamed. Futilely wishing a hole would appear in the ground to swallow her, she was left standing awkwardly as Jose's mother blustered through the explanation.

Jose's expression mirrored her own—a mask of anger at his mother, frustration, and embarrassment. Horrified at the situation, she braced for an awkward scene but was saved when Jose, being the sweet gentleman that he was, took her to the side to explain the situation. She appreciated his candor and chose to leave as surreptitiously as possible. While he'd expressed his dismay over his mother's actions, she'd admitted her mother was just as bad.

She truly thought she'd never see them again, but a few weeks later, she ran into Jose, and he introduced Melanie. Joanne's stomach had dropped at the fear that Melanie would be a raving bitch to *the other woman, who was never the other woman*, but Melanie had smiled widely, shook her hand, and said how happy she was to meet her. From that moment on, an unexpected friendship blossomed between Joanne, Jose, and Melanie.

"Oh, my goodness, Joanne," Melanie gushed, snapping Joanne back to the present. "Jose told me that you were on the boat that was in the news! He said that you were so heroic!"

"No! Believe me, I was terrified!" she protested, dismissively waving her hands.

Melanie placed her hand on Joanne's arm, stilling the motion. "Being terrified doesn't mean you weren't heroic. Bryce told us that you were so caring. I know from listening to Jose talk about other rescues that sometimes *not* falling apart is the best thing a person can do. It makes the officers' job so much easier."

She nodded, but as soon as Melanie mentioned the name Bryce, Joanne was stuck on the image of him standing next to her on the ferry. "Bryce was very nice to me… well, to everyone."

Melanie nodded slowly as she studied Joanne with keen eyes. "You know, he and Jose are really good friends. And I've also had the opportunity to get to know him."

"Oh…" Melanie's cryptic statement piqued Joanne's curiosity, but she struggled to form a coherent response.

"And he's single."

"Oh." Her cheeks heated, but once again, she floundered as she tried to think of a response.

Melanie parted her lips as if to say something, then snapped them closed. "I swear, Joanne, I was going to suggest trying to set you two up, but I know that meddling if two people aren't informed and interested doesn't make any sense." She paused, her gaze intent on

Joanne and her head tilting slightly. "But, if you were interested…"

Fighting the urge to squirm, Joanne finally gave up all pretense and sighed. "To be honest, yes, I am interested. But it feels so weird to put myself out there. I feel like I have the worst dating luck."

"No, you don't. You just haven't met the right person yet. I think you're brave!" Melanie clapped her hands and rubbed them together. "Look… baking a batch of cookies and dropping them off at the station as a thank you to the officers who helped out with the rescue wouldn't be a bad way to see him again. Then just let nature take its course." Melanie winked as she said goodbye, then started to push her cart away when she stopped suddenly and looked over her shoulder. "And by the way, Joanne. I have it on good authority that he's interested, too."

Joanne's mouth dropped open as she watched her friend's back retreat around the corner of the aisle. Then, suddenly coming unstuck, she hurried to the baking aisle to ensure she had the ingredients for chocolate chip cookies. She didn't mind letting nature take its course, but her grandma's recipe for chocolate chip cookies was a surefire way to nudge the fates along.

Bryce maneuvered the rolling cart along the deck, his boots clunking against the wooden planks as he made his way from the station to the docked vessels. A storm was brewing on the horizon, and the officers hustled to get the VMP boats restocked for the next day or in case a nighttime callout occurred. Andy had detected one of the vessels had been slow to start earlier, so Bryce had spent the better part of his afternoon checking the engines, going beyond the usual maintenance.

He cast an eye toward the brooding gray clouds in the west. The storm was not advancing rapidly, and he hoped the working and recreational vessels on the water would have plenty of time to finish and get to safety. Storm rescues were inherently precarious, especially when they could have been avoided.

As he, Jared, and Callan walked back into the station, Bryce felt a heavy sense of foreboding as a blanket of gloom settled over him. At the end of the day, he strode into the parking lot and spotted a familiar figure leaning against his SUV. One look at her and the nagging sense of dread solidified into a tangible reality.

"Well, shit," he grumbled under his breath.

"What the hell?" Andy muttered, echoing Bryce's sentiments. "She's like a bad penny that keeps turning up."

"Can't you get rid of her?" Callan asked, his tone filled with concern.

"Believe me, I've tried." Bryce's frustration was palpable.

"You've done the nice-guy routine," Jared said. "I think it's going to take more with her."

Ignoring her wouldn't work, especially since she was leaning against his driver's door. Long dark hair, thick and wavy. Dark brown eyes. A curvy figure. Everything that had once attracted him to her now paled compared to the lean blonde that had worked her way into his constant thoughts. Not to mention, Allison's abrasive personality had increased with time, making any enjoyment of her company impossible.

Approaching his vehicle, he kept his distance as he asked, "Allison. What do you want?"

She dipped her chin, looked up at him in a practiced coy expression, and twirled a strand of hair. "Bryce, you haven't called me."

"No, I haven't." That was the only response he was going to give her. Cold and impersonal, hoping she'd take the hint. He should've known that wasn't going to work. So far, no strategy had proven effective.

He'd met Allison one night when he'd stopped by the pub to grab takeout before heading home. She was attractive and, at first, had seemed friendly. It had been a long day at work, and he'd enjoyed sharing a few drinks. She didn't seem to mind his quiet demeanor as she chatted excitedly about living in Norfolk and traveling several times a month, dividing her office time between Norfolk and Baltimore. She asked about his work and seemed interested in the coaching he did with the American Legion youth teams.

The next day, he was surprised to spot her hanging along the fence while coaching a baseball game. Foolishly flattered that she'd sought him out, they ended up at her hotel, saying they wanted nothing more than fun. They'd started hooking up when she was in town, but he knew deep in his heart that it wasn't going anywhere permanent. Allison began to see every woman around as competition, spewing snide comments about their clothes, hair, makeup, or anything else she could think of. He quickly realized that she was the kind of person who derived her self-esteem by belittling others.

But when it was just the two of them, he let his dick rule his head. They were just friends with benefits. *Well, more like fuck buddies since they never talked about anything of substance.* He'd never led her on by saying that he loved her and never talked about a future. He thought they were having a good time, but after about six months, she told him she expected something more permanent. That's when he knew he'd screwed up by not continuing to communicate that, for him, the relationship had never changed from when it began.

When she'd tried to cling to him, he was forced to tell her that he wasn't feeling the same connection. Her narrowed eyes, screeching, and throwing a pot toward him before storming out of his apartment was the last he'd seen of her for months. One of his friend's wives had told him that on Allison's social media, she was already involved with someone else in Virginia Beach. Bryce was relieved. Soon after, he moved from his apartment to the house he'd bought and didn't give her another thought.

And now, here she was, smiling widely as she extended her arms out to the side. "Well, I'm back on the shore, and since I hadn't heard from you, I thought I'd just show up to see if you'd like to go to dinner."

"Allison, I didn't call because we have nothing to discuss."

She jerked her head back, her smile slightly pinched. "Surely two old friends can have dinner."

"I'm afraid not."

Her facial muscles instantly tightened. "I thought we'd surely still be friends after all we meant to each other."

"Allison." He stepped closer and lowered his voice, hoping to avoid a scene. "We were never right for each other. Not as friends, and we were never a couple. We went over this months ago."

"That's not true! You said you didn't love me but never considered my feelings! You didn't mind sleeping with me but didn't want to put a ring on it. How do you think that makes me feel?"

"We both knew at that time what we were doing. There were no promises made, so no promises were broken."

"How can you say that? You didn't even give us a chance!"

He glanced to the side, hating public scenes, glad when his friends, their faces filled with sympathetic grimaces, had stepped to the side but stayed in the vicinity if needed.

"You are such a bastard," she cried. "Leading me on, and then you just dump me!"

Fat tears rolled down her cheeks, but he couldn't imagine how she managed to summon them on demand. He didn't believe she was really upset. "I thought you were already dating someone else."

Her lips curved ever so slightly. "You were keeping up with me. I just did that to make you jealous. He means nothing."

"Then you'll understand exactly how I feel. You mean nothing to me."

Her expression morphed into pure anger, and even though he was much larger than she, he stepped back.

She swiped her hand over her face, then looked at a point beyond him and said, "Don't even try it with this one. He's only interested in sex." Looking at him, she leaned closer. "We're not through, baby. Not by a long shot." Allison whirled around and stomped to her car.

Uncertain of what she meant, he stared at her retreating back before he twisted his neck to look behind him, and his breath stuck in his throat.

Joanne stood to the side, a wrapped platter in her hand. She glanced from him to several of the other officers nearby, her eyes wide and face flaming. "I made some cookies for... all of you... for helping the other day with the... um... ferry incident. Um... here." She thrust the platter into the hands of the closest officer, who happened to be Andy. Then she turned and hurriedly weaved through the parking lot past several vehicles before coming to her own.

Bryce shook his head slowly as the others gathered around.

"Fuck," Jose said. "I got a text from Melanie that said she ran into Joanne and told her to make you cookies. What fucking bad timing."

Andy peeked under the wrap, pulled out a cookie, then took a big bite. Chewing, he lifted his brows and offered a chocolatey grin. "Damn, it's good."

Bryce shot him a glare. "Seriously? You're eating my cookies?"

Jared laughed while snagging several. "She said they're for all of us."

He stalked over and grabbed the plate from Andy's hands. "You heard Jose. They were intended for me." The scent of freshly baked chocolate chip cookies wafted by, and he sighed. "Or they were."

"Allison is a psycho," Joseph said, reaching his fingers under the plastic wrap and grabbing a cookie. "I almost went out with her once when I met her a couple of years ago at the bar in Seaside. Thank God my brother knew about her and warned me off. She comes to the shore every couple of weeks and hangs out in the bars to try to snag someone."

"Sure wish someone had warned me. I would have never asked her out."

Joseph shrugged. "When you two started dating, I figured you knew what you were doing."

"We didn't *date*. We were never that, and she knew it," he corrected.

Jose walked over and slid a cookie from the platter.

"Hey," Bryce grumbled. "You weren't even on the callout for the ferry."

"But *my* wife told her to make them and bring them to you."

"Yeah, and look how that ended!"

"You're missing the point, man. At least you know Joanne is interested. It's not just one-sided."

Letting Jose's words move over him, he finally

nodded. "But how do I get her to know that what she witnessed was fucked up?"

"I'd let her know right away," Jared said. "When Billie overheard me in a bad scene with a former hookup, it wasn't good."

"Oh, that makes me feel a fuckton better!"

"Look," Callan said, his mouth full of cookie goodness. He swallowed, then finished his thought. "Talk to Joanne so she doesn't spend any time thinking about it."

Jose walked over and clapped him on the shoulder. "Her phone number and address are on the report for the ferry callout. All's fair in love and all that shit. Go for it."

"Jesus, man, this is worse than middle school."

Jose threw his head back and laughed, soon joined by the others. Bryce offered a chin lift as they headed to their vehicles. He stood for only a moment before he headed back inside the station, sinking his teeth into a cookie. Groaning at what was probably the best cookie he'd ever eaten, he pulled up the ferry report. Jotting down her information, he went back out to his SUV with the platter of cookies in one hand, woefully staring at the pitiful few still left.

Sometimes fate needed more than a little help. Sometimes it needed a fucking push!

8

Why is dating so hard?

That was the million-dollar question that Joanne had been asking herself for years. And now, standing at her kitchen window overlooking the neglected flower beds, the same question still plagued her.

Her recent escapade had only added fuel to her perplexed state. Having thoroughly embarrassed herself by showing up at the marine police station, unannounced and unexpected, only to find the man of her interest engaged in a should-be-private-but-was-very-public discussion with a girlfriend. Or former girlfriend. Or wannabe girlfriend.

A sigh as heavy as her thoughts escaped her lips. She shoved a cookie into her mouth, marveling at her grandma's recipe. The buttery chocolate bite soothed her mood, so she was glad she hadn't given them all away. Swallowing, she filled a glass of milk and drank, deciding that the combination of milk and cookies was probably the best coupling in the world. *Certainly more reliable than my attempts at pairing up.*

Rinsing her glass, she sucked in a fortifying breath as she stared at the yard. Another lesson she'd learned from her grandmother—there was nothing like physical labor to chase away the moody blues. Deciding that she would attack the yard, she headed outside with a pair of gardening gloves.

Her tiny house was just a rental, and she'd only been in it since moving to the shore four months ago. In the summer, she enjoyed working in the yard, and her elderly landlord was thrilled about any beautification she completed. Now, the flower beds were full of leaves, and some late-growing weeds threatened to take over. She used the wheelbarrow he'd left in the shed to haul the raked leaves to the edge of the woods to dump.

After almost an hour of raking, she stood to rest with her hands on her hips and arched her back in a stretch, working out the kinks. While her grandmother had extolled the virtues of hard work chasing away a bad mood, she certainly hadn't warned her about the aches.

Now, with the flower beds ready for the winter, she trudged to the house to fetch the hose, wanting to wash out the wheelbarrow. Turning on the spigot, she dragged the hose closer to the shed where she'd left it.

Suddenly, her peaceful yard work was invaded by a late-season wasp as it buzzed too closely to her head, seemingly fascinated with her. She threw her arm out, but it continued to hover too close for comfort. Her heart raced as she waved her arm again. Ever since she'd been stung as a teenager, she was terrified of any flying stinging creature. "Shoo!" She waved her hand around, fear turning her quiet afternoon into a frantic dance in the yard. The wasp was soon joined by a friend, and they both dive-bombed her head.

"Get out of here!" she screamed while spinning around frantically, spraying the water at the wasps as she raced in a circle. "Shoo! Get away!" Water arced through the air, raining down on her like a downpour. Her chest heaved as she gasped just before she detected the buzz swooping around her head again. "Augh!" she shrieked, leaping around as water continued to spout from the hose, desperate to keep the wasps from getting nearer.

"What the...?"

Her feet skidded to a stop at the sound of a distinctly male voice coming from behind her. Lowering the hose, she swiped her drenched hair from her eyes, and her mouth fell open in astonishment as her gaze landed on Bryce. He stood in her yard, still in his uniform but now with water droplets glistening on his face and his damp shirt plastered against his chest.

She was sure she couldn't feel more embarrassed than when she was an awkward bystander at the scene between him and the pretty woman at the station, but seeing the bedraggled man in front of her sent her embarrassment level into orbit.

Dropping the still-gushing hose onto the ground, she lifted her hands in a feckless effort to wipe away some water, but the hose wiggled like a snake, squirting more water over both of them.

"Oh my God!" she cried out, bending to grab the spurting end when her head collided against something hard and unyielding. Her head throbbed in pain as she tumbled backward, landing on her ass. Clutching her forehead, she squinted up as he grabbed the end of a hose with one hand while rubbing his forehead with the other.

"Jesus Christ, woman!" His exclamation filled the air, a blend of shock and irritation.

Stunned by the unexpected appearance of Bryce in her yard and reeling from the impact of their heads colliding, she stayed on her ass, watching in dumb silence as he jogged over to her house and shut off the water spigot. The water spray slowed to a drip, and the snaking hose settled on the ground.

He muttered something under his breath, and she leaped to her feet, wondering if she could salvage the situation.

She couldn't fathom how it was possible to recover as he approached with a wet shirt clinging to his dampened body and a quarter-sized knot forming on his forehead. Once again, wishing for and not finding a hole opening up so she could fling herself into the abyss, she shrugged and raised her hands to the side. "Um... hi."

Bryce had driven down the sunlit street, noting the small, neat houses along either side. Some with manicured lawns or children's toys scattered about gave evidence to the families that lived there. A few had seen better days, but that was much like most streets on the shore. His heart had thumped against his rib cage, anxious to see Joanne again, hoping they would have a chance to talk without anyone else around.

When he stopped outside her house, which was more like a cottage, he caught sight of her on the side, standing in her yard. The sunlight glistened in her hair, and the messy bun with escaping tendrils gave her a carefree appearance. She had a hose in her hand, and when she turned, his gaze continued to peruse her silhouette. Her faded, long-sleeved T-shirt stretched over her breasts, and her jeans showcased not only her ass but her long legs. The whole package ended with red sneakers. Simple, relaxed, and genuine.

With a hopeful heart that she would give him a chance to explain the awkward scene she'd witnessed at the station, he climbed out of his SUV and started walking toward her. Ready to throw his hand up in greeting, the rush of water from the hose must have kept her from hearing his approach because she never turned toward him. Not wanting to startle her, he stopped several feet away. Just as he started to call out her name, she screamed and waved her hands in the air, dancing in a circle with water from the hose aimed in all directions.

He spied the offending wasp that seemed more fascinated with the water than it was with her, but she appeared determined to drown it. Bryce charged forward to assist when she whirled around again, her hair dripping with water and her eyes closed as she waved her hands continuously. Before he could react, a splash of cold water hit him right in the face.

Jerking, he lifted his hands in protection, but another spin from her sent the water blasting across his shirt.

"What the—" He managed to hold his curse in midsentence as she yelped. She swiped the soaked strands of hair from her eyes with a swift, frantic motion. As her gaze locked onto his, she let the hose slip from her grasp. But with the water pressure on full blast, the hose writhed like a dancing snake, sending another arc of cold water his way.

He lunged forward to grab the hose, attempting to keep it from doing any more damage, but his head surprisingly connected with hers. Through blurred vision, he watched helplessly as she fell backward, as though in slow motion, onto her rear. He swallowed another curse as his fingers enclosed around the hose. Rubbing the pain that slashed throughout his head, he stumbled to the house and turned off the spigot. The water eased to a dribble as he tossed the end of the hose to the ground.

He hustled back to offer her a hand up, but she'd scrambled to her feet. Hands planted on his hips, he stared at the bedraggled but still beautiful woman in front of him. Before he could ask if she was okay, she looked up and mumbled, "Um... hi."

A bubble of laughter formed deep in his gut, then erupted before he was able to hold it in. He leaned back, belting out laughter, glad when she joined in.

As his mouth slowed, he held her gaze. "I think you successfully dispatched the wasp."

She pressed her lips together but was unable to keep more laughter from rushing forward. "I am so sorry!" Red dotted her cheeks, but he wasn't sure if it was from the sun, the exertion, or embarrassment.

"Oh God, you're drenched. Please, come in and let me get you a towel!" She reached out and grabbed his arm, giving a little tug.

Thrilled she was giving him time, he hesitated for only a few seconds before following her through the back door and into a small kitchen.

Her cottage was small, but once inside, it screamed cozy. Bright green and yellow curtains hung over the windows, and various items with a sunflower pattern sat on the counter. She darted over and opened a closet door, exposing a stacked washer and dryer. She pulled a fresh towel from the dryer and handed it to him. It smelled of lilac, the same scent he had noticed on her when they were on the boat. It hadn't dawned on him then that that was from her dryer sheets and not perfume, but the understated scent was now firmly associated with her. She pulled out another one for herself.

"Thanks." He took the towel from her hands and swiped it over his hair and face. There wasn't much he could do for his shirt, but as he handed the towel back to her, she was staring at his chest, chewing on her bottom lip.

"Why don't you take your shirt off," she suggested.

Catching him by surprise, he lifted an eyebrow.

"I can pop your shirt into my dryer, and it'll be warm and dry in just a few minutes."

It was on the tip of his tongue to refuse, his practical side knowing it wasn't necessary. But with the allure of her standing in front of him with an earnest expression, he was swayed to take her up on her offer.

Unbuttoning his shirt, he pulled the damp fabric off his shoulders and handed it to her, catching a flicker in her eyes. She stood frozen, her hands hanging limply at her sides, and her gaze riveted on the expanse of his chest. Her face held a blank expression, and self-doubt slammed into him. Wondering if he should've left his shirt on, he started to slide his arm back into the sleeve.

Jumping as if an electric jolt struck her, she snagged the shirt from his hands. Giving her head a little shake, she murmured, "Sorry. Sorry. I'll just... I... um... got lost... I'll just put this in the dryer."

Confusion and curiosity held him in place as he stood in her kitchen. She tossed the shirt into the dryer, along with a dryer sheet. Flipping the dial, she started it, and the gentle hum of the tumbling machine filled the background. She turned around, her gaze roving over him, and her cheeks pinkened to a rosy blush.

Finally returning her gaze to his eyes, she blinked and blushed more. "I'm gawking."

Eyes widening, he tilted his head to the side. "Excuse me?"

Her hands fluttered like a trapped butterfly. "I'm so sorry, but I've been gawking at you. It's utterly rude. If a man gawked at me like that, I'd probably be offended.

Well, maybe not offended. It's kind of flattering, but not if it was in a creepy way. But I don't want you to be offended because I'm gawking simply because it's like your muscles took lessons from Greek statues. Or was that Michelangelo? Anyway, you're really… kind of breathtaking."

"Breathtaking?" He was confident of his body and had heard his fair share of compliments, but breathtaking was a word he couldn't remember having been applied to him before.

She wiggled her fingers in a whimsical flourish toward him. "You must know it, Bryce. Your muscles look like they have muscles. I don't have any muscles. I'm completely allergic to anything that remotely resembles exercise."

"Except your wasp dance."

Her eyes jerked open wide, and he couldn't keep the grin off his face.

Her lips twitched. "Yes. My wasp dance." She dropped her chin and covered her face with her hands, still shaking her head. "Oh my God. I can't believe you saw that."

"I didn't only *see* it, Joanne. But I was a participant with the waterfall and head knocking as part of the dance."

She lifted her head as she dropped her hands. "I'm so embarrassed!"

"Don't be. I haven't laughed like that in a while."

She lifted her hand and delicately touched his forehead, sweeping a lock of hair from his eyes. "Are you okay?"

"I've got a hard head, so I really should be asking you that question."

Nodding, she said, "Yeah. I must have a hard head, too."

They stared for a moment with only the rumbling sound coming from the dryer, and all thoughts of conversation flew from his mind. Here he was, standing shirtless in the kitchen of the woman he was interested in, and he couldn't think of anything to say. Or at least not anything witty. "Um... I've got a T-shirt in my vehicle. I'll go get it."

She nodded. "I'll stop gawking now and run to change into something dry," she mumbled before hurrying out of the room and into what he assumed was her bedroom.

He jogged outside, heading straight to his SUV. Opening the back, he grabbed his workout bag and jerked a T-shirt from its contents. Giving it a sniff, he was satisfied that it was clean and pulled it over his head. Not wanting to miss out on any time with her, he hustled back inside.

Stepping into the kitchen, he found her exactly in the same spot as where he'd left her, only now she was wearing leggings, a pink sweatshirt, and her feet sported pink fuzzy socks.

"I hope I didn't embarrass you," she said, her blue eyes pinned on him.

Grinning, he nodded. "While being gawked at and called breathtaking did wonders for my ego, I thought it would be more appropriate to throw on a shirt."

They stood in silence for another moment before

she finally tilted her head slightly and asked, "So… um… what brought you out this way?"

"I brought your empty platter back."

Her brows shot to her forehead. "Empty? You ate all those cookies already?"

"Well," he drawled. "They were also given to the other guys at the station. By the time I got to them, I was lucky to get three."

She gasped. "Oh, I'm sorry. I did actually make them for you—" She blinked. "I mean, they were for every-body. But I wanted you to have more…" Her nose scrunched. "Why did you really come out here?"

Stepping closer, he longed to reach out to take her hand in his but hesitated. "I wanted to ask you out, Joanne, but damn, I've never had to work so hard to do so."

9

"Oh."

At Joanne's one-word response, Bryce had no idea what she was thinking. Her brow was furrowed, but her gaze stayed locked on his, and he could feel her unasked questions right in his gut. *Christ, how do I explain all this to her?* Sighing heavily, he said. "You're wondering about the woman."

Now, the heavy sigh left her lips. She nodded, offering a little shrug. "Yes, but honestly, Bryce, it's really none of my business."

"It is if I want to ask you out, and hope you'll say yes. And if that scene you witnessed keeps you from feeling comfortable enough to agree, it is your business."

She remained locked in place, her eyes roaming over his face before she finally asked, "I've got some tea. Would you like some?"

Nodding, he noticed the tightness in his chest loosened slightly since she wasn't kicking him out. "Absolutely."

He smiled but could still see the hesitation in her eyes. After pouring two glasses, she led him to the living room sofa, where she sat down on one end before placing the glasses on the coffee table. Twisting her body, she tucked one bent leg under her ass. He hurried to sit on the other side of the sofa, twisting in a similar way so they were facing each other. He scrubbed his hand over his face. Suddenly, he hated the idea of discussing Allison with Joanne, but he didn't want the misinterpretation of Allison between them.

"Joanne, I don't date a lot," he began, then hesitated again.

"You really don't owe me an explanation," she rushed, placing her hand on the sofa between them.

"Maybe not, but I want to give it anyway." Seeing her nod, he continued. "Dating for me was something that occurred when two people had a desire to build a relationship. Believe me, that's rarely happened. For the most part, a more… random… uh…" His face burned, and he wished he'd figured out a way to discuss the topic in a way that didn't make him sound like a hound. "Shit," he muttered under his breath.

"You had more random physical encounters."

His gaze jerked up to see her gentle smile curving the corners of her mouth. "Uh… yeah."

A soft giggle sounded out as she shook her head. "Bryce, I'm thirty years old. Believe me, I understand the difference between what you hope for and what sometimes actually happens. We all have needs." She shrugged. "Taking care of physical needs is nothing to be ashamed of."

The constriction in his throat eased, and he inhaled deeply as his smile met hers. "Thanks for understanding. Anyway, almost a year ago, I'd gone to a bar one night by myself, not looking for company." He snorted at the memory. "I was focused more on the wings, onion rings, and beer than I was anyone else around."

Her gaze never left his face as she gave all her attention to him. It dawned on him how rare that was. So many people were in such a hurry that they rarely let someone finish a conversation or thought before they had to jump in. And as much as he hated the conversation topic, he appreciated Joanne giving him the chance to explain.

"Allison came over and sat down. It wasn't hard to pick up on her flirting, and she was attractive enough, so I didn't discourage her. I'm not exactly Mr. Exciting or Witty, so her talking so much made it easy on me. She was in town on her way between her work in Norfolk and Maryland. Her company had her travel between the two offices often. I didn't feel anything other than physical attraction, and she kept talking, flirting, hinting that she was up for a night. We went back to her hotel. I left the next morning and hadn't planned on seeing her again unless she passed through town and was interested in another hookup. I was surprised to find her hanging at the youth ball game where I was coaching since I had only mentioned in passing that was where I'd be. When I told her I had plans afterward with friends, she wasn't pissy but seemed dejected. Looking back, I wonder if it wasn't part of her play."

"Guilt," Joanne acknowledged, nodding slowly. "If I had to guess, guilt would be the one emotion that has caused more people to agree to a date or prolong a relationship that they really weren't interested in."

"You sound like you understand?"

Rolling her eyes, she chuckled. "Oh, believe me. I've agreed to so many things because someone has guilted me into it."

"Sounds like stories I wanna hear."

"Maybe later, but right now, I want to hear more about you."

Wanting to conclude the topic of Allison, he continued, "When the game was over, I spoke to her for a few minutes, but that guilt you just mentioned made me do something stupid. She looked so hurt, I asked if she'd like to go to dinner."

"And she jumped right on it."

He barked out laughter. "Oh hell, you better believe it. So we made arrangements for that night. As I was getting ready for the date, part of me wondered if I would discover she was someone I might connect with. I guess there's always that hope. The date was fine, but I still didn't feel anything special."

"Oh, I so understand," Joanne said, her voice indicating she felt his emotion deeply.

He thought about what Jose had said about her many blind dates and figured she knew exactly what he was talking about. "Allison's conversation was all about her. She seemed determined that I would be so enthralled with getting to know her that she spent no time getting to know me. But like an idiot, we ended up back at her hotel. And what happened after that…" He grimaced. "I have no good reason for continuing to see her. Maybe it was just convenient sex, and I know that makes me sound like a royal prick."

Her lips twitched. "I can't imagine you being a royal prick, but then I don't know you well."

"Yeah," he sighed. "She started coming to Baytown almost every other weekend. And since I wasn't seeing anyone else, it was easy just to keep hooking up. I never considered us anything more than…"

"Friends with benefits?"

He blew out a long breath. "Honestly? I didn't really care about her like true friends, so that sounds disingenuous."

"Fuck buddies?" Joanne prompted, her lips still twitching.

He snorted and rolled his eyes. "Still maybe too much. That would imply we were buddies." He shrugged again, then reached to squeeze the back of his neck. "But yeah. That's probably what we were in my mind. We'd go out for dinner, talk some, then end up at my apartment."

Joanne remained quiet, simply nodding as he continued.

"I had a small efficiency apartment while I waited to find a house to purchase. It was tiny, but it was where I felt comfortable." He shook his head and said, "I think she was incredibly disappointed."

"So what finally happened?"

"This continued for about six months, and I knew I needed to end it. She started to leave things at the apartment, which barely held my things. She brought up how we needed to look for a bigger place. And then she told me one weekend that she wanted us to go into Virginia Beach to ring shop." He shook his head and scrubbed his hand over his face. "I was floored. That's when I knew we needed to stop."

Hearing himself tell the story, he felt foolish. He should have stopped seeing Allison months earlier. But he had been so sure that she was on the same *convenient sex* wavelength as he was. "I guess this is where I sound like a royal prick."

"Well, I wouldn't say it makes you sound like a royal prick. But it definitely sounds like the two of you weren't communicating about your expectations."

He barked out a rude sound and nodded. "You've got that right. In hindsight, I admit she was probably dropping hints, but they really weren't striking home. I never told her I loved her. We never talked about a future together. We sure as hell never talked about anything of real substance. My failure was keeping up what I thought was a casual relationship with someone who thought we were moving forward."

"Well, she may have been dropping hints, but she also could've easily initiated that expectation discussion. Dropping hints doesn't take the place of having a real conversation." She cocked her head to the side, her gaze pinned on him. "How did it end?"

"When she dropped the ring shopping bombshell on me, I realized the conversation you were just mentioning needed to take place. I told her, as gently as I could, that I wasn't on the same page. She begged and said that I would get there in time. I told her that I didn't see that happening. She wanted to know why I didn't love her but wasn't happy when I countered and said that she never mentioned love. She said it was implied, and I said that I missed the implication."

Joanne scrunched her nose. "Sounds messy."

"Hell yeah, it was. She stormed out, slamming the door while saying how much she hated me. As bad as this sounds, I was relieved. But then, she showed up the next weekend, acting as though nothing had changed, and I had to reiterate what had been said. I realized that I made a monumental mistake and just wanted it over. I told her at that point that I no longer considered us together in any way. She left with a few more choice words, threats, and slamming doors after she packed up the things she had in my apartment. About a month later, a friend noticed that Allison had posted on her social media that she was dating somebody and had a whole bunch of pictures of her and another guy. Again, I was fucking relieved." His shoulders slumped, knowing how all this might sound to Joanne, but he felt hopeful when her expression stayed relaxed and her gaze held warmth.

"So what happened today?"

He spread his hands out and shook his head. "I honestly don't know. But that entire scene could not have been more fucked up if I had woken up this morning and said I want to participate in one of the most fucked-up things that could possibly happen."

Laughter slipped out, and she shook her head, her

hand lifting to cover her mouth. "It sounded like she truly thought you guys had something."

"I haven't seen or heard from her in months. In at least five months. I have no idea why she thought it was a good idea to show up at my work and pitch a fit about how I was ignoring her when we've obviously moved on." He moved slightly so that his gaze could stay pinned directly on her. "Please, believe me, Joanne, when I say that her timing could not have been worse. If I could have been unencumbered when you arrived with those cookies, I would've had every one of them for myself and would've definitely asked you out then."

"Do you think she got the message?"

He tilted his head back to stare blankly at the ceiling for a few seconds. Sighing, he dropped his chin and turned his full attention back to Joanne. "I don't usually go in for name-calling, but one of the guys said it best when he said something about Allison was kind of psycho. Enough that it makes me a little nervous. But I'm not going out with her, so she'll just have to keep taking no for an answer."

"I can understand that was embarrassing, Bryce. I'm sorry that I showed up unexpectedly."

"No, don't apologize. I'm glad you came to the station." He shook his head slightly and winced. "Well, I'm not glad that you witnessed her rant. What I mean is that it's nice to know that you cared enough to see me again and brought cookies."

She smiled, and his chest eased a bit more at her easy acquiescence. "Anyway, I just didn't want you to think I was involved with her. Or involved with anyone." He reached out and placed his hand over hers. "You're the person I was hoping to ask out."

"I'm glad. Although, I have a feeling that Jose has probably talked to you about me. Right?"

Blushing slightly, he nodded. "He has nothing except the nicest things to say about you. But I'd like to get to know you myself."

10

Joanne thought about the scene she'd witnessed with Bryce and Allison, but it paled compared to trying to sum up her entire dating life, which seemed crazier than his, at least on the surface. Now, faced with trying to explain her thoughts and actions, she realized how ridiculous, and maybe even pathetic, she would sound. Looking at him, she wondered why she felt compelled to tell him anything. *We haven't even gone out on a date.* Yet she felt more comfortable with him than she had any other man in a long time.

"Hey," he said, leaning closer. One of his hands rested on hers, placed between them on the sofa, but with the forefinger on his other hand, he gently soothed along her forehead. "You don't have to tell me anything you don't want to, Joanne."

"It's not that I don't want to, Bryce." She snorted. "But your story with Allison was much more simple than trying to explain how I've approached dating. Or, more rightly stated, how I've been pushed into approaching dating. Believe me, my story goes much further back than when I met Jose."

"Then start at the beginning."

She sighed, pressing her lips together. She had remained quiet while he gave his explanation, wanting him to have the ability to gather in and speak his thoughts. As he was silent now, she realized he was giving her the same opportunity.

She dragged her tongue over her bottom lip, casting her mind back. "My parents were in love." Seeing his raised eyebrows at her pronouncement, she smiled. "I guess that wasn't where you expected me to start."

Now, he chuckled and squeezed her fingers. "Go for it, Joanne. I want to hear it all."

The tension left her shoulders as she settled back against the comfortable cushions. "My parents were in love. Really, truly, madly in love. I would've thought my mom had exaggerated if I hadn't witnessed it myself. But it was true. My dad adored my mom, and she would've done anything for him. My dad died when I was seventeen years old." She felt Bryce's hand tighten around her fingers. "He had a heart attack, but we got to see him at the hospital right before he died, so we had a chance to say goodbye."

"I am so sorry," Bryce said. "That must have brought up a lot of memories when you were with Saul."

Pressing her lips together, she nodded. His eyes also held pain, and she knew instinctively that he had also suffered loss. *I hope he shares the cause with me sometime.*

"The only reason I tell you that now is because it truly has to do with how I, and my mom, have viewed dating ever since. I planned to go to the University of Virginia, but I didn't want to leave my mom. I completed my associate's degree at Old Dominion University and lived at home. I had a good time, but the loss was hard on my mom for the first couple of years, and I wanted to be there for her. I finished my counseling and administrative degree at Old Dominion University, so I was still close to her. I still didn't date a lot. By then, I wasn't interested in frat parties or drunken tailgate football parties. I went out occasionally, usually with an older graduate student, but never more than a couple of times. If it didn't seem long-term, I didn't want to continue the relationship."

"Sounds reasonable. Sure as hell more reasonable than I was with Allison."

She chuckled. "Once I earned my master's degree, I was twenty-four years old and focused on work. Mom moved to the Eastern Shore, where she had grown up, and I had a job in rural Virginia at a small, private university for a few years. Again, I would date, but never for more than a couple of months. I wondered if I was too picky or not destined for love, but I hated trying to force myself into a relationship that I knew wouldn't last. Then, I ended up working at VCU in Richmond. A big change for me—from rural to urban, from a small college to a large university, and from not a large dating pool to a much bigger variety."

Her voice trailed off, and she didn't realize her expression had changed until Bryce gently squeezed her hand. She sucked in a quick breath, feeling more in that simple touch than she had in a long time.

"It sounds like there's more to the story."

Snorting, she nodded. "Not a good story. I met a guy who actually lasted more than a couple of months. Chad and I dated for almost two years. We talked about ring shopping. Talked about the future. My mom was excited. I thought everything was good. And then, as cliché as it sounds, I came home one weekend to visit Mom, but she had a church charity event to attend, so I returned to our apartment a day early."

Bryce sucked in a hasty breath, the hissing cutting through the silence. "Shit... no way."

Lifting her brows, she nodded. "Yep, you guessed it. Walked in, and like a bad scene in a movie, there was a trail of clothes from the door to the bedroom. Believe me, though, I wasn't a wilting flower. I was hurt... so unbelievably hurt, but mostly, I was pissed as hell. I marched in, saw them going at it in bed, and stood there with my arms crossed. She was his assistant, so I knew her. And I got to know her even more because she was naked. Well, obviously, they both were. Then, finally, they noticed me standing there. They scrambled to cover themselves as he tried to tell me she was nothing. That just pissed her off, and she began screaming at him. Looking back, it's rather comical." A heavy sigh left her lips. "Of course, after she hastily grabbed her clothes, dressed, and ran out, he tried to talk to me. I threw some of his clothes out the door and told him that if he also didn't leave, I'd throw all his clothes out. He'd had to go to his car in his skivvies."

"Damn, woman. That's impressive."

She bit her lip, then sighed again, feeling the

emotional memory weighing on her shoulders. "I was badass at the moment, but there were a lot of tears and wine later on." Holding his gaze, she admitted, "It wasn't that I really missed *him* because I never want to be with a cheating bastard. But, it was the idea of love. I'd allowed myself to hope that I had something special, and the obliteration of that hope was tough. Plus, he made it worse."

He tilted his head to the side, his gaze penetrating. "How so?"

"He couldn't accept that he had fucked up irrevocably and that I wasn't going just to forgive, forget, and take him back. He wouldn't stop calling, texting, coming by my place, and then stopping at my work. So much so, I had to take out a restraining order."

"Holy shit, Joanne!"

"That finally got him to back off. I haven't heard from him in about six months."

He continued to hold her hand, his thumb rubbing over her knuckles. The slight touch moved through her, soothing the rough edges of the memories.

"Anyway, I wanted a change of pace. I was able to get a job as a counselor at the community college here on the Shore and moved back. It was then that my mom decided it was her life goal to make sure that I had the opportunity to experience what she and my dad had. Thus began months of her setting me up."

"And that's how you met Jose."

She dropped her chin and shook her head, moaning. "Oh God. That was so embarrassing." Looking up again, she curved her lips. "My mom is active in several women's groups, charitable organizations in the area, her church, and even the American Legion Auxiliary. Believe me, she has a vast network of other women trying to set up their sons, nephews, grandsons, and let's not forget the *Oh, he's a nice man who lives next door to so-and-so.*"

Laughter belted out from Bryce, and she was glad he found it amusing and not pathetic. "She had met Jose's mom, and Mary called and invited me over for an informal barbecue to celebrate her grandson's birthday and for me to meet her son. I agreed, assuming that Jose knew about it. I happened to arrive before he did, so I was inside the house helping his mom. She was so sweet and encouraging, and I thought, maybe, just maybe, this might be the one. He drives up, and as I'm walking outside with his mother, Jose climbs out and reaches into the back seat. I thought he was getting a food platter or something like that. Instead, he pulls out an infant carrier! And then walks over, holding hands with a gorgeous woman. If I could have ordered a meteor to drop into the yard, creating a massive hole so that I could have thrown myself in, I would have!"

"I know you didn't know this then, Joanne, but Jose's mom was always trying to set him up on blind dates. Believe me, I know he understood."

"I could tell the woman he was with was embarrassed, and then Jose introduced his family to her and the baby. The scene was about to get crazy, and I just wanted to get out of there. Thankfully, Melanie was so gracious and stepped to the side with the baby while Jose walked over to me. I assured him that I had no idea he didn't know I was there. He was embarrassed but just as gracious as Melanie. I told him I would get my purse and slip out. He tried to protest by saying he hated for me to leave since none of this was my fault, but I told him that he gave me the impetus to tell my mom to stop trying to set me up on blind dates."

"He's a good man."

"He absolutely is a good man, and he's with a wonderful woman. And I have to say that his mom called me the next day to apologize. It's all good. I've ended up becoming friends with Melanie."

"How did your mom react?"

Joanne barked out laughter, rolling her eyes. "It slowed her down for a while. Actually, William and his boating day from hell was the first blind date she has set me up on since then." Shrugging her shoulders, she added, "Of course, you had to witness the end of that horrid date."

They were quiet momentarily, and she continued pulling her thoughts together. Pressing her lips tightly, she rubbed them back and forth before lifting her gaze to his again. "You see, the thing about my mom is that she's not trying to set me up on blind dates because she thinks I can't find someone on my own, or she's desperate for grandbabies, or she's just a manipulator. In truth, she's just a hopeful romantic who wants her daughter to find the kind of love she had with my dad."

"And your other blind dates? Jose hinted that most weren't good."

Puffing out her cheeks as the air expelled from her lungs in a rush, she nodded. "Don't get me wrong. They weren't all horrible. But I knew right away that they were nothing special. Some talked just about themselves or talked over me. Some seemed to want to jump to a physical relationship before the first date ended."

He grunted, but she just laughed. "Well, you've been hit on by women just interested in a hookup."

"True that." He nodded, smiling as his fingers continued to rub over her hand.

"And even if a guy was nice, polite, interesting, or I actually went on a second date with them, there was no spark. And I'm in my thirties now… if it's not special, I don't want to drag it out for them or for me."

"But you keep trying?"

It was hard not to wince at his words even though his tone was gentle. "I guess I keep going on dates, partly out of guilt because my mom has set them up, but also because somewhere deep inside, I'm a hopeful romantic also." She didn't want to sound needy or desperate, but she also wanted to give him total honesty because what she felt for him was more than what she'd felt with any other guy… hope.

11

Hopeful. Hopeful romantic.

Bryce heard the words brimming with promise from Joanne's lips. While other men might have balked, cynically dismissed, or run in terror at hearing the candid confession from a woman looking for love, her words resonated deep inside his heart. It wasn't about chasing the fairy tale but yearning for something deep and enduring. He might not want what his parents had—or didn't have—but he sure as hell wanted what Aunt Debbie and Uncle Bernie showed love could be.

Her vulnerability was palpable, crowding the space between them as she averted her gaze, casting her eyes to the side. Still cradling her hand, he gave it a reassuring jiggle, drawing her attention back to his face. Her gaze, filled with dreams and hopes, was exactly where he wanted it to be—on him. "I get it."

Her brow furrowed as she sucked in her lips. "Get what?"

"Hopeful."

Her eyes stayed full of uncertainty.

"No, really, Joanne. I get it." He knew she'd given a lot of herself by what she'd told him. And even though they'd never gone out on a date, so it was pre-emptive to say they were starting, he still felt like something was happening between them. Suddenly, a chirp rang out and interrupted their conversation, alerting them that the dryer cycle had finished.

She startled, then smiled as she let go of his hand and stood. He watched her move to the dryer and pull his shirt out. Her hand moved over the material, and she looked over her shoulder. "It's ready."

Moving to her, he took the now-warm and dry material from her hands and shrugged it on over his T-shirt. The scent of lilac filled the air, and he didn't mind, knowing it would remind him of her. "Thanks. I appreciate this."

"Well, it was my fault you got wet in the first place."

"I don't know about that. I think a case could be made for it being the wasp's fault."

Her eyes sparkled as they widened. "Yes, I prefer that explanation!"

He hesitated, unable to think of a reason to prolong his stay. "Well, I really should be going, I guess."

Her smile slipped. "Oh yeah. Sure."

He walked to the door, kicking himself for not thinking of more to say. Turning quickly, he barely had time to grab her shoulders to keep her from running into the back of him.

"Sorry!" she exclaimed, eyes wide and cheeks pinkening.

"No, it was my fault for stopping so quickly."

"Was there something else?"

He looked into her face, her eyes intently holding his gaze, her lips parted ever so slightly. "Yes. Would you do me the honor of letting me take you to dinner?"

Her lips now curved once again as she nodded. "I'd love to have dinner with you."

"Would you think I was crazy if I suggested now?"

She blinked and inhaled a quick gasp of air, but the smile stayed on her face. "Now?"

"Yeah... I was going to ask you out for tomorrow, but I'm having such a good time getting to know you that I hate to wait even a day." He grabbed the back of his neck and squeezed. "I guess that's too soon—"

"No, no! I'd like to."

"Really?" With his barked-out question, he didn't sound cool but didn't care.

"Well, I have to eat dinner, and I suppose you have to eat dinner, too... so..."

"Yeah," he said, nodding, feeling relief flood throughout his chest. Suddenly thinking about his cats, he grimaced. "I need to run home first. I've got to feed my cats."

"Oh... okay... well, I could meet you—"

"Come with me. We can run by my house and then get dinner somewhere."

"Okay." Her hasty agreement was quickly squashed when she glanced down. "Oh, I need to get my shoes and fix my face."

Not wanting an opportunity to pass, he jumped in. "How about you stay just as you are, which is beautiful, and come to my place. I can pull something out of the freezer to heat…" As soon as the words left his mouth, his face fell. "Sorry, Joanne. That's so not what I wanted to do. You deserve to be taken out to a nice restaurant for a really good date, not—"

"Stop right there," she said, her hand covering his mouth.

His lips twitched at the feel of her fingers on his flesh, and he had to maintain his composure when he really wanted to lick her fingertips. She inhaled deeply, and he waited to see what she would say.

"Bryce, I've been on a lot of first dates. Dates that almost never resulted in a second date. And if they did, they never progressed much further. After my experience with Chad, I knew that I didn't want to waste time with someone when I knew it wasn't going anywhere. Still hopeful, but not naive or stupid."

"Okay," he mumbled against her fingers.

"I don't need to be wined and dined. I just want to spend time with someone who I'm interested in and is interested in me." She shrugged, dropping her hand. "Any food at your place is fine. Actually, it's more than fine."

He smiled, her words settling deep in his chest.

"Tell you what. If you give me ten minutes, I'll be ready and can follow you to your place."

He started to insist that he'd drive but wanted her to be comfortable with her exit strategy if needed. He just hoped she wouldn't feel the need. "Take your time. There's no hurry. My cats will wait."

Laughing, she shook her head. "If you can look at me

the way I am now and still ask me out, I'm not going to worry about trying to beautify myself too much. Honestly, I'll be ready in a few minutes."

She turned to walk down the hall, but he grabbed her hand, gently pulling her to a stop. She looked over her shoulder, a question in her eyes.

"Just wanted to say… you're beautiful the way you are right now."

Her smile widened until her face lit, and her eyes sparkled. He let go of her hand and watched as she hurried down the hall, disappearing into a room. True to her word, ten minutes later, she reappeared, her hair brushed and pulled back into a low ponytail. Jeans that weren't skintight but showed off her curves. And a bright pink T-shirt paired with a pale pink sweater.

"Ready?"

Her face showed an eagerness that he felt inside, and she nodded. "Absolutely."

As she trailed Bryce's SUV, elation pulsed through her veins. She entered his address into her GPS but appreciated his conscientious driving, ensuring she wasn't left behind. Eagerly looking around as they pulled onto a rural road, the older neighborhood with sprawling lots and quaint houses was in contrast to where she'd imagined a bachelor would live. The ambiance of the family-oriented neighborhood reminded her of childhood memories. And while she hadn't spent any time conjuring a mental image of

Bryce's home, the reality was unexpected... and delightful.

He parked outside a one-story rambler that appeared L-shaped from what she could see. It was painted pale yellow, with white shutters and a white front door. She had never thought of a single man dwelling in a yellow house but didn't know why that struck her as unusual. Yet the way the evening light shone over the trees, the house seemed to glow, and her heart lifted at the beauty before her.

A tap on her window caused her to jump, yanking her from her reverie. Embarrassed to have been caught now gawking at his house, she hastily flung open the door, placing her hand in his, allowing him to assist her out of the car. "Your house is so beautiful!"

His broad and genuine smile hinted at the pride he took in his home and her appreciation of it. "I bought it a few months ago after renting an apartment for several years. It was perfect timing, actually. The owners had just finished making some upgrades when they decided they no longer wanted to live on the shore, so I got a great deal since there were still more upgrades to complete. Come on in."

His hand remained wrapped around hers as they walked over a crushed oyster path lined with low hedges to the front porch. No sooner had they stepped into the cozy foyer leading to the living room when a welcoming committee of several cats came trotting from the back hallway. Their tails stood straight in the air, and a chorus of loud meows greeted them.

"Oh my goodness! You weren't kidding when you said you had cats!"

His gaze jumped to her. "I didn't even think to ask if you were allergic."

Seeing the worry crease his forehead, she smiled and shook her head. "Nope, I adore cats!"

She bent to a squat and held out her hand. Immediately, three of the cats came to her, sniffing her hand before allowing her to pet them. The smaller cat stayed back, still swirling around Bryce's legs.

"What are their names?"

"Pumpkin for that guy," he said, dipping his head toward the large orange cat. "Mixer for the tabby cat over there. Creamsicle for the orange and white cat, but he usually just gets called Sickle."

Still squatting, she twisted her neck and looked up at him, her brow furrowed. "Interesting names." She laughed. "And very original." Inclining her head toward the black cat, still hovering by his legs, she asked, "And that one has to be Blackie or Midnight, right?"

He chuckled and shook his head. "Uh… no, this one is Princess."

She wobbled while still in her squat, barely managing to keep from landing on her ass in the middle of his foyer. "Princess? You've got a Pumpkin, Mixer, and Sickle for your boy cats, obviously based on their coloring. But Princess?"

He reached his hand down, and Joanne eagerly allowed him to help her to her feet. "As the only female, her personality was so different right from the beginning. And it didn't take long to figure out that she was absolutely a little princess."

Her heart melted at his explanation and seeing the gentle way he petted each one. "I love cats. This must be how you charm all the women you bring here." As soon as the words left her mouth, she realized they sounded like she was fishing for information. Giving her head a little shake, she winced. "That's not what I meant—"

"I don't bring women here."

She stood, barely breathing as their gazes never wavered. "Oh…" she finally said, unable to think of anything else to say while being secretly thrilled.

The cats continued to meow loudly, still swirling around their legs, and he laughed. "Right now, they're pretty demanding. How about I show you the kitchen, and I'm sure they'll lead the way."

The cats held their tails high as they led the way down the short hall ending in the eat-in kitchen. The living room spread across the entire front of the house, and a large kitchen with room for a table was directly behind.

He quickly fed the cats with an obviously practiced hand, placing their food dishes on the floor.

While the cats ate, she looked out the sliding glass door and realized the house was U-shaped, with wings going back on each side and a stone patio courtyard directly out from the kitchen.

"This is amazing! I've never been in a U-shaped house before."

"It was built to be a duplex years ago. Each side was a two-bedroom house and was a mirror image of the other. But the couple I bought it from had knocked out a few walls and turned it into one house. So in the front, the living room is so large and wide because it used to be two, same for back here. They kept one large kitchen and turned the other duplex's kitchen into an informal dining room. He inclined his head toward the right and said, "There are two bedrooms with a bathroom between on that side. And on the other side, they created a larger owner's bedroom with an en suite bathroom and a smaller bedroom that could be an office, if needed."

She really wanted a tour, but just then, her stomach growled, and she hoped he hadn't noticed. But the grin on his face indicated she wasn't so lucky.

"If you give me a few minutes to change clothes, we'll have dinner."

She wondered what he was serving since they hadn't stopped on the way home. True to his word, he was back in just a couple of minutes, a T-shirt stretched across his chest and arms and a pair of jeans. Loving the casual look, she asked, "Is there anything I can do to help?"

"I still want to take you out to dinner sometime soon, but for tonight, I'll heat something quick so we can focus on us as we get to know each other."

Her smile widened, and she nodded. "Sounds good to me."

He opened the freezer and pulled out a dish before taking it to the microwave and popping it in. Turning back to the refrigerator, he pulled out the fixings for a salad. Looking over his shoulder, he invited, "Have a seat at the counter." He winced, then added, "I'm afraid I only have water or beer to offer you to drink."

"Beer is good." She sat on one of the barstools at the counter, eager to watch him in his natural element. It dawned on her that usually, first dates occurred out somewhere. But here, Bryce was comfortable as he quickly chopped vegetables for a salad. The four cats sat in the middle of the floor as they washed their paws and faces. Her heart warmed as he relaxed, and she really liked what she saw.

Soon, he plated a chicken, cheese, broccoli, and rice casserole. With the salad and slices of chocolate cake for dessert, she was wide-eyed at the spread he'd laid out.

"Before you ask—no, I didn't make the casserole. Some American Legion Auxiliary women will bring food to the local law enforcement facilities. As one of the single men, it just so happens that I get to snag a few for my freezer."

She took a bite and groaned as her eyes rolled back. "This is really good! I love to cook, and I'm all about easy, comfort food." Glancing at his counter, she grinned. She stood and grabbed a bag of potato chips, then turned, and asked, "Do you mind?"

"No, not at all."

She felt certain that he wasn't expecting her addition to the recipe. Crushing some of the potato chips over the top, she lifted a brow toward him. Gaining his nod, she did the same over his plate.

The added crunch had both of them groaning again. "I know that might seem silly, but my grandmother not only had the best cookie recipe but she indulged in the potato chip crunch on some of my favorite foods. Not healthy, but oh, so good!"

"Damn, you're right!" He wiped his mouth and grinned. "I can cook if I have to, but I confess that sometimes when I come home from work, especially if it's been a long, busy day, it's nice to grab a home-cooked meal that I didn't have to fix. Other than that, I'll hit up some of the restaurants for takeout."

"You would think that since I've been around the Virginia Marine Police twice in one week, I would know more about what you do. But I confess, I'm woefully ignorant about your job."

"It's law enforcement on the water," he began. "We're the largest division of the Virginia Marine resources commission. We do search and rescue, ensure people follow boating safety laws, respond to emergencies on the water, and investigate boating, accidents, and criminal activity. The duties can change depending on where you are. Those near Norfolk can provide counterterrorism patrols to the shipyards. We monitor our area of the Chesapeake Bay in the same way."

Fascinated, she took a sip of beer as she listened. "I am so impressed, Bryce. I had no idea. I can imagine that for you, every day is a little different."

"Absolutely. Some days, it feels like all I do is fix boats, check for recreational fishing licenses, or inspect commercial fishermen for compliance. Another day, we may have to deal with pulling people out of the water from boating accidents."

"I remember reading about a woman and a man who went over the bridge a couple of months ago."

He was already nodding, and she leaned forward with interest.

"Believe it or not, that woman, Ivy, is now engaged to the officer who pulled her from the water. Actually, Ivy and Andy knew each other in high school, but that incident on the bridge when she saved a baby was what got them together."

"You're kidding!"

He smiled and shook his head. "Honest to God."

Magnetically drawn to the curve of his lips, she unabashedly stared, smiling in return as her heart beat faster. The longer she was around him, the more his smiles appeared authentic—genuine reflections of his happiness. And as the hours passed quickly with laughter and stolen glances, she had more fun with him than on any previous date she'd had. Perhaps, for the first time, she was dancing on the edge of something truly special. *A girl can hope!*

12

When Bryce confessed to Joanne that he'd never had any women in this house, it was the truth. Granted, he'd only lived in this house for a few months, and after Allison, he'd vowed to be careful who he invited. The last thing he wanted was someone to start treating his house like their place when that wasn't what he felt. Inviting Joanne after only a few hours to get to know each other was a bold leap. But everything he learned about her, the intimate details and quirks, had already set her apart, placing her miles ahead of any past flings or fleeting attractions.

She radiated genuineness and generosity. Her laughter was infectious, and her descriptive tales gave life to her stories. While he'd certainly heard about how she met Jose, he'd only been given the bare bones of what happened. But hearing it from Joanne, the tale was filled with emotion, imagining Jose's scowling irritation with his mom and Joanne's red-faced embarrassment.

But even in the retelling, it was easy to see that she greatly understood human nature.

With their meal devoured and the dishes placed in the dishwasher, he wanted to prolong their evening. "How would you like another beer and sit outside to continue to enjoy the evening?" The storm that had been expected had veered north, and the sky was clear for now.

"I'd love it," she said, her voice soft. She rinsed their empties, and he tossed them into the recycle bin before grabbing two more from the refrigerator.

He guided her through the sliding glass door that opened up to a stone patio of the courtyard. The unique U-shaped design of the house flanked them on three sides, cocooning them with privacy. And as they sank into the cushioned Adirondack chairs, they enjoyed an unobstructed panorama of twinkling stars.

"This is so nice," she whispered. "It's like our own little world here."

"It's one of the reasons I chose this place. It's great for having friends over, but when I want to be alone, it's the perfect oasis." He rolled his head to the side and held her gaze. "Your house is nice, too."

She offered a delicate shrug. "My place is more of a little cottage. It's a rental. The price is right, and the space is fine for now." She twirled her forefinger in a circle and added, "This place, on the other hand, seems like it would be perfect for a family."

"Yeah, the couple that had the duplex turned into one larger home had planned on raising a family here."

"I'm curious, though. It seems a little large for one

person. Was that a concern when you bought it? Or did you see it as a good investment?"

He was quiet for a moment, thinking of his answer. Her question may have been simple, but if he had told the truth, his answer would have been complex. And revealing.

He stared at her face, seeing the gentle curiosity in her gaze, and wondered how much to divulge. Essentially, they were on their first date. And while he didn't usually talk about his family, he felt the desire to share. "My parents were never together."

Seeing her blink, she filled her eyes with confusion.

"God, that came out wrong," he muttered. "What I mean is that they weren't anything more than a teenage hookup."

Joanne's touch on his arm was gentle, but she radiated empathy. Her fingers offered a soothing presence. "Oh, Bryce," she began with a soft tone. "You don't have to talk about this. I should never have asked such a personal question."

His gaze shifted to where her hand lay, and he felt anchored by the connection. "It's alright. It's not like it's a big secret." His first statement was genuine, but his second statement held a veil of untruth. While his closest friends were privy to a few tidbits about his background, he seldom allowed anyone to know his story. He had no reason to keep it private, but it also wasn't something that normally came up in conversation.

Yet, with Joanne, the answer to her innocent question about the size of his house was ultimately tied to his past. And while her curiosity wasn't invasive, he wanted to share a part of his past.

"My parents met in high school. I can't even say that they were really a high school romance, but more like a high school hookup. Mom got pregnant with me when she was sixteen. She dropped out of school but finished getting her diploma at a night school that catered to pregnant teenagers. I know that nowadays it's not a big deal, but the school preferred not to have pregnant teenagers roaming the halls." He shook his head but was surprised at the outburst from Joanne.

"That's so ridiculous! They let the father stay in school but make it so uncomfortable that the mother had to have a separate program just to get a high school diploma!"

He chuckled at her vehemence and nodded, completely agreeing. "Anyway, my parents didn't stay together. The politest way to put it is that I was a surprise pregnancy. The reality is that it was very much an unwanted pregnancy. My dad wanted her to get an abortion, and my mom refused. My grandparents let her live at home until she got her diploma, but then they wanted her to get a job. She had just turned seventeen when I was born, but it wasn't easy. My dad halfheartedly tried to help out some, but they hadn't been dating steadily when I was conceived. I think it broke Mom's heart, but she knew that he would never be faithful and never be husband material, much less dad material. My grandparents helped out as much as they could, but they were older when they had my mom and had just retired. My granddad died when I was about three, and my grandma died a couple of years later. Mom had to sell their house just to cover their medical and funeral bills. Honestly, it was really my aunt and uncle that raised me."

Joanne had seamlessly adjusted her position so that her body was facing toward him. She tilted gracefully against the wide, flat arm of the chair nearest to him. A deep desire stirred within him, wishing they were still inside, nestled on the cozy sofa without the interference of furniture between them.

Suddenly, as though his thoughts had the power to conjure up the weather, clouds moved in and obscured the stars, and the rumble of thunder sounded in the distance. "We better go in," he murmured, rising and extending his hand with an urgency born from more than just the impending rain. He wanted every opportunity to touch her, even if it was just the mere brush of their fingertips. Her acceptance was evident as she eagerly reached out each time and allowed his fingers to wrap around hers.

The wind increased, urging them back into the kitchen. With their hands still entwined, he led her into the large living room and over to the plush, deep, cushioned, sectional sofa that curved in one corner, angled toward the wide-screen TV. He'd hosted a few game-day parties in this room with his friends, but never anyone he wanted to impress more than Joanne. His nerves eased when he noted that when they settled, she oriented herself to maintain their proximity.

The cats quickly jumped up to make themselves comfortable among the humans. Pumpkin and Sickle curled up on the ottoman, and Mixer found a place on the back of the sofa, curled up in the corner. Princess waited, then snuggled up next to Bryce's thigh.

Joanne laughed at the menagerie and turned her attention back to him. "You were going to tell me more about your aunt and uncle?" Her voice held a tinge of curiosity, bringing him back to the story he had been divulging.

A nostalgic smile tugged at his lips as memories moved through his mind. "Mom had an older brother about ten years older than her. My uncle Bernie and his wife, Debbie, weren't able to have kids, but they had a nice house, so Mom and I moved in with them."

"How old were you then?"

"I started first grade living at their house, so I must've been about six. It was great because they had a big yard and lived in a neighborhood where there were other kids my age. Mom was about twenty-four but never really had a chance to be a young woman without a baby to lug around. At the time, I didn't know what was going on. I just knew that Aunt Debbie made sure I had a bath at night, and Uncle Bernie helped me with my homework."

His voice faded as darker memories threatened to shift forward. Joanne must have sensed the change because her hand began to gently smooth over his arm. Grounded by her meaningful touch, he held her gaze and felt some weight lift off his chest. "When I was eight, my mom had been out partying with someone, and they were in a car accident. The guy she was with was drunk, and they ran off the road. My mom was killed, and he was paralyzed."

Joanne's sharp intake of breath marked her shock, and she shifted closer on the sofa. He wrapped his arm around her shoulder as she leaned closer, bridging the gap between them. Her gaze stayed on him, and he delved deeply to see what emotions passed through her eyes. There was undeniable sadness swirling, yet it lacked the sting of pity. There was genuine concern, but it was devoid of the morbid curiosity he'd encountered when others found out about his family. She leaned so close that her hands landed on his thigh, her fingers squeezing slightly. It was a gesture of pure consolation, a balm he gratefully accepted.

"As next of kin, Bernie and Debbie applied for and received custody of me. From the time I was eight, although you could count from when I was much younger than that, they were my parents."

"They sound amazing," she declared. "Are they still…?"

"Aunt Debbie is," he answered without her having to finish her question. "Uncle Bernie died not too long after I joined the Navy. He ran a boat mechanic shop in Maryland, and I hung out there every day after school and on weekends. I wanted to graduate from high school, get some world experience, which I decided to do in the Navy, and then come back and work for him. But I never got the chance. He died before my first year in the Navy was over. I told Debbie that I would get out and come home to be with her, but she insisted I serve out my enlistment."

"Are you still close with her?"

Laughing, he nodded. His hand drifted to her shoulder, his fingers gliding through the ends of her hair. At that moment, he wanted nothing more than to bury his face in her neck, smelling her sweet lilac scent and feeling her silky hair against his skin. "Oh yeah. We talk almost every week. I ended up doing two tours in the Navy, and during that time, she sold the business, which made sense. She had asked me if I wanted to take it up, but I honestly couldn't imagine doing the job without Bernie around."

"Did she ever remarry?"

"No. At first, I was a selfish prick, probably secretly putting out the juju vibes she wouldn't even date. Of course, now, I'd love for her to find someone. I know Bernie would want her to be happy."

"You implied that your story was tied into this house that you bought," she gently reminded.

So mesmerized by staring into her face, he'd forgotten what his original explanation had indicated. "Oh yeah." He dragged his attention away from her momentarily and cast his gaze around the room. "I don't know when I'll get married and have kids, but I hope that's part of my future. With the right person, of course. And I wasn't willing to wait to find a place I could claim as my own. My house. My yard. My sanctuary. All ready for when that future walks through the door."

The words made him vulnerable, and he swallowed deeply, turning his gaze back to her. So far, she'd proven to be an exceptional listener, understanding and offering comfort. But he had no idea what her honest reaction might be.

"I think that's wonderful, Bryce, what you've done with your life. Accepting the love that came from others and not becoming bitter about what you didn't have."

"Never knew my dad, and he's never made an attempt to contact me. I had Grandpa and Bernie... two dads who were the best men I've known. Both showed me what a family and true home should look like."

"And your mom? Your memories of her?"

"I remember I thought she was beautiful. She would sing to me, laugh with me, and play around with me. Looking back, I understand that I was probably more of a little brother to her that she loved, happy to leave the parenting to my grandparents, Bernie, and Debbie. I'm not resentful. It's just the family I had. But it's taught me about the kind of family I want."

Inhaling deeply, he knew their conversation had moved to a place he'd never been before and probably should have been terrified at the idea that he'd laid such heavy onto Joanne during their first date. But it was too late to take anything back now, and he found that he didn't want to.

By now, they had both inched closer, allowing his arm to curl around her shoulders, and her body leaned against his. Her face was right in front of his eyes, making it easy to see the dash of pale freckles across her cheeks and the way her blue eyes had a ring of indigo. Her lips were plump and moist, and he couldn't wait to find out if she tasted as good as she looked. But he hesitated. As much as he wanted to claim her mouth, he needed to know she was on the same page.

Her gaze held intensity as she stared at him, then she leaned forward and whispered, "I already know you're the kind of man who won't try to take what might not be yours. No games. I'll be up front." Her tongue darted out to swipe over her bottom lip, and her sweet breath washed over his face. "I'd really like to kiss you."

His lips curved, thrilled that they were on the same page, but more than that, ecstatic that she didn't hold back.

The arm around her shoulders tightened, pulling her closer and erasing the space between them. He angled his head ever so slightly, then brought their faces together, his lips moving over her slightly before sealing his mouth to her. He'd planned on taking it slow... sweet kisses, small nibbles, easy movements. But he hadn't expected that the little gasp from her lips would shoot straight to his cock. Or the way she melted into his embrace. Or the way her breasts pressed against his chest.

He lifted his head, stared into the abyss of her eyes, and fought to catch his breath like he'd run a marathon. "I... I planned on slow..." he managed to say, his gaze never leaving hers.

She dropped her gaze to his mouth, ran her tongue over her lips, then said, "I don't want slow." Her hands slid from his arms to the back of his head as she straddled his lap and pulled him closer.

His tongue plunged into her warm mouth, tasting everything unique and tantalizing all at once. With one hand, he cupped the back of her head to keep their noses from smashing together as he maximized the angle, wanting her mouth against his. His other hand slid to her ass, then up under her shirt to skim his fingers along the warm, soft skin of her back.

Her fingers held his shoulders, the grip firm as though she was afraid she might fall. As his tongue drifted and explored every nook, her tongue dragged over his, creating a velvet friction that made his already straining cock threaten against his zipper.

Determined not to allow himself to be carried away, he continued to direct the kiss with his mouth and hands. Finally, he dragged his lips away from hers, their ragged breathing pouring between them.

"Joanne," he groaned, leaning forward to rest his forehead against hers.

"Yeah?" she answered, her voice deep and needy.

"I didn't invite you over here to have sex." Watching her blink slowly, he hastened to add, "Not that I don't want to because you can probably feel how much I do." He was sure as tightly as she was pressed against him, she would have no trouble recognizing his erection, but just to make his point, he pressed his hips upward slightly, and the doubt in her eyes rolled into lust.

"It's important for you to know that you've been on my mind since I first laid eyes on you. But I want to do this right. We've spent some time digging into our past. I want to spend some time with you in the present. I don't want to be another one of your regrets."

13

I don't want to be another one of your regrets.

Of all the things Bryce could have said to Joanne, those words struck home straight to her heart. As hot and bothered as she was from just grinding herself on him and their kiss, she knew she would be putty in his hands if they had sex. If he wanted, she would easily sleep with him, but the fact that he cared enough about her not to want to be a regret meant everything.

Dragging in a deep breath through her nose with her lips pressed together to keep from begging him for more, she nodded slowly. Still keeping her hands on his shoulders, her tight grip loosened as her fingers relaxed. She shifted backward, still straddling his thighs but putting some distance between her crotch and his groin. Finally, letting the air out slowly, she glided her hands to his stubble-covered jaws and traced his cheeks with her thumbs. "As much as I wanted to ride you into the sunset, you were right to slow us down. Because while I cannot imagine that having sex with you would ever be a regret, it's not worth the chance."

His gaze penetrated deeply into her eyes. "You don't hate me?"

A snort slipped out, and she rolled her eyes. "Well, my body is going through the Bryce-happy-dance withdrawal, but no, I don't hate you."

His brows lifted with confusion. "The Bryce-happy-dance?"

"Come on, you know what I mean. You're built, you're gorgeous, you kiss like it's what you really want to do and not just to placate me. And my body is primed and ready for anything and everything."

He blinked slowly, eyes widening, and she winced at the verbal flood. "Sorry, that was—"

"Fucking fantastic," he rushed, his grin widening. Her body moved as he shook with laughter.

"It was too much, too soon, and made me sound desperate."

Shaking his head, he palmed her cheek. "It was great. Seriously, Joanne. What guy wouldn't want to hear that?" They stared for a moment, neither speaking. Finally, he said, "But there's something in there that I don't understand." Before she could ask, he said, "About kissing."

"Oh, that…" she muttered, dropping her gaze away from his intense perusal.

With his thumb, he applied just enough pressure on her chin to lift her head so that her eyes were back on him.

Shrugging, she said, "A lot of guys will want to kiss just to… um… move things along." Seeing his lifted brows, she continued. "Not like they really want to kiss someone or show affection, but as though they assume it's what the woman wants before sex. You didn't do that. It felt like you really wanted to kiss me."

"I did. I do," he mumbled against her lips as he kissed her again. This time, she swept her tongue over his, exploring his taste, memorizing each nuance.

Pulling away, she sighed. "But you're right. I don't want to be one of your regrets either."

Even though she didn't want to leave his lap, she felt sure his cock could do with a respite. She was suffering from the female version of blue balls and could only imagine that he had a raging case of the real thing.

As she swung one leg over, he held her waist and guided her gently until she sat next to him. Suddenly unsure, she glanced to the side. "I suppose this is where we end the evening."

"Please don't go on my account."

Her gaze jumped up to his, her brow furrowing slightly.

"The evening is still young. We could watch a movie, drink another beer, listen to music, and keep talking. There's a lot of things we could do because I really don't want you to leave now."

The air rushed from her lungs, and she nodded in relief. "A movie sounds great. I'm not fussy, so pick anything you want. Do you mind if I get a glass of water?"

"While I look for a movie, grab anything you want for yourself. I've got filtered water in the refrigerator. A glass for me would also be great."

She stood quickly with a swift motion, desperately hoping he didn't notice the slight waver as she straightened. The small chuckle rumbling in his chest indicated that he'd seen her almost stumble but was kind enough to let it pass. She dashed into his kitchen while he searched for a movie, retrieved the water pitcher from the refrigerator, and poured two glasses of chilled water.

Reentering the living room, she was suddenly unsure where she should sit. The sofa was wide and deep and could easily double as a bed. Uncertain if she should sit beside him, maintaining a distance or nestle closer to him.

Pressing up against him might look like she was trying to make him regret his decision for them to slow down. Throwing caution to the wind, she opted to sit close. As she glanced over, she noted his finger hovering over the remote. "What did you choose?"

"I almost settled on an epic tale but realized it might seem stupid to you."

She tilted her head, curiosity filling her. It really didn't matter what movie he chose since she figured she would be too aware of his proximity to even pay attention. "Honestly, Bryce, you can put on whatever you want."

Seeming to make up his mind, he flashed a grin, reclined against the cushions, and clicked on the remote. A moment later, an old classic filled the screen. As a delighted squeal emitted, she could feel his gaze staring at the side of her head. Turning, she grinned. "This is perfect."

He held his glass with one hand, and the other arm curled naturally around her shoulders, pulling her close. "Yeah, it is."

They watched the movie, their bodies slowly relaxing into the deep cushions. Amid the scenes, she discovered he'd read the books years ago. They chatted enthusiastically about scenes in the books that had been left out of the movie version and shared favorite passages. As the moonlight filtered through the front blinds, her eyes began to close, and she struggled to stay awake, not wanting the date to end.

This was the best date she could ever remember, including her early days with Chad. In fact, he was nothing more than a distant memory, settled into the box of regrets she kept in the back of her mind. Her eyes continued to grow heavy, and she knew she needed to head home. But with her body molded against his and their legs stretched out onto the ottoman, the last thought she remembered having was, *I'll just rest for a moment in his arms.*

One of the cats was at his side, two others were at their feet, and one slept on the back of the sofa. As the movie progressed, Joanne's body grew increasingly heavy as the gentle pull of gravity drew her closer to Bryce's sturdy embrace. He deftly stretched out his free hand, snagged the remote, and changed to a channel with soft music. Lowering the volume, he let the soft tones create an ambiance of serenity. The kitchen's illumination barely reached the living room, allowing them to be cloaked in shadows. He shifted delicately so her back was straight, not wanting her to wake with a stiff neck.

He could have woken her to suggest she head home and plan their next date. But instead, finding their position too precious to disrupt, he closed his eyes as she snuggled against his side with her head on his shoulder. Unsure if he would be able to sleep, he didn't care. He'd just spent the evening with a beautiful woman who had turned out to be funny, interesting, and oh, so sexy. It was the best date he'd ever had, and he didn't want their time together to end.

Moved by instinct, he traced soothing patterns up and down her back, loving the feel of her in his arms. And peaceful sleep came.

"Umph!" he grunted as something hard landed on his gut, causing him to jerk. Blinking his eyes open, he was surprised to see the room was lighter from the sunlight coming through the blinds. And he wasn't in his bed.

"Sorry," a mumbled sound came from his side.

Jerking his head, he spied a blinking, hair-tangled Joanne with a sleep crinkle running along her cheek. Her hand had landed on his stomach as she pushed herself up. He couldn't believe that despite his sofa feeling as comfortable as a bed, he'd fallen asleep there.

Or that he'd slept with Joanne pressed against his side even though having her there felt right.

"Oh God, I can't believe I fell asleep!" she said, one hand still resting on his stomach as the other pushed her hair from her face. "What time is it?"

They sat up together, and he looked at the time on the TV. "Six o'clock."

"Oh God. I've got to get home so I can shower before work," she groaned, climbing over him.

His arms snapped around her and pulled her close. "Kiss first."

"I have morning breath!"

"Don't care," he muttered against her lips. Taking the kiss deep, he remembered what she said last night about kissing. She was right on more than one account. Sometimes kissing was just a precursor to sex, but with her, it was just because he wanted to kiss her.

Finally separating, he grinned and said, "Now, that's the best way to wake up."

She laughed as she rose from the sofa and looked around before leaning over to grab her shoes and purse. She plopped back down next to him as she slid her shoes on. Then she looked around more before snagging her phone from the coffee table.

He leaped to his feet as she stood and placed his hands on her shoulders. "Be careful going home. I didn't mean to keep you here all night, but I'm glad to have spent time with you. When can I see you again?"

She smiled, her eyes twinkling. "No bullshit with you, is there?"

"No," he agreed, tucking a strand of hair behind her

ear. "Not ever, but especially not when there's someone I want to spend time with and get to know better. And unless you have an objection, I don't want to waste any time. So the sooner I can see you, the better it'll be."

"My schedule is easy." She shrugged. "I work Monday through Friday, no weekends unless there's a special event at the college. Basically, my evenings and weekends are always free."

"Mine involves some weekend shifts, and sometimes I'm on call during the night. I'll text you my schedule for the next few weeks."

She smiled and nodded. "I hate to leave, but I've really got to run. You can check your schedule and let me know when you'd like to see me again—"

"Tonight?"

Her chin jerked down, and her eyes widened with surprise, but her smile gave him hope.

"I get off at four," she said. Glancing over her shoulder, she said, "If we need to be here for the cats, I can bring what we need and fix dinner here."

"You don't have to do that—"

"I want to," she shot back. Before he had a chance to protest, she shook her head. "I like to cook, Bryce. Cooking for one isn't a lot of fun, so I usually save it for when friends come over or my mom and I are together. Cooking for you in a kitchen that isn't minuscule? Perfect."

He wrapped his arms around her as they stood by his front door. "Can't argue with that." Bending, he kissed her deeply. When they finally separated, he walked her to her car and watched her pull out of his driveway.

Once he was back in his house, the four cats swirled around his legs while meowing as though he needed reminding they wanted to be fed. Grinning, he said, "Come on, you all. Let's get breakfast to celebrate the best date ever."

14

Joanne stood on the worn wooden dock, waiting to climb aboard the ferry going to Tangier Island. Trying not to let the fact that she wasn't on Saul's boat dampen her mood, she reminded herself that he was recovering at home. Several other ferrymen shouldered the extra passenger loads, promising to give a tenth of their sales to Saul and his wife to help with medical costs until he could return. She closed her eyes and tilted her face skyward, allowing the sun to offer a respite against the nip in the air.

As she stood on the dock, her mind cast back over the changes in her life since that last fateful ferry ride. Since meeting Bryce, their moments together had woven into days of memories and getting to know each other. She loved his large kitchen and made him dinner at his place for their second date. She found they had even more to talk about, therefore dispelling the wonder if their attraction was just a flash. He'd invited her to the youth ball game to watch him coach on Saturday morning. Her mother was working one of the Auxilliary bakesale booths, and she wasn't ready for her to know she was seeing someone. She'd only stayed long enough to see him in action but was moved by the dedication and rapport he exhibited with the kids, parents, and friends who were also coaching.

As she'd scanned the bleachers that day, she was relieved not to spot Allison, hoping the other woman had finally accepted the message that Bryce wasn't interested. But while looking over the stands, she'd also seen Melanie boisterously wave while grinning at her, and she blushed, certain that Bryce had told Jose that they were starting to see each other. Melanie sat with a huge group of women who Joanne recognized from the few American Legion Auxiliary meetings she'd attended with her mom.

She'd winced, hoping that her friend wasn't telling others. She yearned for her and Bryce to stay in their bubble a little longer. It wasn't that she wasn't proud or excited, but starting a new relationship had enough pressure without everyone's scrutiny of them.

Melanie had offered a reassuring smile followed by a subtle shake of her head, conveying a silent promise—their secret was safe.

She'd only had a chance to see Bryce from afar, but he'd offered a chin lift and smile toward her, causing her stomach to flutter and her heart to melt.

He had duty on Sunday, so she'd visited with her mom. But she and Bryce managed to squeeze in dinner the other evenings. She was ready to jump him, but he'd set a slow and deliberate pace each time. It was evident by his actions that his interest was genuine. She wasn't averse to the idea of a casual fling, but her past experiences had been unfulfilling. She thought her sex life with Chad had been good, but realized what she had with Chad wasn't close to the fireworks she felt from just making out with Bryce.

She boarded his boat at the sound of the ferryman's call, then moved toward the front to find a seat. This boat held about twenty people and looked like it would be close to being filled.

"Is this seat taken?"

She jumped slightly as her eyes snapped open to see a man standing close by, his head inclined to the empty seat next to her. "No, please, feel free to sit there."

He settled in next to her, and she offered the type of smile you gave when you felt the need to be pleasant, even if the person was a stranger.

"Is this your first time over to the island?" he asked.

"No. I come over for business fairly often." He nodded politely, then they both looked away as many of the other seats filled.

Suddenly, she thought of Brian from her last trip. So much had happened that she hadn't given him another thought. *I still have the money in my wallet.*

Most of the other ferry guests appeared to be tourists, but she waved at one of the visiting nurses she often saw on the ferry. She was sitting across from her.

"It feels weird, doesn't it?" the other woman said. "I'm so used to Saul."

Joanne nodded, but when the engines started, it

drowned out her ability to converse with anyone who wasn't right beside her.

"I hadn't thought about that, but I guess you see some of the same people over and over, don't you?" the man sitting next to her said.

"That's true. Most of the islanders have to come over to the shore occasionally for various reasons, and then there are those of us that go over regularly for work."

"It's my understanding that I need to pay close attention to the ferry schedule."

"That's right because most of them only make a trip over and back each day. There are multiple ferries, so you could probably catch another one if you missed this one. But you definitely will want to make sure you don't lose track of time on the island."

"They're not exactly overrun with hotel vacancies, are they?" He chuckled.

"No. In fact, last week, there was a man I met going over, but he didn't make the ferry coming back. Of course, that meant he missed the terror of our captain having a heart attack."

"I heard about that! You were on that boat?"

"Yes, I was. But the Coast Guard and police came and took care of the captain and the rest of us. I guess maybe it was good that the other passenger missed that ferry. I'm sure he just caught another one."

"I'm Matthew, by the way."

"Joanne," she said.

The man pulled out his phone and was soon engrossed in texting someone. Joanne was relieved, too tired to make conversation with a stranger after having sat up so late with Bryce. In fact, thinking about Bryce was all she really wanted to do, anyway.

She finished at the school earlier than she anticipated and ran by the diner to grab a sandwich before going back to the dock to wait on the ferry.

Eating alone, she sat at the counter to avoid taking up table space. It was a counter that faced one of the windows, so she had a view of the beautiful day while enjoying her sandwich. Most people walked, rode a bike or scooter, or drove a golf cart on the island, and she found the traffic moving past the window to be fascinating.

"Hey, Joanne!"

Turning toward the call of her name, she smiled at one of the servers.

"Hey, Carolyn."

"Who was that handsome man you were with last week? I had just come on duty and saw the two of you sitting together."

"Oh, he's no one special. I just met him on the ferry."

"Were you on Saul's ferry?" Carolyn asked, her eyes widening.

"Yes." They chatted for several minutes about Saul before Carolyn needed to hustle away to serve other patrons. As Joanne was paying, she asked, "By the way, have you seen the man who I was with? Has he been back in?"

"Not on my shifts, and I'm here almost every day." Carolyn looked behind Joanne and laughed. " You have the magic touch, lady. That man has been standing on the sidewalk, staring in for several minutes, and I swear he's looking at you."

Joanne twisted her head around to see who Carolyn was talking about and spied Matthew. Offering an awkward wave, he waved in return before walking down the street toward the harbor.

"Don't tell me that's somebody else you met coming across on the ferry today!"

Rolling her eyes, Joanne said, "That's exactly what happened. Believe me, there's nothing there other than just a friendly person."

"Well, he seems interested."

"Maybe, but I'm not." Carolyn's eyes grew large, and she gasped, "You're seeing someone? Someone your mother didn't set you up with?"

Joanne rolled her eyes again at the reference to her mom's blind date attempts and nodded. "Yes, I am. He works for the Virginia Marine Police."

"Then he can come to save you if you need help. Sounds delicious!"

Carolyn had to check on her other patrons and said goodbye, which was fine with Joanne. She pulled out her card to pay and noticed the money still in her wallet from the last time she was here with Brian. She started to put the whole amount in the tip jar but decided to hold on to it for another week in case she ran into him again.

Making it to the harbor with plenty of time, she spied Matthew sitting on one of the wooden benches.

Standing nearby, she said, "I see you heeded the advice of not missing the ferry going back to the shore."

He looked up and smiled. "Your advice was well taken. I made sure my business was finished and even had a little time to walk around the island." He blushed slightly and added, "I hope you don't think I was stalking you. I was walking past the diner and thought I recognized you sitting there. I certainly didn't mean to make you uncomfortable."

She waved her hand dismissively and shook her head. "Don't worry about it. If you keep visiting the island regularly, you'll see many people repeatedly. But if you ever want a decent meal, that's the place to go."

"Good to know. Thanks for the recommendation."

They both turned at the sound of a boat horn and made their way to the ferry. It was a full boat going back, and as it turned out, she and Matthew were not seated close to each other. That was fine, as she yawned, knowing that making conversation would be too taxing. Closing her eyes, she let the boat's movement lull her as her thoughts wandered to Bryce.

Under the cloudless, blue skies over the bay, Bryce, Jared, and Andy engaged in routine checks of fishing licenses. They spent extra time chatting with some of the local fishermen who wore their sun-beaten faces with pride. He reveled in this aspect of his job, not feeling that it was beneath him to be active in something that, to some, might appear mundane. When he was younger, his uncle knew all the fishermen in their area, getting to know the ones who brought their boats for him to work on. Bernie taught Bryce that it was as important to understand the owner as it was to understand the vessel.

"These are the people who go out every day, in all kinds of weather, to bring in the food from the sea, just like the farmers in the field. Their work is vital to the economy and vital to the ecosystem. It's sure as fuck vital to our business."

Just as they were about to wrap up with the last fisherman and ready to return to the station, the dispatcher radioed. Callan started the engine and responded with their location and ETA. Looking at the others with a serious expression, he said, "Some teenagers were fishing just north of us. Seems they caught something." He hesitated for a second, then finished. "A body."

"Shit," Bryce muttered, his stomach churning at the news. He hastened into the wheelhouse, grabbing the tether lines and ensuring he had the necessary equipment. Although the bay didn't frequently serve up such macabre discoveries, it wasn't as uncommon as many people would think. The distressing element was that teenagers stumbled upon the chilling occurrence.

In a matter of minutes, they reached the designated inlet. Another VMP vessel carrying Joseph, Ryan, and Jose was also on its way. The dispatcher radioed that the North Heron Deputies would join them shortly, arriving at the closest land location.

Surveying the area, Bryce saw a small rowboat. Inside, two teenage boys sat, visibly shaken. The pallor on one boy's face had taken on a greenish hue, and Bryce assumed that if he'd seen the body in the water, the young man had probably lost his lunch. The other boy appeared only marginally better, managing to keep his composure but held terror in his eyes.

"We need to have these boys checked out," he called out to Callan. The other officer nodded and said, "Hate like hell for them to have discovered something like this."

Coming close, he shouted out, "Where is the location?"

The less-green boy pointed at the embankment. "We almost didn't see him, sir. We were just heading out in the bay when we noticed something over on the side. As soon as we got close, we could tell it was a body—"

The other boy leaned over and retched again. Bryce called, "We're going to tether your boat to our vessel and bring you aboard."

He looked up to see several deputies arriving by land and pointed at where the body was entangled in some of the tree limbs bending low over the water. They began securing the area as a possible crime scene.

"We gotta stop meeting like this," someone shouted from the side.

Bryce looked over at Sam Shackley, one of North Heron's detectives. "Tell me about it," he jerked his head toward the boys still sitting in their boat as it was being secured.

"We've got the boys here. Need to check out the one that became sick to make sure he's not dehydrated. Andy will have the station call their parents."

The scene soon buzzed with activity, and Andy shepherded the boys to the other side of the vessel, keeping them shielded from the grim sight. Bryce leaned over the edge, his attention riveted to the approaching detectives.

Sam was close to Bryce's age, but the years of detective experience were etched into his face, making him appear older than he was. "There's no trace of footprints on this side of the embankment and no disturbance at all on the land. He probably wasn't dumped here. From the looks of it, my guess would be that he floated here."

"Looks like he came in with the tide," Bryce said, his sharp gaze noting the area. "The Coast Guard can estimate the tides and currents."

Sam climbed aboard the VMP vessel, directing his attention to the shaken boys. Ryan arrived in the other VMP boat, quickly taking charge of the boys. As the father of teenagers, he had an evident paternal instinct. Bryce had no doubt Ryan felt the boys' anguish and wanted to get them to their parents as soon as possible.

Once Sam had finished with his initial questions, the boys were transferred to Ryan's vessel after their parents had been contacted.

As the scene on the embankment progressed, Bryce's gaze shifted back to the gruesome discovery. Upon Sam's instructions, the deputies gingerly turned the body over. The bloated visage, now distorted by water and time, made it hard to identify, yet it would be mostly skeletal if it had been in the water for longer. As it was, the deceased must have washed up fairly quickly after death.

The body would be transported to the hospital, where the medical examiner would determine the cause of death. The possibilities ranged from an accidental fall from a boat to more sinister foul play. There had been no reports of anyone missing, and the body didn't appear to have been in the water for long before washing up on the shoreline.

"Going by the clothes, I'd say male. And wearing a suit, I'd say he wasn't out fishing," Sam surmised, shaking his head.

"We haven't had any reports of anyone falling over-board," Bryce noted, his brow furrowed.

Sam snapped his notebook closed and placed it in his coat pocket. "We'll know more once the ME completes his evaluation."

They remained at the site, providing support to the sheriff's department even after the body was removed for transport to the hospital's morgue. But with the sun dipping lower and a final nod from Sam as the detectives finished combing the area, the VMP crew knew it was time to head back to the station. With the roar of their engines, they sailed back to the Baytown Harbor, the weight of the day heavy on their shoulders.

Positioning himself at the boat's bow, Bryce shoved his hands deep into his pockets. He easily managed the boat's movements with his legs firmly planted apart. The vast expanse of the clear sky stretched above, and the breeze helped clear his mind as he focused on something much more pleasant. The idea filled him that he could spend another evening with Joanne, sitting outside under the stars.

They had managed to hide their burgeoning relationship from prying eyes. The only people who knew they'd started seeing each other were Jose and Melanie. Joanne hadn't even told her mother, which Bryce knew would have to change soon, or her mother would orchestrate another blind date. Bryce knew Joanne wouldn't be tempted, but he didn't want her mother to waste her time trying to set something up now that he was the one who would have all her dates.

A part of him was ready to shout from the rooftops that he and Joanne were together, but they jointly decided it was best to start slowly and quietly. He'd never been a big fan of a public spotlight shining on his private life, and he wanted to fiercely guard their growing bond as they learned more about each other.

With each passing day, he delved deeper into the layers of Joanne. A smile escaped his lips as he mused over their compatibility. The more he learned about her, the more he liked. Snorting, he shook his head. What he learned about her, he loved. While the adage claimed that opposites might attract, he was a steadfast believer that shared values and interests were the real glue in a relationship. Going out with women who were excessively extroverted and always wanting to be with a lot of people had never resonated with his more introspective nature. But Joanne was different. She liked cooking meals side by side, watching old movies, gazing at stars, and lounging around as they spent time getting to know each other.

Their little bubble of privacy would soon pop, but he was prepared. It might have only been a short time, but Bryce knew he was ready to face the world with her. Lost in his thoughts, as he stood and looked out over the bay, his hand gently rubbed his chest over his heart, and he smiled.

15

Joanne entered her mom's duplex through the front door. Her parents grew up on the Eastern Shore, but after marrying, they'd moved to Portsmouth. After her father died, she and her mother stayed in their home. But once Joanne moved away, her mother sold the home and moved back to the Baytown area. She rented one side of a two-story duplex. The landlord lived next door and would take care of the yard and maintenance. Charlie was a few years older than her mom, and Joanne sometimes wondered if something more than friendship would develop between the two. But, so far, they were just friends.

"Mom!" she called out.

Her mother walked from the kitchen with a smile on her face while wiping her hands on a dish towel. Joanne breathed easier. She knew if her mom had already heard about Bryce, she would not be smiling but would be immediately quizzing her.

"Joanne, sweetheart, I was hoping you would come

by today. I got in from the church meeting and had a nice conversation with Mrs. Hennesy. Her grandson is coming for a visit now that he will soon graduate from law school. I know he's younger than you, but I thought—"

"Mom, stop."

Her mother's mouth stayed open for a couple of seconds, then snapped shut. Her expression was blank, her emotions hidden. Speaking softly, she said, "I'm sorry, Joanne. I know you told me no more blind dates, but it's just so hard to meet someone nowadays. Bars. Nightclubs. They even have all those dating apps, but you don't know anything about those people. At least, this way, you know he has family in the area, and surely, Mrs. Hennessy wouldn't try to get an introduction for her grandson if he was a serial killer!"

She laughed and reached out to grab her mom's hand, giving a little squeeze. "How about a cup of coffee?"

Her mom's face brightened, and she nodded. "Come on back. I've already got a fresh pot ready."

A few minutes later, she sat at the kitchen table across from her mom. "The reason I don't want you to try to fix me up with anyone is because it's not needed. I know you worry about me and want me to find the kind of love you and Dad had."

Her mom's face was no longer blank but held the same sad and dreamy combination whenever they talked about Joanne's dad. Her mom had always said that she wouldn't look for another love when she had the greatest love for so many years. "You're right, sweetheart. I do want you to find the kind of love your dad and I cherished."

Squeezing her mom's hand again, Joanne smiled. "What I need to tell you is that I'm dating someone."

Jerking slightly, her mom narrowed her eyes. "I just saw you a week ago. How on earth did you go from not seeing anyone to seeing someone in a week?"

"It's still new, but we've seen each other almost every day for a while. I just wanted to keep it a secret until I felt like the relationship was more developed. I have no idea what might happen, but we are dating exclusively."

Her mother's brow lifted. "Do I know him?"

"He's a friend of Jose and Melanie. He works for the Virginia Marine Police, and so he knows the other officers, their wives, and even Jose's mom."

Her mom's face brightened considerably at the mention of his employment. "Oh my!" She leaned forward and placed her hand on Joanne's arm. "I know you think I've been terrible at all my attempts at matchmaking." Before Joanne had a chance to respond, her mother lifted her hand while shaking her head. "I should say *all* my terrible attempts at matchmaking since they were all unmitigated failures."

She shook her head and placed her hand over her mother's. "Mom, you and Dad had an amazing relationship and gave me such a wonderful example of what love can be. And believe me when I tell you that that's the kind of relationship I want to have too. And because I truly wanted that kind of love, I was more than willing to go on all those blind dates. Because one of those men might spark something special inside, and it's okay that they didn't. I just wasn't willing to keep going on. I could always tell it wasn't right. And I know what I have with him is something special. Even though we're new, I found what I had searched for. I always told you I'd rather be alone than be with the wrong man. That's still true."

"And you think Bryce is the right man?" her mom asked with a specter of hope in her eyes.

Shrugging, she answered honestly. "I don't really know, Mom. It's too early to say. But I can tell you that I feel more for him during this time than I have for any person I've ever been with." Suddenly, her whole body jerked. "Wait... I didn't mention his name. How did you know—"

Her mom held up her phone, wiggled it back and forth, and cocked one eyebrow.

"Oh God, Mom! Shit! You already knew!"

"Hard to keep many secrets here on the Shore, Joanne."

Tears stung her eyes as she reached out to clutch her mom's hand. "I'm so sorry. I never meant to keep you out of it. I just... I was so nervous. I really like him and hated to give you hope when it might turn out to be nothing special."

"Don't apologize, sweetheart." Her mother's smile wobbled slightly as she looked down at her coffee cup. Taking a deep breath, she lifted her head and held Joanne's gaze. "Moms try to do the right things and make things better for their children. That's easier when kids are little... skinned knees, kissed boo-boos, braiding hair, and buying school supplies. And when your father died, I tried so hard not to fall apart. I didn't want you to take care of me, but I know you made decisions because of me when you went to the community college and then finished college in Virginia Beach to stay near me. And since you've been back, I guess I've just wanted to do whatever I could to help you be happy."

"Mom, you make me happy just by being my mom. And you don't have to try to fix whatever you're afraid Chad broke. Believe me, he made me angry but didn't break anything in me."

Her mom smiled warmly, then leaned back in her chair. "I'm so glad you left Chad. I'm so glad you are strong enough to be alone rather than with a man who is not right for you. And now, because I don't want you to be alone, I'm thrilled you've met someone." Grinning, she took a sip of coffee. "It looks like Mrs. Hennessey will have to find someone else for her grandson to go out to dinner with."

Laughing, she nodded. "Absolutely. He can find his own dates because I've got mine!"

16

Dinner out. At a restaurant. In public. Those thoughts slammed into Joanne. She was so ready to go out on an official date with Bryce. She'd loved the privacy they'd created with their dates at each other's houses while getting to know each other, but she was ready to step out into the world and not worry if anyone saw them.

As they pulled into the parking lot of El Plato Caliente, she turned to him and smiled. "Does it sound weird that I'm excited?"

A deep chuckle filled the vehicle, coming to rest in her heart. He looked toward her and grinned. "No weirder than knowing I'm just as excited."

"This changes things, you know." As soon as the words left her lips, she crinkled her nose. "God, that sounded so melodramatic. I'm sorry."

"You're not melodramatic in the least." He laughed. Sobering, he held her gaze. "But I know what you mean. So far, we've spent our time alone, and the only ones who really know anything has started between us are

Melanie, Jose, and now your mom. It's been a nice way to build our foundation."

She nodded, then looked through the windshield toward the restaurant. "At least this isn't in Baytown."

"No, but between the sheriff's department, other law enforcement, and the American Legion, odds are we'll see someone we know." He dipped his head, staring into her eyes. "Is that okay? Because I'm ready to let it be known that I'm dating you, but I want you comfortable."

Her smile curved until she grinned widely. "I'm so ready, Bryce."

He leaned forward and placed a soft kiss on her lips. Pulling back, he grinned. "I'll come around and get you."

She sat in Bryce's SUV as he walked around the front to her door. Once opened, her smile remained in place as her hand rested in his. He assisted her down, then linked fingers as they walked into the restaurant. She had heard about the food here but had never been. So much had changed in the years since she used to visit her grandparents on the shore. Back then, there were a few diners, several bars, and precious few restaurants.

They were met at the door by a smiling hostess, who escorted them to a booth, comfortably padded in red vinyl seats against the tall, dark wooden backs that gave them a private feel. Once his beer and her margarita had been delivered, they leaned toward each other, hands held in the middle of the table, still smiling.

"This is so crazy," she said. "We're in our thirties, yet it feels as though we're teenagers sneaking around."

"Everyone will soon get used to seeing us together.

Our friends will be happy, and since I think I made my point to Allison, that shouldn't be an issue."

"I haven't dated anyone here other than several blind dates."

"I've got to tell you, I was nervous about you talking to your mom. Glad… but nervous."

Her mouth fell open. "Why?"

"Because I really want her approval."

Joanne rolled her eyes and snorted at the same time. "Bryce, she'll love you. Believe me, she's more likely to scare you off!"

Now, it was his turn to scoff. "There's no way she could."

"You don't know my mom! Since I haven't made it to date number two with anybody in a long time, she'll already have me walking down the aisle just knowing that you and I have been dating."

She was unsure she should have mentioned "walking down the aisle" but could've sworn he wasn't bothered at all by the possibility of her mom planning.

"My aunt Debbie would probably do the same thing," he said, causing her to breathe easier.

Their food was soon delivered to their table, and they settled in to enjoy their meal. Just like every time they'd been together, the conversation flowed. No awkward silences. No desperately searching for another topic to discuss. No looking at the time, wondering how long it would be before she could escape. Instead, she barely tasted the delicious food as her gaze stayed riveted on him, and she noticed how he stared back at her, too.

"I thought the food was spicy, but seeing you two look at each other, I think all the flames may come from here."

She jumped, swinging her head to the side to see Lisa standing next to their booth. Blushing, she laughed. "Bryce, this is one of my coworkers, Lisa. Lisa, this is Bryce." Lisa knew of her penchant for lousy blind dates, and she didn't want her to think Bryce was another one of those. Yet she had no idea how to refer to him in an introduction.

Bryce lifted his arm to shake Lisa's hand. "It's nice to meet you, Lisa."

Lisa quickly motioned for him to keep eating. She looked over her shoulder and said, "Richard and James are also here. We were just having drinks."

Richard and James walked up behind Lisa, and both men greeted Joanne before shaking hands with Bryce. She noticed Bryce's easygoing manner with Richard, but a slight scowl moved over his face when James shook his hand. Sure that she hadn't imagined it, she pushed her curiosity to the side as she said goodbye to her coworkers.

"Well, I guess that's our first foray out into the world as a couple," she said, smiling.

"James wasn't happy you were out with me."

She blinked, staring at Bryce. Unlike Chad, who'd often have a snide comment to make when another man looked at her, Bryce's face was open, with no accusing look in his eye. "I... I don't know what to say to that."

He reached over and placed his hand gently on top of hers. "There's nothing to say. It's not your fault, and for that matter, it's not his that he likes you. I can't blame him for that. He did try to give my hand the 'my dick's bigger than yours' handshake, but I can blow that off since you're the one sitting here having dinner with me. Of course, if it happens again…"

Eyes bugging, she shook her head. "I'm sure you must be mistaken. He's never asked me out."

"That's why he's probably pissed at himself right now. I got here first. He recognizes that, and is now kicking himself that he didn't ask you out."

"I wouldn't have gone out with him, anyway." Seeing Bryce's lifted brows, she said, "I would never date a coworker. That's a surefire way to have a miserable time at work."

"Can I ask if you were interested?"

"Asking if you can ask is already like asking, isn't it?"

He blinked, then laughter barked out. "I guess you're right."

She grinned and shook her head. "I'm glad he never asked me because I would've said no. And not just because we work together, but because I didn't have any interest in him in any way other than a coworker." She scrunched her nose as she thought.

"Don't worry about it. He's now seen us together, and I didn't back down from the handshake."

"Is that some kind of archaic man talk?"

Bryce laughed and nodded. "To be honest, I would've respected him more if he hadn't tried to do the hard grip. I'm not gonna break his hand, but I gave it right back. The message was received and sent. Now, everything should be cool. He can just be your coworker, and if he wishes he asked you out before I came into the picture, that's on him."

It sounded a little harsh, but she knew Bryce was right.

"Hey, man, I heard you called out for that body."

She jerked as both their heads turned to the young man standing nearby. Not recognizing him, she turned her attention back to Bryce, finding him glaring at the intruder.

"Part of my job," Bryce said curtly.

"They got me on traffic duty. Can't wait until I put in enough time to go on callouts like that." The young man grinned widely, then tossed a wave as he walked away.

Bryce's jaw was hard as he muttered, "Fucking rookie."

"I don't even know what to say to that little conversation," Joanne said, still astonished.

Bryce sighed heavily before lifting his gaze to hers. "That guy is a rookie deputy. Hasn't learned to keep his mouth shut about cases, and at this rate, he'll still be stuck on traffic until he does."

She placed her hand on his arm and soothed her fingers over his tight muscles. "I'm sorry you had to go on a case like that." She had no idea what had happened but could only imagine if he'd seen a body, it couldn't have been pleasant.

His arm relaxed as he continued to hold her gaze. "A body had floated onto the embankment in one of the inlets. The sheriff's department handles the investigation."

Offering a gentle nod while still rubbing his arm, she

said, "I'm really sorry." Looking around at the other patrons, she said, "Well, I guess we really are out together, aren't we? At least I don't see anyone else I know, so maybe we can continue to enjoy our time."

Bryce's voice, low and sincere, pierced the silence. "You know, Joanne, I'm invested in us. I'm not going out with anyone else."

She blinked as his unexpected statement caught her by surprise. "Um... I'm not seeing anyone else either." She wasn't sure why he made the pronouncement, but it was nice to hear that he wasn't going out with anyone else while seeing her. Cocking her head to the side, she swallowed her vulnerability and asked, "Is this about commitment?"

His expression relaxed as his lips curved slightly. "No, not really. While I know you could easily have an entourage of admirers, you don't strike me as the kind of woman dangling a string of multiple men."

The idea of trying to finagle more than one relationship at a time sent a burst of laughter from her. "I'd never be able to handle it!"

"I realize at our age, the terms boyfriend and girlfriend can sound juvenile. But considering our recent conversations, I need you to know unequivocally that when I'm with you, I'm not with anyone else. I might not have had a dad to show me the way a man should be, but I had my uncle Bernie as a compass in life. And for him, it was only Aunt Debbie. And I know you've had a relationship where those boundaries got obliterated. Words can be cheap, but I just want it to be said that I consider us to be together, and there isn't going to be another woman when I'm with you."

At his declaration, her heart raced, pounding with a hundred thundering horses. "Do you want to get out of here?"

His gaze was locked on hers, holding her captive. A slow, tantalizing grin curved his lips, and she was ready to see that smile when they were alone and not holding back anymore. She wanted all of him and could feel the heat of his anticipation. A fire built between them, and she couldn't wait to stoke it.

Without breaking eye contact, he summoned the server, tossed his card at her, and signed as soon as she returned with the bill. Still not losing Joanne's eyes, he stood, and his hand reached for hers. Drawn like a magnet, she eagerly grabbed on and felt the warmth from his fingertips. She missed the connection once she was inside his SUV, and he walked around to get into the driver's side.

The drive to his place was silent. Emotions communicated through the touch of their hands and the glances they shared. The journey was short, but her mind was distracted by anticipation. Suddenly, they were parking in his driveway. She rushed out, no longer waiting for him, meeting him at the front.

Once inside, he kicked the door closed, then, with eagerness and reverence, he twirled her around so that her back was against the solid door. He hesitated for only a few seconds, handing control over to her. Her gaze moved from his dark, lust-filled eyes to his mouth. She knew what those lips could do to hers and couldn't wait to find out what other parts of her body could be set on fire. With a nod, she whispered, "Yes."

She thought he was going to bend for a kiss, but instead, he grabbed her waist, hoisted her up with her back still pressed against the wall, and brought them face-to-face. Her legs wrapped around his waist, her ankles hooked around his ass, and her hands clutched his shoulders.

His body pressed against hers, and while being sandwiched between the door and the hard planes of his chest, their lips met. This was no slow kiss but a wild tangling of lips and tongues, noses bumping, and wild passion that was messy. And she loved every second. He dragged his lips from her mouth, kissing and sucking and nipping his way down her neck. She jerked back to give him more access, banging her head on the door, but felt no pain.

His hand under her ass slid around her thigh and under her dress until his fingers danced slightly over her crotch. Slipping underneath the scrap of silk, he glided his thumb along her sex. Tingles vibrated throughout her body, turning into full-blown shivers.

The inferno was stoked by licks of flames from his tongue, dragging down her neck and across the upper part of her chest. Their clothes only served to be in the way, and she wanted them gone. With his chest pressed tightly against hers, she had no way to maneuver her fingers between them, so she slid her hands down his side and to the back, grabbing the bottom of his shirt and jerking upward. All she managed to do was get it out of the waistband of his pants, barely making any progress.

"Clothes," she moaned as his tongue traced along the upper curves of her breasts. "Need them off," she mumbled before his lips moved back to hers, stealing her words and her breath.

With his arm supporting her, he shifted backward and began to walk. Not caring if their first time was hanging over his comfortable couch, she realized he walked down the hall toward his bedroom. *Good! His bed will be even better!* She hadn't had sex in over six months, not since Chad. Primed and ready, she felt sure she would combust as soon as their clothes were off.

When they entered his bedroom, he stalked to the bed, turned, and fell backward, causing her to land on top of him. Stradling his hips, she scrambled to her knees and grinned as she pulled her dress over her head. His hand slipped underneath her bra, palming her breast as she unfastened the back, dragged the lace down her arms, and tossed it to the side. Now topless, she leaned forward, giving him ready access, a gift he took quick advantage of.

"Christ, you're beautiful," he said, his gaze roving from her face to her taut nipples.

"You're still too covered up," she groaned, her hands making short work of unbuttoning his shirt.

In a flash, he rolled, and she landed on her back as he slid from the bed. Shrugging the shirt from his arms, he let it fall behind him. She propped up on her elbows and stared at his naked chest. He might have said she was beautiful, but the show of tanned smooth skin stretched over muscles that rivaled any bodybuilder model she'd seen on a romance cover, she knew she stared at beauty. The air dragged into her lungs with difficulty, and she licked her lips in anticipation.

"Keep looking at me like that, Joanne, and this won't last long at all." He chuckled, then clarified, "At least the first time."

The idea that they'd have sex more than once during the night caused another full-body shiver. Her gaze never left him as he shucked his shoes, socks, pants, and boxers, then leaned over to the nightstand to grab a condom.

She thought she was ready, but seeing Bryce's totally naked body with his impressive erect cock jutting proudly as she lay in just panties, she suddenly felt inadequate. "I don't exercise."

He jerked slightly, his body stilling, eyes narrowing. "What?"

"Um... I don't exercise. I never have. I actually hate sweating in a gym where other people are around. And the only way I'd run was if I was being chased during a zombie apocalypse." His lips twitched, but she kept going. "I try to be health conscious with what I eat, but I don't look like the kind of woman who would be on the cover of a health and fitness magazine."

He reached out his hand and gently dragged his fingertips along her leg in a soothing motion. "What are you really saying, sweetheart?"

She tried to ignore that he used an endearment that sounded real and not a throwaway. She sighed and said, "I'm sorry. That was probably a mood killer, wasn't it?"

She glanced down at his still impressive erection, and a giggle slipped out. "Or not."

Laughter burst out as his shoulders shook. "Gotta tell you, it'll take a lot more than that to be a mood killer for me." He leaned forward and snagged her panties, drawing them down her legs as he bent to kiss each thigh, knee, and foot. Standing again, he said, "For the record, I only care about what's on the inside of a woman. But if I had my druthers, I'd rather them look like real women, no matter their size or shape, instead of a photoshopped version of what somebody thinks I want to look at. And even more honestly, I can't think of a body more perfect than yours right now."

His words washed over her, and she smiled. Lifting her hands, she wiggled her fingers slightly, beckoning him in. And, thank God, he acquiesced with a grin on his face.

17

Bryce knew Joanne was a confident woman, but he could only imagine the way Chad broke her trust and ripped a bit of her confidence away at the same time. He was up for the task of letting her know she was perfect.

He crawled over her body but kept his weight off her, reveling in the smile gracing her face. She reached up and clung to his arms, her smile widening. "You look like you have a secret ready to burst out," he said.

"Your body is perfection. But I confess the first time we met, I focused on your glorious, muscular arms. I don't know a woman alive who doesn't love strong arms."

Bending his elbows ever so slowly, he lowered his body until his chest barely brushed hers. A hiss escaped between her teeth. "Of course, right now, I'd have to say that your chest is in competition with your biceps. But then, so are your legs."

He settled his hips between her thighs, pressing his cock against her sex. Applying a little more pressure, he ground against the sensitive nerves, eliciting another hiss from her lips.

"Okay," she whispered. "Now, your cock has to be the number one body part, followed by your arms, your chest, and your legs. But I should clarify that those last three are in no particular order."

"Well, if we're going for the best body parts, I need to get in on the action." His lips moved over hers, his tongue splashing through her mouth, finding the velvety softness, making his cock even harder.

"Oh, you're getting in on the action," she muttered.

"Your beautiful face and those lips are on the top of my list." He grinned, then kissed his way down her chest. Shifting slightly, he latched onto one nipple, sucking it deeply into his mouth. Her fingernails dug into his shoulders, but he moved between her breasts, barely taking a breath. Still mumbling, he said, "Okay, your breasts are right up there among my favorite Joanne parts."

She laughed as he kissed her stomach, and her legs fell open in what he hoped was anticipation and an invitation. Slowly, he kissed her mound before dragging the flat of his tongue over her wet folds.

She was no longer hissing but moaning loudly as her fingers clutched the slightly longer hair on top of his head.

"Now, I may have found nirvana." He continued licking and sucking, then moved up to her clit, inserting a finger inside her sex. She was tight, and he couldn't wait to feel her around his cock.

Adding another finger, he crooked in just the right

spot, where her hips bucked off the mattress, her short fingernails dragged along his scalp, and she cried out as her body shattered.

Riding out her release, he dove in again and lapped her essence, memorizing the feel, the taste, and the scent.

Kissing his way back up to her lips, he grinned as he stared down once again. "Oh, yeah. I'd say the whole fucking package that makes up *you* is my favorite."

She laughed and pulled him closer. Wanting her to feel in control, he rolled them until she was once again straddling his hips, only this time with no clothes between them. Her breasts tantalized, and he palmed them first, pulling lightly on her nipples.

She grabbed a condom, ripped the foil, and rolled it on his eager cock. Lifting on her knees, she settled him at her opening and then slowly eased down. His eyes nearly rolled back in his head, but he forced himself to keep his gaze on her, not wanting to miss out on one second of their lovemaking.

If he thought her sex was tight with his fingers, his cock felt strangled, but in the best way. It was all he could do to keep from wanting to move, but he forced his body to still, making sure everything that happened was what she wanted.

Once fully seated, she leaned forward, placed her hands on his shoulders, and began to ride him as she rocked up and down. She alternated between fast and slow, then shallow and deep, until he thought he'd go mad with desire for her. After several minutes, she began to slow, and a blush crossed her cheeks.

"Are you okay?"

"I told you that I hate exercise, but now I see why I need to take up running."

"Don't worry about it, babe. I've got you."

With his hands banding her waist, he lifted her slightly to give his hips room to move. He began pistoning up and down, and in this position, he was able to slide one hand between them to her bundle of nerves. As he pinched slightly, she threw her head back and cried out as her body began to shake again. His cock felt strangled by her inner muscles and had never been so affected during sex ever before.

Continuing to thrust, he felt his balls tighten before he gripped her hips. His fingers dug into the flesh of her ass, and he roared through his own release. He could've sworn that the word orgasm truly meant little death.

When she flopped forward, he was grateful he could move, and his arms wrapped around her back, holding her tight. Their breaths were ragged, and their chests heaved. For several long minutes, he fought to see clearly and have his racing heartbeat slow down. Knowing he needed to take care of the condom, he hated the idea of pulling out.

They had just started seeing each other, but he wanted to broach the subject of going bare as soon as they could. Her thoughts must've been running along the same vein because as he pulled out and shifted her to the side, she said, "I haven't been with anyone since… well, since my last relationship. Naturally, I got tested right after I caught him with someone else. Thank God, it came back clean, but I don't mind getting tested again. I'm on the pill, but…" She blushed. "Sorry… I guess that was too much, too soon, wasn't it?"

"Don't ever be afraid to bring up anything with me," he said, lifting his hand to push back her hair from her face. "To be honest, I was just thinking about the same thing. I'd love nothing more than not to deal with condoms if you didn't want to, either. But if you want to keep using them, that's fine with me. Just so you know, I also get tested for my job. My last test was a month ago, and I haven't slept with anyone in the past six months, either."

Her grin widened, and she said, "I trust you and want you to trust me, so I'll get tested this week."

He leaned over and kissed her again. This time, the heat of passion had slid into the warmth of affection—an emotion just as powerful and much more long-lasting. He climbed from the bed and hastened into the bathroom. While there, it dawned on him that he should have ensured she knew the night was young and he didn't want her to think about leaving. Afraid of finding her half dressed, he hustled back into the bedroom, thrilled when his gaze landed on her still lying on the bed in all her glory. Grinning at the way her eyes seemed to devour him, he crawled back onto the bed.

"I was afraid you were going to run for the hills while I was gone."

She wrapped her arms around him and lifted her brow. "Do you want me to?"

"Hell, no! I want you right here, in this bed with me all night. Maybe even all day tomorrow."

She crinkled her nose and sighed. "I can stay all night, but I'm supposed to help in the concession booth tomorrow for the youth game. It'll be my first time working there, and I hate to give them the excuse that I have to stay in bed with this gorgeous man, although, looking at you now, I'm ready to call it in!"

He laughed and pulled her closer. "We can go together. I'm coaching tomorrow anyway."

She was quiet for a moment, and he asked, "What are you thinking?"

"I'm thinking that if we show up at such a public event together tomorrow, we will have truly given up our private bubble."

He had tucked her head close on his chest but now pushed back slightly so he could peer into her eyes. "Is that okay? How do you feel about that?"

She was quiet for just a moment, then finally smiled and nodded. "We already started the process of coming out together tonight at the restaurant. As long as you're okay with your friends seeing you with me, I'm good, too."

"I'm more than proud to be seen in public with you as my girlfriend."

She reached out and placed her palm on his cheek as they lay facing each other, her thumb drifting lightly over his skin. He closed his eyes and leaned into her touch.

"Then here's to tomorrow, going out together, putting everyone's matchmaking skills to rest."

"Thank God for that!" He leaned in, his mouth sealing over hers. With their bodies pressed together, it didn't take long for the flames to consume them once again.

As they finally lay tangled together, he knew he would be dragging at the game with little sleep. And his last thought before drifting away was that he didn't care as long as Joanne was in his bed.

The following morning, it didn't escape his notice that all eyes seemed to be on him and Joanne as they walked hand in hand from the parking lot to the ballfield. The smiles being sent their way also didn't miss his notice.

"I feel like I've just walked into a dinner party with the back of my dress tucked in my underwear," Joanne whispered. "Everyone is staring in our direction with a smile."

A deep chuckle erupted as he looked down. "First, I have to ask if you've ever actually gone to a dinner party with your dress tucked in your underwear?"

She elbowed him in the stomach. "No, thank God! But you know what I mean. It feels strange to be on display."

"I've never liked being in the spotlight, but in this case, I'm proud that it's because I'm with you."

"Unfortunately, in my case, everybody's probably wondering if this is a blind date and is the first time we've been together."

"Nah," he said, shaking his head. "You would never walk into a ballfield holding hands with a blind date."

Now, it was her time to laugh. "You're right about

that! Most of my blind dates make me want to hide under the table."

Once they'd come to the opening in the fence where the kids and others gathered, he looked at her and jiggled her hand slightly. He wanted to kiss her but wasn't about to take advantage of her nervous feelings. Catching him by surprise, she lifted to her toes and lightly pressed her lips to his. His chest swelled as he kissed her smile in public.

"Go coach the kids." She laughed as she settled back on her heels.

"I know you have to go make popcorn and hot dogs, but make sure to cheer some, too."

"Absolutely," she agreed, smiling as she turned and headed to the concession stand.

He looked up into the stands, already seeing lots of wide eyes and smiling faces. Turning to jog onto the field, he caught the same from the other coaches. He'd been correct when he'd said he wasn't one to search for the spotlight, but right now, he didn't mind who saw him with Joanne. A thought passed through his mind, and he faltered. *Of course, there is her mother...* And he hoped he'd have her approval.

18

The crowds began to swarm the bleachers at the ballfield, and Joanne was stunned at how many people came out to support the kids and the teams. When she'd been in high school, she'd gone to games, but they were always school-related. This was a volunteer program by the local chapter of the American Legion and was structured so that all children had a chance to play sports regardless of their athletic ability or their parents' ability to pay. The Legionnaires covered the costs, and the AL Auxiliary handled the concession stand, with those profits also going to the teams.

Her mother had joined the Auxiliary when she'd moved to the area and had easily convinced Joanne to participate. Multiple booths were set up, and she would have felt overwhelmed if she hadn't met so many people from the Auxiliary. She recognized Tori Evans, whose hands were full of a three-year-old and a one-year-old. Tori's in-laws, Nancy and Ed, swooped in, each offering to take a grandchild off Tori's hands, and by the smile on her face, she was grateful for the respite. Corinne and Eric McFarlane also had their hands full of grandkids, with Katelyn's little boy, Brogan's little girl, and Aiden's little boy and girl. A whole group of women sat together in the stands with babies and toddlers. She couldn't help but smile, knowing she wanted children one day. And then the idea of her and Bryce having children hit her, and her smile widened. *God, I've known him for a short time, and here I am, thinking of what-ifs!* But staring into the crowd, she felt a sense of community, realizing how many people she had already recognized.

"Hey, Joanne!"

Turning, she spied Melanie strolling Suzette toward her, and she waved. "Good morning."

Melanie walked with several other women, and they stopped with her. Melanie said, "I know you are still getting to know people in town, but I wanted to introduce you to Judith, one of the doctors in town. And this is Shiloh, Billie, and Ivy. Their husbands all work with Jose and Bryce."

"Oh," she said, feeling a blush hit her cheeks. All four women were beautiful, each wearing smiles as they moved in closer. Billie had wavy blond hair cut at her shoulders and blue eyes that twinkled. Shiloh hung back slightly, a shy smile on her face.

Melanie leaned closer. "Don't worry. It wasn't me who let the cat out of the bag. These men talk as much as any women do. Bryce told Jose, and then it just got around to the other officers—"

"And naturally, they told us that Bryce was off the

market." Ivy laughed. Her auburn hair was pulled back in a ponytail, but tendrils around her face bounced free.

Joanne rolled her eyes, shaking her head. "I wondered how people would start finding out we were dating."

Judith said, "Ryan and I are having an impromptu get-together tonight. We'll plan what the station will want to do for our holiday project this year, and I want you to come, too." Judith was a little older than the others, but her beauty shone through as well. Joanne had already met her as one of the doctors in town but had no idea she was married to Bryce's boss.

"Ooh, I can't wait for the holidays!" Billie said, enthusiasm pouring from her.

Joanne wasn't sure what kind of project they referred to, but a tingle of excitement moved through her at the idea of being out with Bryce and his co-workers. Unsure what he might say, she replied, "I think that sounds great, but I don't know if he—"

"Already asked him," Judith interjected. "And he said he'd be thrilled to have you there with him."

Jerking slightly, Joanne laughed. "Well, then, I guess I'll see you tonight."

The other women grinned widely, but just then, the crowd in the stands cheered, and everyone's attention swung to a little boy pumping his arms as he raced toward first base. As the others made their way into the stands, she hurried back over to the hot dog stand.

"Joanne, hello!"

She turned to see Jose's mother buying hot dogs for

what looked like all of her children and grandchildren. "Mrs. Martinez. How nice to see you again."

Jose's mother smiled pleasantly, then leaned forward and said, "A little bird told me that you were seeing Bryce."

Blushing again, she said, "It seems like there are lots of little birds here."

Mary leaned closer and whispered, "Because Bryce is such a close friend with my Jose, I can tell you that he's a good man."

"Thank you for that. I happen to agree with you."

Patting Joanne's arm, Mary scolded, "I saw your mother just yesterday, and she didn't mention you were seeing anyone."

Knowing where the conversation was going, she said, "Don't worry, Mrs. Martinez. I asked her to keep it quiet until we were ready. We just wanted time to be together first without everyone else knowing."

"Very smart, Joanne. We moms don't always know the right thing to do and say, but our hearts are in the right place." With a wink, she paid for her hot dogs and turned to hand them to her husband before they walked back to the stands.

By the time she finished her hour shift at the concession stand, she realized that most of Baytown had seen her there, and it seemed like most people knew she was with Bryce. She walked over to the fence, glad the game was over. She grinned as the children cheered and clapped for each other before the next game began. Bryce jogged over, a smile on his face, and seeing him in his AL T-shirt stretched over his chest and arms, She was tempted to grab him and pull him in for a kiss. Deciding to keep the PDA to a minimum, she kept her hands clutching the top of the fence.

"It looks like you guys have a lot of fun," she said, her gaze locked on him even though she was aware of the cheering, happy children around.

"We do." He nodded. "We might even have more fun than the kids." He tilted his head to the side, his eyes moving over her. "Is everything okay? You look like you're about to tell me there's no Santa Claus."

Shaking her head, she laughed. "No, believe me, there is definitely a Santa Claus, and he gave me exactly what I always hoped for."

Bryce wiggled his eyebrows and said, "He gave me the same gift, Joanne."

Her smile faltered as she continued, "But I really need to go see my mom. I know we were going to spend the afternoon together, but so many people now know that we're together. I'm gonna be lucky if my mom hasn't already heard it. And I desperately want Mom to meet you so her feelings aren't hurt."

"Absolutely! In fact, since my kids have just finished playing, I don't have to stick around. Is your duty at the concession stand over with?"

"Yeah, I just had the first shift."

"Then let's head back to my place, and you can get your car. Talk to your mom and set something up."

She lifted a brow. "And what about Judith and Ryan's party?"

He had the grace to blush. "I was going to tell you

185

about that, but I wanted to make sure you were comfortable first."

Laughing, she looked around. "If I'm not comfortable after this, I don't know what will make me that way. Yes, we can definitely go to the party." They stood for a few seconds, staring at each other. "You know, I really want to lean forward and kiss you, but we're standing in front of an entire set of bleachers full of people probably staring at us."

"Mom first," he reminded.

"You're right. And then… watch out, Buddy, because I won't be able to keep my hands to myself!"

"I like your style, babe." He grinned. He jogged down to the gate, walked through, and met her on the sideline. He slung his arm around her shoulders, and they walked back to the parking lot.

19

"Told you Joanne was nice," Jose said, grinning as Bryce walked into Ryan and Judith's den.

"Couldn't believe my eyes seeing you with Joanne at the game. Gotta say that when I spied Allison hanging around, I was afraid you might not get out of there alive!" Jared halfheartedly joked.

Bryce's head swung around. "Allison was there?" he asked, keeping his voice low while glancing into the kitchen to see Joanne standing with the other women, smiling her bright-eyed smile.

"Yeah. I saw her standing near the end of the bleachers. She had her eye on the two of you, and when I looked back, she was gone," Jared said.

"Damn. I really hope she gets it through her head that there's no going back to what we had, which wasn't anything special anyway."

Joseph handed another beer to Bryce. "Been there, man. It sucks. But Joanne has a good head on her shoulders. She won't let Allison throw her."

Bryce knew that when Joseph was interested in Shiloh, a past hookup of his was determined to rock their boat. "I just don't want her to have to put up with anyone's shit, especially because of me."

Their conversation halted as more people walked into the room. Jose gently lifted Suzette out of Melanie's arms. "Go ahead and get a plate, sweetheart, while I take care of her."

Callan walked in with a little bundle in his arms and his smiling wife, Sophia, next to him. Their baby boy, Phillip, named after Sophia's brother, was born two months ago, and this was his first official VMP outing. The women all cooed as they swarmed around to see the tiny sleeping boy and offer hugs to Sophia.

"Oh, I'm so glad you brought Phillip!" Judith said, walking over with her teenage stepdaughter, Cindy. "With both sets of grandparents living in Baytown, I thought you might leave him at home."

"I wanted everyone to have a chance to see the littlest officer." Sophia laughed.

Andy, Jared, and Joseph stood to the side with Ryan's son, Trevor, and talked about the Navy. Trevor said he wanted to keep his post-graduation options open but was considering the military. Ryan walked to them and rested his hand on his son's shoulder, joining the conversation.

Jared's wife, Billie, and Andy's wife, Ivy, worked near the Chesapeake Bay and had their heads together, discussing conservation measures. After Cindy left the baby adoration group, she stood, and the two women easily enveloped her in their conversation.

Bryce's gaze searched and easily found Joanne standing near the counter dividing the kitchen and family room, talking with Shiloh, Joseph's wife. Shiloh was quiet, and while she always seemed to enjoy the get-togethers, he was sure Joanne was an easy person for Shiloh to talk to. Smiling at how Joanne easily fit into his world, his chest expanded once again.

The good feeling from the night before fell away as Ryan stopped in the hall, his words cutting through the end-of-shift jocularity of the officers. "I need everyone who worked the rescue off Tangier Island of Saul's ferry to stay. And everyone else can continue their duties."

Raised brows mirrored Bryce's when he looked around the room, but they all hustled to obey. He headed into the workroom and saw Sam walking in with Ryan. Greeting the group, he wondered what was happening.

As soon as they were seated, Sam jumped in. "We don't have an ID on the body found the other day. The medical examiner determined he was dead before going into the water. And the body wasn't in the water long. He was killed and dumped close to where he was found washed up on shore. The cause of death was due to strangulation. While the body was clothed, anything of identification was removed—wallet, keys, phone, money, watch. His brown suit was off the rack department store brand. Nothing with his clothes would aid in identification. The medical examiner found no tattoos and what looked like an appendectomy scar from many years ago." He pinned the others with a hard stare. "But whoever stripped his ID missed one item. Shoved into his inside jacket pocket was a ferry stub."

Sitting up straighter, Bryce homed in on what Sam was reporting. Thinking of Ryan's request for who stayed and the day they rescued Saul when he had his heart attack, Bryce said, "Shit. Was the date when Saul had his heart attack?"

Sam nodded. "Yep. Saul's ferry on the day you had to rescue him. I went to the hospital to ask Saul if he remembered the man based on the description of the suit." He rubbed his chin and shook his head. "Saul's wife nearly bit my head off for asking him the question."

"What'd he tell you?" Jared asked.

"Nothing. He can't remember that day at all."

"Joanne…" Bryce groaned, his heart falling into his stomach. Seeing the others, he said, "She was on that ferry."

"Shit, that's right!" Jose nodded.

Sam looked at Bryce, and he explained, "Joanne Norris. The woman I'm dating. We weren't dating then, but started right after that."

"Does she often take the ferry?"

"About every other week, although the days can change based on the weather and the students' needs." Seeing the look of confusion, he said, "She works for the community college and goes over to counsel the teenagers at the school on Tangier as to their plans for after high school."

"I see," Sam muttered, tapping into his tablet.

"No man fit that description on the ferry," Callan added. "Unless he was on the one that morning."

Sam looked at Bryce. "Was Joanne on that one?"

He nodded slowly, and his gut churned. "Yeah. She was there."

"I'll need to speak with her. Will she be at the community college?"

He looked at the clock on the wall. "She was coming here to meet me when she got off work. We were going to have dinner in town before I went to the American Legion meeting tonight. She should be here any moment—"

BettsAnne, the intrepid station receptionist, stepped to the door. "Actually, she's here now."

Sam looked at Ryan, who twisted around toward the door. "Show her in." Looking back at the others, he said, "You all are dismissed."

"I'd like to stay," Bryce said.

"Fine by me." Sam looked at the others. "I've got the Coast Guard looking at the tides and currents on that day and a few days afterward. That'll give us an indication of where he might have been killed. If you think of anything else, let me know."

The other officers stood and left the room. Bryce watched as they sent nods and tight smiles down the hall and assumed they were greeting Joanne. Blowing out a long breath, he stood.

She followed BettsAnne into the room, her eyes filled with uncertainty until she spied Bryce. Her lips curved, although uneasiness continued to emanate from her. "Hey, what's up?"

He headed straight to her, pulled her into a hug, and placed a kiss on her forehead, hoping to lessen the tension. Turning her to face the table, he said, "This is Joanne Norris. You've met my chief, Ryan Coates, and this is Sam Shackley, a detective for the North Heron Sheriff's Department. Detective Shackley needs to ask you about the day of Saul's heart attack—"

"He's okay, isn't he?" she asked, her eyes widening as her hand landed on her chest.

"Yeah, as far as we know. Come on, let's sit down." Bryce ushered her to a chair, and he sat down next to her once she was settled. Before Sam started, he asked, "Do you remember me telling you about a body we found?"

She jerked slightly as her gaze shot toward him. "Yes…"

He hated hearing the timidity in her voice. "Detective Shackley has some information and some questions for you."

"Me?" she squeaked. Her eyes bugged out as she looked first at Bryce and then toward Sam.

"Ms. Norris," Sam began. "We're investigating the death of an unidentified male. The only evidence we have at this time is a ferry stub for Saul's ferry on the day that Saul had a heart attack. No one matching his description was rescued by the VMP, so we think he may have been on the earlier ferry that morning. About five feet, eleven inches. Brown hair. Brown suit—"

She sucked in a gasp. "Oh, God. Brian."

Bryce jerked his head to the side and stared at her. "Who's Brian?"

Her chest heaved as she shook her head. "I don't know."

His mouth opened then snapped shut as he looked toward Ryan and Sam, their expressions showing the same confusion on his face. Pivoting in his chair to face her, he gained her gaze and said, "Tell us whatever you think you know."

She let out a long breath, then nodded. "I go over every couple of weeks to Tangier, never on the same schedule because of the weather or what's happening with the students or what's going on at the college. It's a little more frequent now because if their plans include furthering their education, they have to start that process now."

A wince crossed her face. "I'm sorry. You don't really care why I go over."

"We want to hear everything, so don't worry about it," Sam encouraged.

Nodding, she continued, "I usually take Saul's ferry simply because his was the first one I rode on, and he was so personable that I just stuck with him. Every trip is different... different people, some tourists, and occasionally, I've started recognizing a few people from the island." She winced and shook her head. "I'm probably not making any sense."

Sam said gently, "You're fine, Ms. Norris."

"Please, call me Joanne."

"All right, Joanne. You said Brian. I assume you met someone fitting the description I gave you."

"Yes. He sat next to me on the ferry, and we chatted." She lifted her hand and rubbed her forehead. "I can't even remember much of what we talked about. Let's see... he said he remembered seeing me before, and I also remembered seeing him a few weeks earlier. Um... he asked about my work, and I explained why I was going to the island. I'm embarrassed, but we didn't talk about him other than his name."

"Did he give his full name?"

"No, just Brian."

"Did he carry anything with him?"

Blinking, she cocked her head to the side. "Um... yeah. He had a briefcase."

"Okay, and you just saw him on the ferry going over? No other time?" Sam asked.

She blushed and shot a side glance toward Bryce. Cocking his head to the side, he waited to see what she was going to say.

"Well, actually, we had lunch together that day."

Bryce blinked, her unexpected answer surprising him. A flash of jealousy moved through him, but he quickly tamped it down. Obviously, he and Joanne hadn't started dating at that time, yet he hated the thought of her with anyone else, even just having lunch. And blanking his expression, he waited to see what else Sam would say.

"And did you meet him for lunch?"

She nodded and sighed. "I'm afraid it was quick, not very interesting, and he left rather abruptly."

"What I'm going to do, Joanne, is ask you to elaborate. Things that might not have seemed very important at the time, or even now to you, could be very important to this case. Give us as much detail and timeline as you can."

"We met at the Crab Shack on the island, and I got there before he did. This was about two o'clock. He saw me and came inside. We ordered and sat together in a booth. He gave no indication as to what he'd been doing on the island other than saying he had business there. After I told him what I did, I figured he would tell me if he wanted me to know. Since he didn't, I didn't want to pry. Instead, he asked about my visit with the teenagers."

"Did he seem distracted? Interested in what you were saying? Just killing time?" Sam asked.

"Sort of. He kept looking down at his phone. He didn't seem very interested in what I was saying, but believe me, it wasn't like a date. We were just two fellow travelers sharing a meal before heading back, and I knew it was a workday for both of us, so I figured he had work-related issues to keep track of on his phone."

"You said he left abruptly, and he didn't take the ferry back, did he?"

"I was surprised he didn't make it for the return trip, but we weren't together at the end of the meal because of the phone call he received."

Bryce scrubbed his hand down his face. "What phone call?"

"Halfway through the meal, he got a phone call and apologized, saying he had to take it. He was only on for a moment and then grimaced, tossed some money onto the table, and said he had to go. He walked away, and that was the last time I saw him."

"And you didn't see him on the dock at all?" Sam asked.

"No. I kept watching in case he came when Saul was just pulling out. Not that I had any reason other than I hated for someone to miss the ferry. I looked for him the last time I went but didn't see him. I was hoping to see him on my next trip."

"Why are you so anxious to see him again?" Sam asked.

"I wanted to give him back the money."

Sam's brows lifted. "What money?"

Bryce caught Ryan covering a slight smile, knowing Joanne's roundabout way of telling the story probably had scrambled Sam's notetaking.

"He left way too much money on the table. Two hundred-dollar bills! I wasn't going to have him pay for my lunch, and I didn't want the server to have to make change. I kept it simple. I paid the server with my credit card, then took the two hundred dollars to give back to him when I saw him on the ferry." She sighed. "Now, I don't really know what to do with the money."

"Let's get back to the phone call," Sam prompted.

Her face fell. "I don't know anything about it. Um… it came in about two thirty… maybe a little after. He just said, 'Yeah, yeah, got it.' Then he disconnected, stood, and tossed the money onto the table while apologizing and saying he had to go. That was all that happened."

"Did you see which way he went when he left the restaurant?"

She closed her eyes for a few seconds, then said, "He was walking in the direction of the harbor. But, as I said, he was nowhere to be seen when I got there." Her eyes snapped open. "Oh, wait! I do know his last name. Saul asked if any of us had seen Brian Atwell." She let out a long breath. "You don't think he died that day, do you?"

"We don't know yet, Joanne," Sam said. "The medical examiner is still working. We just wanted to establish his identification, and you may have provided us with that." He turned his tablet toward her. "Is this the man?"

Bryce leaned forward at the same time Joanne did to see a Maryland driver's license for Brian Atwell. He looked to the side as she nodded. "Yes, that's him."

"With this information, we'll be able to have the medical examiner determine if the deceased is this man. And if so, then we will need to come up with a timeline of his activities and whereabouts. You've also helped us with that. Thank you."

She leaned back in her seat, looked at the others, and said, "I didn't know him. We were just two travelers who passed one day and shared a conversation and part of a meal. Yet it feels so weird to know that if he's the body that was found, I might've been the last person to talk to him."

She shuddered as Sam thanked her for her information. Bryce stood as she did and wrapped his arm around her. He didn't mention that there was no way she was the last person to see the man alive. That distinction would belong to the murderer.

Keeping his mouth shut, he shared a look with Sam and Ryan, knowing they had the same thought, before walking Joanne out of the room.

20

Joanne stayed in the parking lot of the VMP station, leaning on Bryce for several minutes after they left the meeting. He'd whispered words of comfort, then kissed her goodbye. They had planned on grabbing dinner somewhere in town, but now he needed to go back inside and see if there was anything else Sam or Ryan required from him. No longer feeling like dining out, she'd said she was going home. They agreed that he'd go to his house to feed the cats and meet her at her place.

Her grip tightened around the steering wheel as she pulled into her driveway. Making no attempt to get out of her vehicle, she stared at her cottage, but her mind was not on the comforting sight of home. Instead, she was ensnared in the memory of the lunch with Brian. *Maybe it's not actually his body they found.* She sighed heavily. *But it was still a body... someone's son, or father, or brother.*

She had pushed Brian to the recesses of her memory since that day, but now every second she'd spent in his presence resurfaced. She hated to think that someone she knew might have died so horribly. *If it was him, did he catch a ride with someone else and fall overboard?* Shaking her head, she realized that if that had happened, it would've been reported.

A heavy sigh left her lungs, and she climbed out of her car and walked to the front door. Before she had a chance to get her keys out, the quiet serenity was disrupted by the crunch of tires on the oyster shell driveway behind her. Her face lit as she hoped Bryce had gotten away from the station quickly and had come straight to her house.

Her smile fell when it wasn't his SUV that was parked behind her vehicle. Squinting into the evening sun's glare off the windshield, she didn't recognize the car, and it wasn't until the driver emerged that the air rushed from her lungs as her confusion shifted swiftly to alarm and exasperation.

He was as she remembered—tall and lean, with his dark brown hair meticulously styled. Black slacks and a white button-up shirt with the sleeves precisely rolled up to give an affected casual look.

Before he could advance to her porch, she grimaced and threw her hand up, palm out in a clear indication for him to halt. "No, Chad. Absolutely not. I can't believe you're here."

He stopped several feet away, offering a slight nod. "Hello, Joanne." His voice once seemed endearing but now felt manipulative.

"You must remember that I took out a restraining order after we broke up." As the words left her mouth, it suddenly dawned on her that the order's time limit would have passed.

"I know, but you wouldn't talk to me. I would never have done anything to hurt you. But I know that continuing to hassle you wasn't the right thing to do, and believe me, I'm not here to cause a problem."

Each word hung heavy in the air, a reminder of their tumultuous ending. Her shoulders slumped. "Then why are you here, Chad, and how did you find me?"

"I know this will piss you off, but one of your former coworkers told me that you had moved to the Eastern Shore. I knew you had probably moved closer to your mom, and it doesn't take much online looking to find someone's address."

"Well, that makes me feel safe," she muttered, holding his gaze. "But that doesn't tell me *why* you're here."

"I've done a lot of thinking in the past six months."

Her brows lifted, and an incredulous scoff barked out. "Oh, have you? I suppose that's what you do with your time between banging your sidepiece?"

He sighed and shook his head. "I know I deserve that—"

"Oh, you deserve a lot more than that, but I think I probably said everything to you that needed to be said six months ago when I kicked you out of my apartment. So unless you have something new to say—"

"I wanted to say I was sorry."

She dropped her chin and stared at her feet for a moment before lifting her head and pinning him with another hard stare. "Chad, I'm tired. It's been a long day, and I really don't have time for—"

"No, seriously, Joanne, I'm really sorry. What I did was unconscionable."

Memories of finding him in bed with another woman raced through her mind, but she found they didn't carry the power they used to. *Enough time has passed to lessen the blow? Probably. Knowing that Chad's infidelity was not my fault? Definitely. And maybe, just maybe, the knowledge that Bryce was interested in me on my own? Absolutely!*

She nodded. "Yes, it was absolutely unconscionable."

His expression fell, but he nodded. "And it had nothing to do with you. It was all me. My weakness. My fault. My horrid mistake."

Choking back a derisive snort, she said, "Again, I agree, Chad. At the time, it was hard not to see if there was any reason I could've given you to cheat, but that was ridiculous. You bear the brunt of that decision alone."

His shoulders hefted as he sucked in a deep breath, then his hound dog expression morphed into the almost cute look that she once had fallen for.

"I know you had a restraining order registered where we used to live because I didn't handle the breakup well. But I'd really like to make amends. I'd like to take you to dinner. Somewhere in public so you feel comfortable. And we can just talk—"

His words hit her, and she jerked slightly. "Are you serious?"

"We had something special, Joanne. I fucked it up—"

"Yes, by fucking someone else," she muttered. "Then by trying to tell me it was my fault and then threatening that it would be a mistake for me to break up."

He winced. "I never meant that as a threat. But I'm a different person now. I've looked at myself. I thought about what made me do things that even I didn't like. I'd just love to have the chance to sit with you for a little while and talk."

"Chad, that's not going to happen. For one, if you're truly here to apologize, fine. I accept your apology. But I've moved on. A new place to live. New job. And a new man in my life."

The instant she said those last words, she could tell they struck him hard. He may have found her address, but since she didn't put anything on social media, he had no idea about the rest of her life.

The cute little expression on his face fell away. "A new man?"

"Yes, a new man. I have no desire to have dinner with you even if I wasn't dating, but since I am, the answer is definitely no."

A dark expression crossed his face, sending a chill through her. Yet she couldn't be sure with the distance and the evening shadows falling over her front walk. The expression disappeared before another little smile was sent her way.

The sound of tires once again on her drive drew her attention away from Chad, and this time, she breathed a sigh of relief, recognizing Bryce's SUV. As his sharp and discerning gaze flickered to Chad, his eyes narrowed slightly with protectiveness. She watched as he took in the situation, and she beamed her smile toward him as he alighted from his vehicle and stalked toward her. His warm gaze stayed on her as he passed Chad and jogged up the front porch stairs straight into her arms.

"Hey, sweetheart," she said, the pet name flowing out naturally, although she was aware of its dual purpose since she wanted to stake her claim in front of Chad. Lifting on her toes, she placed her hand on Bryce's chest to offer her mouth. He took her invitation without hesitation and kissed her.

Wanting to drag Bryce inside her house and settle them in a cocoon against the world, she definitely didn't want to give Chad any more of her time. Waving her hand dismissively toward the interloper still standing on her walk, she said, "This is Chad. He just stopped by to tell me he knew where I lived and to say he was sorry. Again. He was just leaving."

Bryce's brows lifted, and she saw the tightening of his jaw. "Chad? I thought there was a restraining order on him."

"It was for only six months. But if he remains in the area, I have no problem getting it renewed here."

"Well, Chad," Bryce began. His arms held Joanne while he turned his now-glacial gaze toward the other man. "I guess I really should thank you. If you weren't such a fuckup, then I would've never met Joanne. But as it is, I think I'll just take my girlfriend inside. And I *will* be watching to make sure that you leave."

With his arm still wrapped around her, Joanne opened her front door, and they disappeared inside, closing the door behind them. She let out a long breath as Bryce stalked to her window, jerked back the curtain, and stood in plain sight with his hands on his hips, not moving until Chad's car disappeared from sight.

Kicking off her shoes, she walked over to Bryce and wrapped her arms around his waist. "I can't believe he was here."

Bryce swung around, his jaw still tight. "How did he know where you lived?"

"He ran into an old coworker of mine and found out that I had a job in Eastern Shore. He knew my mom lived out here, having visited with me a couple of times. As far as how he found out this address, I guess anything can be found on the Internet."

"I want you to go in tomorrow and fill out another restraining order."

"Do you really think that's necessary?"

"Yes, I do. While it might not seem like he's escalating, the fact that he came out here shows that he is."

"I'm not afraid of him, Bryce. I just want him gone out of my life."

"I get that, babe. But you should still consider it."

She nodded slowly but was too exhausted to think about anything beyond the moment. "I've got to go to Tangier Island tomorrow." Dropping her chin, she leaned her forehead against his chest, and he pulled her close. "God, what a couple of hours it's been."

"I know, babe, and I'm really sorry."

They remained standing with their arms around each other before he finally said, "I confess I actually felt a bolt of jealousy when I spied Chad."

Her laughter turned into more of a chortle. "Believe me, there's nothing to be jealous of."

"I guess I just can't imagine a man having you and then being such a dumbass."

This time, she face-planted against his chest as her shoulders shook with mirth. "That's because he always was a dumbass, and I just didn't realize it." She leaned her head back and said, "This is embarrassing and doesn't sound like a very self-assured, liberated woman, but the truth is, I kept hoping that a relationship with him would be more... would feel more. I guess I was in love with the idea of being in love more than I was in love with him. Because now, looking back, what I felt for him was not love. It was companionship that never turned into love."

"I don't think that sounds bad at all. I know a lot of men think it's unmanly to want that kind of forever relationship. Or maybe that's just what they say because they think that's what they're supposed to say. I always knew I wanted what Bernie and Debbie had."

Leaning back, she held his gaze and sighed. "Obviously, when I walked in on Chad and his assistant, I was angry and felt betrayed. But I discovered it was easy to walk away from him. My tears were not because I had lost him but more because I had spent so long with a man who didn't deserve that time from me. But maybe he's finally gone. He showed up, apologized, and that's it."

"I hope you're right, Joanne. But I've got to tell you, I don't trust him. He searched to find where you lived and where you worked and had the audacity to show up under the pretense of apologizing. To me, that's not a man who's moved on. That's a man who's still looking to make a statement."

She didn't like hearing what Bryce had to say about Chad, but she also couldn't deny that maybe he was right. Sighing heavily again, she admitted, "He did say he wanted to take me to dinner—"

"What?"

Her fingers gripped his waist tighter. "Honey, I said no. And your arrival was perfectly timed. He now knows that when it comes to me, he missed the boat—" She gasped as her mind jumped. "Oh God... I didn't mean... damn, Bryce. How horrible if that body is Brian."

"Joanne, honey, let's forget about everything for a little while. When I drove up and saw Chad, I forgot all about dinner. One of the town ladies dropped off a huge pot of homemade chili. We divided it up, and I have a big container in the car. Let me go get it."

"I can make a batch of cornbread to go with it."

"Sounds good."

She tilted her head back to meet his lips in a soft, lingering kiss. Unable to resist, she watched as he jogged out to his SUV, loving how his body moved as he walked. Powerful, graceful, and captivating. Bryce was quietly confident, not cocky. He was a big guy but seemed to have complete command of his body. He was not flashy nor threatening.

He had just opened the door of his SUV when he pulled his phone from his pocket and looked down. His features, usually calm and reassuring, darkened. His expression showed evidence that he wasn't happy with whoever was calling. Hoping he wasn't getting called in to work for some emergency, she watched in fascination as he jabbed at his phone, then put it to his ear. Whoever he talked to was not getting the sweet Bryce she knew. His face registered anger, and his body was tight as his arm jerked around with sharp movements. Finally jabbing at the phone one more time, he shoved it into his pocket. With his fists planted on his hips, he tilted his head back, closed his eyes, and stood for a moment in the driveway. Even from a distance, she could see the tension in his body.

Finally, he shook his head, then reached inside his vehicle and pulled out the large plastic container. Jumping slightly, Joanne snapped back to the task at hand. Hurrying into the kitchen, it struck her that she already knew he was trustworthy. The feelings she had for him and about him were vastly different than she'd ever had with Chad.

Hearing the front door open, she called out, "In the kitchen!"

The cornbread was a boxed mix, but she whipped it up quickly, poured it into a greased pan, and popped it into the oven. Bryce set the container on the counter, and when he pulled off the lid, the tantalizing scent of the chili spices tickled her nose.

She turned to face him, finding his hips leaning against the counter, his arms crossed over his chest, and his gaze firmly focused on her. The raw tension she'd witnessed through the front window appeared to be lessening, and a little smile curved her lips.

Walking over, she rested her hands on his waist, then leaned her body forward so that he fully supported her, a silent testament to the trust and safety she found in his embrace with her body and her heart. "Are you okay?"

"Yeah. I just got a call from Allison." His body tensed again. "Fuckin' Allison."

Closing her eyes, Joanne wondered if the day could get worse.

21

Joanne's eyes closed, and her chest deflated as all the air left her lungs. The weight of her sigh was palpable, and Bryce hated the defeat rolling over her. His heart constricted, cursing himself for even breathing Allison's name. But the foundation of their relationship was built on honesty, and he wasn't going to start by leaving Joanne in the dark. His fingers tightened around her, drawing her in, trying to shield her from the frustration while wanting to chase Allison's words from his mind.

"I know you think you have someone else in your life, Bryce, but I won't take your betrayal lightly. You used me, then tossed me aside just because I allowed myself to fall for you."

"Allison, what betrayal? What did we say when we first started hooking up? That was all we wanted to do, right? You know I'm right."

"Maybe at first. But hookups can turn into more. And I loved you."

"What we had wasn't love. Think about it, Allison. We

didn't do anything together. We never acted as a couple. You left a few things at my apartment because it was convenient. But we didn't live together. We didn't go out together. We didn't date. I was a convenient hookup for you on your job travels. You were a convenient hookup for me since it was occasional. But what we weren't was a couple."

"But—"

"No buts. Get this in your head. I am with someone now, and you need to accept that our hookups are over."

"Tell your new girlfriend to watch her back!"

"Don't threaten her, and don't threaten me. We are done."

He sighed, feeling the weight on his shoulders. "She's delusional. It's not like I broke a promise to her. But somehow, she's got it in her head that what she wants is what she'll get."

Joanne pulled back just enough to look into his face. He could swear nothing was more beautiful than staring into her eyes. In the midst of everything going on, she radiated understanding and undeniable strength. He loved that feeling of calm he received just by looking at her.

"Bryce, she may not have ever gotten a promise of a future with you, but she knows what she's missing out on. Her fantasies are born from a missed opportunity. I was with Chad for a year and wouldn't care who he's seeing now. But having been with you for even such a short period, I know that not having you would hurt. I think, for Allison, just a hope that she could've had something with you is driving her to act irrationally."

He swallowed hard, hesitating for a moment as he contemplated his words. Once again, the desire for transparency won out. "There's something else. The last thing you need is for more shit dumped on you, but if Allison approaches you, I need you to let me know."

Joanne's eyes previously reflected fatigue, but now they held a shadow of concern. She tilted her head slightly to the side, still peering up at him. "Huh?"

"She made a bitch comment about you watching your back. I don't think she'll be dumb enough to do anything because I laid into her and told her that she not only needed to stay away from me but also stay away from you."

"Oh, good grief! What does she think this is? Middle school? Some teenage drama showdown?"

The indignant expression on her face almost caused him to laugh, but Joanne wasn't finished.

"This is like *Alexander and the Terrible, Horrible, No Good, Very Bad Day!*"

Now, he couldn't hold back his laughter. "What? Who's Alexander?"

Her nose scrunched adorably. "Didn't you ever read the book by Judith Viorst when you were a kid? That was the title—*Alexander and The Terrible, Horrible, No Good, Very Bad Day*. Mom used to read it to me when things went wrong."

Nodding while still smiling, he felt the pressure on his chest ease. She stepped from his embrace at the sound of the kitchen timer, moved to the oven, and pulled out the piping hot cornbread. "Let's eat and pretend that everyone else in the world has just disappeared."

Grinning, he loved how easy Joanne made everything. "Sounds like the best plan I can think of."

They spent dinner engaging in small talk as they enjoyed the food, but he knew it was all for show. Joanne's eyes, normally bright and expressive, were now clouded with worry. Her lips were taut and bracketed by lines of concern. She wore her emotions on her face, and it was obvious that they couldn't avoid all the negative topics. Allison and Chad were banished from the conversation—permanently if he had anything to do with it. *But Brian Atwell?* That name lingered between them, threatening to shatter the peace of the evening.

She finally laid her spoon down and sighed. "We need to talk about the... well... Brian, don't we?"

He followed suit, his spoon clinking against his bowl. "Have you thought of anything else you didn't say at the station?"

She slowly shook her head, then reached up to rub her forehead. "No, but I guess I can't help thinking about it."

"What thoughts are weighing you down?"

She pushed her bowl forward and rested her elbows on the table as her chin rested in her palms. "I've never known anyone who's been murdered. Not that I *knew* him. But still..." Her voice trailed off before she finished, "It just seems weird."

She nibbled on her bottom lip, and he reached over to smooth the reddened flesh. "Remember, Joanne, the medical examiner will determine whether it was him."

"How will they do that?"

"Sam will investigate Brian Atwell to determine

where he lived, worked, and family. Then get dental records for the ME to compare." As he talked, he stood and picked up their bowls and saucers and walked to the sink, rinsing them out. Turning, he waited as she placed the leftovers back into the refrigerator.

Looking over her shoulder, she asked, "So we might not know for a while?"

"They'll work fast. It'll be quicker than you think. Once the ME determines whether it's him, there will be more questions for you."

"But... like what?" The worry lines deepened.

He rubbed his hand over his chin. "Well, to see if you've remembered anything else."

"Before I had my run-in with Chad, it was all I could think about."

He remained quiet, giving her a chance to get her thoughts together.

"It was a slow morning for the ferry. Two other couples seemed to be together, and Brian and me. That's probably why he sat next to me and started chatting a little bit since the other four people seemed to know each other. It wasn't flirty. And I'm not saying that so you won't think it was. He really wasn't flirting. We just chatted about nothing in particular, and I remember he made a comment about not wanting to miss the ferry going back because there wasn't a hotel on the island."

"And that's why you noticed when he didn't return."

"Yes. When we met at the Crab Shack, it was just a chance to have something to eat before we headed back. When he got the phone call and left so abruptly, I was surprised but certainly didn't get my feelings hurt. I hated that he left so much money on the table and figured I'd see him on the ferry returning to the shore. I kept watching but didn't see him at all. I thought I might see him running toward us when we pulled away from the harbor. But no. The last time I saw him was when he left the restaurant."

She pressed her lips together and then asked, "Bryce, what are the odds that the body found was him?"

"Oh babe, you're asking the wrong person that question. When we find a body, we investigate the situation and surroundings, but it's up to the detectives to determine that."

"But what if someone was killed at sea? Like if they were on a boat when found."

"If someone is killed at sea, then we have investigative authority, but we rely on the medical examiner and Coast Guard's investigators."

He gently reached over and linked fingers with her, giving a little tug. "Let's go watch the stars." She had bought two chairs so that they could continue their stargazing ritual whenever they spent the night at her house.

He grinned and watched with satisfaction as a slow, tender smile curved her lips. After the events of the evening had cast long shadows over dinner, he was relieved to see her smile.

"Well," she said, her eyes gleaming with a newfound sparkle. "I like the idea of getting lost in space for a while."

They sat side by side in the chairs, leaning back, their gazes lifting upward to the nighttime sky and their fingers entwined, binding their connection. When the chill of the air became too cool, he stood and gently pulled her up with him. "I'm wiped, and I know you are too, babe."

"Bedtime?" she teased as she held his gaze with exaggerated wide eyes.

"Can you think of a better way to finish taking our minds off the world's cares?"

Shaking her head slowly, she confessed, "Sleeping with you makes everything better."

Her words struck deep within. "That's all I want to do, babe. Make everything for you better."

They moved together, and after he flipped off the lights in the kitchen, he led her into her small bedroom, where they quickly got down to the business of focusing just on them—and worshipping her body was at the top of his list.

——-

Bryce walked into the station to find Sam and Ryan waiting for him, along with another detective from the sheriff's department. Instantly on alert, he tensed. "What have you got, Sam?"

"The ME gave a positive identification based on fast-tracked dental records. The deceased is Brian Atwell."

By now, the other VMP officers who had arrived for their shift crowded around.

"He wasn't local, was he?" Callan asked.

Sam shook his head. "No. He lived in Baltimore. Not married. Had a small apartment. I've been in contact with a Baltimore PD detective who sent some of his officers over to check out the apartment. Very little there. Some food in the refrigerator, clothes in the closet, and toiletries in the bathroom. Had a TV and a few worn paperbacks, mostly mysteries. The guy lived simply, which isn't surprising since, digging into him, we can't find that he's had a steady job in the last nine months. Before that, he worked as a salesman. No credit card and not a lot of money in his checking account. But he did have about fifty thousand dollars in a savings account."

"What the fuck?" Bryce's hands landed on his hips.

"And I found where he'd stay at the Seaside Inn when he was in the area."

"Is there a possibility that he could've had a heart attack and died before falling into the water?" Andy asked.

"According to the Coast Guard, the rain and winds that came in the night Joanne had lunch with him could have easily sent his body toward the shore. The state of the remains gave enough for the ME to see that he didn't drown. He could also tell that the hyoid bone in his neck was broken in a significant way, usually occurring with strangulation. What I'm going on now is that Brian Atwell was involved in something or with someone on Tangier, made several trips over to the island, and then whoever he was meeting with possibly killed him. Right now, I don't have much more than that. But it's early days in the investigation."

"What the hell business was an unemployed salesman with a shit ton of money in his savings account doing over on Tangier Island?" Bryce asked, his suspicions heightened and wondering about Brian's contact with Joanne.

"That's why we're here. I arranged with Ryan to be taken over to the island, along with Deputy Mark Robbins. Ryan suggested you might also want to go."

"Absolutely," Bryce agreed. "Joanne is taking the ferry today. She said it was earlier than she was supposed to, but she has meetings all next week and couldn't make the trip when normally scheduled."

"Jose, you're on duty with Bryce at the island," Ryan said, receiving a chin lift from both men.

It didn't take long to get the vessel out onto the water since each boat was meticulously prepped at the end of each shift, ready to be used at a moment's notice. Soon, the breeze on the bay rushed past them as they plowed through the water on a VMP motorboat. They made the distance in an hour. During that time, Sam prepped them with what he needed to accomplish while on the island.

"Jose, I know you need to stay close to the harbor with the vessel, so I'll have Mark take a photograph and start combing the fishermen and businesses nearby. I need to canvas some other businesses, including the Crab Shack, where we know he was with Joanne."

As they approached the island, Sam's eyes widened. "Never been out here before. This isn't what I expected."

Bryce looked over at the harbor, which was not like Baytown's Harbor at all. A road ran along part of the island with multiple dockings all along, most with wooden structures built on them. Plus, there were many small docks with sheds out in the water among the marshes. "Almost everyone here has a crab hut to bring their catch in." He pointed at a long wooden dock. "That's where the ferries dock when they come in. Some of the private boats as well."

Once they reached the island, they moored the boat to the harbor, and he and Sam climbed into a waiting golf cart. Sam had already explained the situation to the one police officer who worked on the island, gaining cooperation and the accommodation of the cart.

"Did the officer know anything?"

"No," Sam replied. "The one who'd been here for a while retired, and they just hired someone else. It's hard to find someone qualified to fill the position. They have to live on the island, so they usually get someone near retirement. But, he said he'd never seen or heard of Brian."

It only took a moment to arrive where several shops were located. They started on separate sides of the lane, each with a copy of Brian's photograph. Thirty minutes later, Bryce met Sam at the end, finding that the detective had no more luck than he had in locating anyone who had ever seen Brian.

A sense of urgency propelled them onward. Next, they made their way to the few restaurants but again had no luck with anyone remembering Brian. Bryce drove them to the Crab Shack, where they found the server who remembered seeing him there with Joanne.

"She comes in a few times when she's over on the island," the server said. "But I remember this guy because I've never seen her with anyone before. Only he didn't stay long. I remember she was a little flustered because he suddenly had a phone call and then left quickly." The server then laughed. "But I don't think Joanne will miss the attention. Some other guy was watching her the next time she came over. Let's face it, when you're that pretty, you naturally get attention."

Bryce wasn't thrilled to hear that someone else had been staring at Joanne. "Have you ever seen the second man before?"

The server's nose scrunched, then she shook her head. "I know all the locals who live here, but we get a lot of repeat customers who come over from the mainland. But I'd never seen that man in the picture before that day he had lunch here, nor the man I saw staring at Joanne the next time she came."

Leaving the restaurant, Bryce asked, "What about the B&Bs? There are a couple of them on the island, and if he missed a ferry and got stuck here, he might have stayed at one."

"Let's check them out," Sam agreed.

There were only three, and it didn't take long to stop by each one and talk to the owners. Every person they encountered studied the photograph of Brian carefully, but no one recognized him.

Stopping at a few more establishments, they made their way back to the harbor.

"Well, that was a bust," Bryce grumbled.

"Not really," Sam corrected. "The one thing it does tell us is that he didn't make a habit of eating or staying over on the island. He didn't shop there. And he wasn't seen walking around like most visitors."

"You think he came over specifically to meet with someone who is probably near the harbor."

"That would be my guess. Let's get back and see what Jose and Mark have found out."

They returned the golf cart and met the other two officers.

"None of the ferry pilots recognized him, but then, if he'd only gone on Saul's boat, that would make sense. I checked out a number of the businesses around there, but no one had any dealings with him," Mark reported.

Jose walked over and said, "Okay, I just talked to some of the fishermen. A few recognized Brian and pointed me toward one of the local fishermen near the end of the harbor. Steve Harlow. Lived on the island all his life, the same as his parents. Fourth generation fisherman. He's the one that Brian talked to. He started to go into more detail, but I told him to wait. Sam, since you're the investigating detective, I thought you should be the one to interview him."

"Thanks, Jose," Sam said. "If you wanna wait at the vessel, I'll take Mark and Bryce with me."

Bryce was glad to be included but wondered why Sam was having him tag along.

As though he could read his thoughts, Sam looked over and said, "As law enforcement, there's no reason you can't be with us for the interview. But I figure you'd want to know everything with Joanne being one of the last people around him. Whoever spent time with him might have seen her."

"Fucking hell," Bryce cursed. He glanced at the time, then said, "She was supposed to be on the ferry coming here today. I'll send a text and tell her to go straight from the school back to the harbor, where she'll be in sight of others for safety."

Even as he said those words, they sounded pitifully inadequate, and he wanted nothing more than to jump back in the golf cart and drive straight to the school. Scrubbing his hand down his face, he gave a little shake, then followed Sam and Mark to the other end of the harbor, where multiple wooden buildings lined the docks.

An older fisherman met them near the end of the wooden dock where two boats were moored, their hulls faded and bobbing in the waves. His skin was weathered and tanned, and the deep creases emitting from his eyes gave proof of a life working on the water and in the relentless sun. His waders were old and faded, telling their own stories of countless tides and fishing expeditions. He stood with his arms crossed over his chest as they approached, giving off an air of wariness.

"Mr. Harlow?" Sam asked.

"Yep."

"I'm Detective Shackley from the North Heron Sheriff's Department. This is Deputy Mark Robbins and Virginia Marine Police Officer Bryce Townsend."

"Guess you came back to talk to my son like the other one did."

"We are interested in anyone who talked to this man," Sam continued, holding out the picture of Brian.

"I don't remember him, but I reckon Steve did." He turned and called out. A younger version of the older man stepped out of the wooden building nearby.

Bryce's eyes narrowed as he watched Steve approach. The younger man's eyes darted around, shifting from his dad to the officers. His shoulders were hunched, and he wore an expression of discomfort. It felt suspicious, but Bryce understood that anyone walking toward three members of law enforcement might feel on edge. He fixed his gaze on Sam, determined to watch and learn everything he could, especially with a case that involved the woman he cared for. With a neutral expression covering his turmoil, he focused on the scene in front of him.

After Sam's formal introductions, he pulled up the picture of Brian and turned his phone toward Steve. "I understand you've identified this man as someone you've talked to. I hope you can help us. We're trying to figure out where he was and what he was doing the last time you may have seen him."

Steve glanced at his dad before looking back to see him, his gaze guarded. Rubbing his chin, he asked, "What's the man done?"

"Well, we don't know that he's done anything," Sam said, his demeanor casual and easygoing. "But he was found dead, and we're just trying to piece together what might've happened."

Steve gave no outward appearance that hearing Brian was dead seemed to be a surprise, but Bryce knew that could be because he didn't know him well or didn't care. Still watching carefully, Bryce continued to listen.

"I can't help you with anything about that. Last time I saw him, he was alive and well," Steve said.

"Tell us about your dealings with him," Sam prodded. "That'll help us know what he was doing over here on the island."

"Well, that I can tell you. He came over to the island hoping to hire a fishing boat for some buddies. We just talked the first time he came over, and I gave him some prices. The next time he came over, he asked if he could go out with me on the water. That was the last time I saw him."

"Did he say if he was used to fishing? Or used to being on a boat?" Sam asked.

Steve shrugged, his eyes shifting down to his boots before lifting again. "He said he didn't know anything about fishing. He also didn't talk much, so I didn't learn anything about him. But I did take him out."

"What was he like?"

Steve shifted his weight from one foot to the other, rocking back and forth, almost antsy as though uncomfortable. "He mostly just sat in the boat and watched. I was pulling nets that morning, and he didn't offer to help. Of course, he was looking to have me take him and his buddies out for recreational fishing."

"Did it seem strange that he went out with you on a commercial run?"

Steve snorted and shook his head. "When we talked the first time, he told me he'd never been out on the boat. I figured if he was going to be puking his guts up, he had to learn about that before he paid big money to take some friends out." He shrugged again. "As it was, he seemed okay. We got back to the harbor, and that was the last I saw him. I was busy dealing with the catch and didn't hear from him again. I just figured he decided that fishing wasn't his thing."

"And do you remember what day that was?"

"Normally, I wouldn't, but I remember it was the day old Saul had a heart attack on the ferry trip going back. I figured he may have been on that ferry and, after that experience, decided he didn't want to get on boats anymore."

"Do you often take people out on recreational fishing trips? I know others here advertise that, but you don't."

Steve dragged his tongue over his bottom lip before catching it with his teeth. "Nah. Not really. Sometimes, though. I guess maybe someone gave him my name. I didn't ask. Money is money. Figured if he was willing to pay, I'd take him and his buddies out."

Sam thanked him and left his card, and the three officers turned to walk away. Bryce wondered if Sam had gotten anything relevant from the interview.

Suddenly, Sam turned back and asked, "One more question. Did he carry anything with him when he was with you?"

Steve faltered, his face scrunching.

"It's just that he was seen earlier with a briefcase. Did he have that with him?"

"Well, not that I recollect. Maybe. Yeah, maybe he did. I didn't really notice."

Thanking him again, Sam offered a wave, and then the three officers walked back down the harbor toward the VMP vessel where Jose waited.

"Bryce!"

He turned at the sound of his name, and relief seared through him at the sight of Joanne jogging toward him. She greeted him with a wide smile and exuberance. He wrapped his arms around her and hugged, then she stepped back and looked at the others. She greeted Jose and Sam, then turned toward Mark as he was introduced.

"I was surprised to get your text," she said. "But I finished early at the school and was already heading to the harbor to wait for the ferry."

There was no doubt she knew why they were on the island, and as much as he wanted to tell her what they'd learned, he was glad when she didn't ask any questions.

A horn sounded, and she looked over her shoulder before turning back to him. "That's my ferry's call. I'll head back to work, and then I'll see you tonight." She lowered her voice and smiled. "Your place?"

Nodding, he grinned. "Yeah." He reached into his pocket and pulled out his keys. "In case you get there before me, you can go on in."

Handing her the key, he heard the sharp intake of air as her eyes widened. She looked up and said, "Thanks, honey. You can trust me with this."

"I know." Kissing her lightly, he watched as she jogged over to where the ferry was boarding. Turning back to the others, they climbed onto the VMP boat.

Speeding away, Sam looked over and said, "My guess is that Steve Harlow knows a fuck of a lot more than he was letting on. He knows something, whether he was part of it with Brian or just the transportation." He looked at Bryce. "Start asking the fishermen you know in the bay. Find out what you can about the Harlows. I'm going to look into him, as well. Banking. Associates. Whatever I can find."

Nodding, Bryce was determined to do what he could to keep Joanne safe. Once at the station, he shook hands with Sam and Mark, then turned to Jose.

"You okay, man?" Jose asked.

"I don't know," Bryce answered honestly. "It's weird as fuck, but there's almost no doubt that this Brian guy was up to something. And the idea that Joanne could be linked by someone who would want their involvement quiet… I don't have a good feeling."

22

Joanne walked out of the community college, feeling the weight of the day's responsibilities bearing down. James had given her the silent treatment for most of the day, but she had no idea what his problem was. Cheryl was out sick, and Richard always seemed to be unable to cope when the secretary wasn't in the office. She would scream if she had to hear one more time that he didn't know how to transfer calls. Chad hadn't made another appearance, and Allison had been quiet so far after her last call to Bryce. She had heard nothing more about Brian, but then she also hadn't asked Bryce about the case.

The dimming sky was streaked with shades of orange and purple as the shorter days of late fall were upon them. Evening shadows already cast long fingers over the few vehicles left in the parking lot. She hadn't meant to stay late, but James had left early, abandoning a report that should have been finished.

After climbing into her car, she started the engine

and pulled onto the road. Anxious to get home, change, and grab what she needed to take to Bryce's house, she slowly noticed her steering wheel tugged at her hands, pulling her attention from her thoughts. Gripping it tighter, she heard a *whomping* sound added to the car's vibrations. Cursing under her breath, she pulled off the road, parked, and climbed out to investigate. She dropped her chin to her chest in frustration as her gaze landed on the flat front tire.

Though she knew how to change a tire, she wasn't sure she had the strength to do the job properly. There was a garage in Baytown that would be able to change a flat for her, but looking at the time, she wondered if she could call Bryce.

While deliberating, a car slowed down and came alongside her. The driver's window rolled down, and a man called out, "Do you need some help?"

Under normal circumstances, she would have taken him up on his offer, but uneasiness slid through her, and she shook her head, lifting her phone out of her purse. "Thank you, but I'll be fine. My boyfriend is on his way," she lied. *Well, it's not really a lie... more like a shield. As soon as I call him, he'll be on his way.* The man did not immediately drive on, his hesitation adding to her uneasiness.

Offering what she knew was a wobbly smile, she was lifting the phone to her ear when another car came by and stopped. Seeing Lisa in the passenger seat, she breathed a sigh of relief. Waving at the first man, she called out, "Thanks for the offer!"

Filled with relief when he pulled back onto the road

and kept going, she slumped against the driver's door. Lisa hopped out, and much to Joanne's surprise, James was the driver. Lisa caught her looking toward him and swallowed deeply before turning back to Joanne. "We started carpooling since we don't live too far apart."

James slid from the driver seat and lifted a brow as he looked down at her tire. "Did you not notice it in the parking lot?"

Irritated with how he'd managed to get back to carpool with Lisa but not finish his report, she wanted to snap that if she had noticed a problem, she wouldn't be driving on it. Instead, with a forced smile, she said, "Obviously not. But I know it didn't look like this when I started out. The air must have been going out a bit slowly."

Just then, her phone vibrated, and she answered quickly after seeing it was Bryce.

"Joanne, are you okay? I'm home, and you aren't here yet."

"Yes, I'm fine. I have a flat tire. Right now, two of my coworkers are here." With a lower voice, she added, "I'm not sure he'll be much help—"

"I'm on my way. Where are you?"

She rattled off the road name, then disconnected. With a genuine smile now firmly on her face, she turned toward Lisa and James. "Thank you for stopping and offering to help, but Bryce is coming."

"Okay," James said, climbing back into his car.

Lisa shot him a confused look. Turning back to Joanne, she said, "We'll wait until Bryce gets here."

Once again grateful, she nodded. It only took a

moment for Bryce to drive up in his SUV. He waved toward James and Lisa as they pulled away, then walked over to Joanne, pulling her into his embrace. "Let's get you sorted, and then we can get home."

She hated to leave the comfort of his arms, and it didn't pass her notice that he didn't say *his* home, but just *home*. For a few seconds, she wondered if she'd lost her mind, already being so deeply involved with a man she'd only been with for a short time. Yet everything about him felt right. Letting him go, she nodded.

"I'm glad I had offers of help. Before Lisa and James came by, another man stopped by to assist. I told him you were coming, but he stayed." She scrunched her nose and added, "I've gotten so jumpy that I looked at him with suspicion, but he was just being nice."

His eyes narrowed. "Did you know him?"

She shook her head and shrugged. "But it's not like I know a lot of locals. Most people are friendly and helpful."

Bryce grunted, but he didn't appear happy. "Maybe." He let out a slow breath, shaking his head before turning back to her car.

She hovered nearby as he knelt to stare at her tire.

"What the fuck?"

Not expecting that response from him, she dropped down to squat and stared at the tire. "What? What's wrong?"

"This tire has been cut. Cut carefully so that the air didn't leave it immediately, but allowed it to leak out slowly."

"I don't remember running over anything. What

could've done that?" Still staring at the tire, she had no idea what she was looking for and twisted to find his intense gaze on her.

"Joanne, babe, you didn't run over anything. This was done with a knife."

She gasped, and only his hand on her arm kept her from falling backward onto her ass. "Are you sure? That makes absolutely no sense!"

He didn't say anything, but he assisted her to stand as he stood too. Jerking his phone out of his pocket, he placed a call. She wanted to ask more questions, but the thunderous expression on his face made her decide that staying quiet was the best thing to do.

She heard him talking, his voice clipped and full of anger. After hanging up, he placed another call. After that, he jammed his phone back into his pocket, stalked over to her, and asked, "Are you okay?"

"Sweetheart, I'm fine. You're the one I'm worried about because you're really angry, and I don't understand what's happening."

He nodded slowly, kissed the top of her head, then let out a shaky breath as he leaned back to hold her gaze. "I called Sam, and he's having a couple of deputies come and look at your car. They're going to see if there are any fingerprints around the wheelbase in case someone placed their hand on the side of your car when they knifed your tire. I've also got a friend, Jason, who owns the garage in Baytown, and he's going to come out and haul your car back to his place."

"Why? Can't he just change the tire here?"

"Since your car was sabotaged, I want him to take it

back to his shop and look it over. He's going to check the other tires and everything under the hood and the car to ensure that no one else has done anything."

Her brain felt sluggish as she struggled to make sense of his explanation. "I don't understand. Why would anyone do this to me?"

"Let's just take care of your car first, and we'll talk when we get home."

She wanted to beg him to talk now because she hated waiting for something important. But as she stared up at his face, usually filled with strength, determination, and kindness, she now observed fear and anger. Pressing her lips together, she nodded. If her acquiescence would give him a modicum of peace, she'd give it willingly.

"Mom, I'm fine. No, really, I'm fine. It was just a flat tire, and Bryce is taking care of it. He's even having the garage check the others." Joanne and Bryce had watched as Jason towed her car, then headed to his house after running through the local drive-through to grab burgers. Once finished, she'd called her mom to chat.

"Well, I want you two to come to dinner. If anyone else asks me if I've met my daughter's boyfriend, and I have to pretend I have, then I'm going to go crazy!"

Joanne looked over at Bryce as he got off the phone with Sam. She mouthed, "Can we have dinner with my mom tomorrow?" and received his smile and nod. It was the first smile she'd seen on him since he'd looked at her tire.

"Mom, how about tomorrow night?"

"Really?" The squeal of delight had Joanne chuckling.

"Yes, we'll come tomorrow night."

"Is there anything he likes or doesn't like?"

"Anything you fix will be perfect. We'll see you about six, okay?"

"Oh, Joanne, I'm so excited!"

After she said goodbye, her smile was still on her face as Bryce walked over and braced her against the counter with his arms on either side.

"Sounds like tomorrow will be the big introduction," he said, his gaze warmly roving over her face.

"Are you okay with that?" She wasn't sure why she asked since Bryce had never indicated that they weren't starting something real, but meeting parents was a big deal whether you were a teenager or a grown adult. It somehow signified a certain level of commitment. He stared at her with intensity, and she held her breath.

He leaned forward, his weight resting on his arms, but his chest pressed against hers. "Joanne, meeting your mom will be an honor for me. What we have is something special. Sure, it's new, but we're not a couple of twenty-year-olds still trying to find ourselves. We know what we want, and we know what we've had in the past that sure as hell wasn't right. So, yeah... I'm okay meeting your mom. That tells me you're in the same place I am with us as a couple."

He kissed her lightly, and she pulled him closer,

wanting all of him. During dinner, he'd told her of his fears and concerns about what happened to Brian. Adding in the threats from Allison and the implied threat from Chad being in the area, she felt as though she were on anxiety overload. And as his lips met hers, she wanted the world to disappear, leaving only the two of them.

Her fingers dug into his shoulders, and her hips moved forward, his erection pressing into her belly. Matching his movements, she ground herself against him and swallowed, the groan slipping from his lips.

His hands spanned her waist, and he lifted her onto the kitchen counter before stepping between her open legs. The new height caused his erection to press against her hot core. She clutched his jaws, tilting her head so that their mouths were sealed.

Wild abandon took over, and the kiss was wet and messy as they pressed tighter together. Bolts of electricity moved between her aching breasts and inner core, creating a need only he could meet.

When they'd arrived at his house, he had changed out of his uniform into a T-shirt and sweatpants. Now, glad for easier access, she tugged at his shirt, pulling it up over his washboard abs. Their mouths separated long enough for him to lean back and lift his hands like a child. She continued to jerk and pull the T-shirt up and over his head and arms. Once she tossed the T-shirt to the floor, his thick arms encircled her as he stepped closer, and his body gave evidence that he was no child.

His unrestrained cock had more freedom in the sweatpants that he was wearing, and they were tented in a delicious way that had her drag her tongue over her lips. His gaze dropped to her mouth, and he dove back in for another kiss, his hands now working to pull her shirt off.

Sitting on the kitchen counter in only a bra, he deftly unfastened the front hook and allowed her breasts to hang free. He kissed his way from her jaw to her chest, taking his time, sucking each nipple deeply. Her fingernails scratched along his back, digging in slightly as his mouth worked wonders, and she thought she'd go mad if they didn't get naked soon.

Glancing behind her, she spied the blinds over the sink open. Gasping, she said, "Not here."

He banded his arms around her, and she hooked her ankles at the back of his waist. He lifted and, with their bodies pressed together, turned and walked into the bedroom. Here, behind the privacy of the closed windows, he placed her gently on the bed.

No longer willing to go slow, she scrambled up and slid her hands down into the waistband of his sweatpants and slowly pulled them down, careful as she unleashed his cock. Continuing to sink to her knees as she dragged his pants to his ankles, he placed his hands on her shoulders as she freed his legs from any material.

Leaning forward, she licked his cock from base to tip, swirling her tongue around the top. His fingers dove into her hair, lightly squeezing her scalp.

Urged on, she slipped her mouth completely over the tip, taking as much of him as she could. With her hand at the base, she alternated pumping, sucking, licking, and teasing.

As his groans filled the room, she loved every sound and felt the heady power of being in control.

"Babe," he said, his voice low and guttural. "Not gonna last."

She continued, shocked when he stepped back and shook his head.

"You know I want this. I want nothing more than to come and have you swallow me down. But tonight, I want to come while buried deep in you." He grinned. "At least for round one."

He assisted her to stand, then turned and fell back on the bed. She crawled over him. He was still giving her the power she needed, as though knowing with her life spinning, she required this.

But she didn't want him to think she just needed sex or control. As she climbed over him, she dipped low so that her breasts dragged along his chest and kissed him. Then settling her entrance over his cock, she confessed, "I need *you*." She lowered herself, inch by inch, loving the way his face contorted with need and pleasure until she was fully seated. His hands gripped her hips, his fingers digging into the flesh of her ass.

She started to move, slower at first, and then faster and faster. She lifted up and down and rocked back and forth, altering her position slightly to maximize the friction. After the blow job, he might come quickly, and she wanted them to come together.

Bending low again so that the pressure was on her sensitive nerves, she soon flew apart, her inner muscles clamping tightly on his cock. Her fingernails were making little crescents in his shoulders, but she had no doubt she would have little bruises on her ass from where he gripped her. In the middle of her release, his face reddened, and throat muscles tightened as he thrust upward, then roared out.

She continued to ride him until she had no strength left in her arms and barely managed not to flop on top of his chest. Their sweat-slicked bodies slowly cooled, and their panting eased into normal breathing. Lifting her head, she stared down at him and smiled. "Thank you for making a sucky day a lot better."

"Thank you for making every day a lot better."

She bit her lips as tears sprung into her eyes and blinked furiously to keep them from falling. "How did I get so lucky?"

His hand cupped her cheek, and she leaned into his warmth.

"Same as me, sweetheart. I looked up one day, and there you were. Now, I have exactly what I'd always hoped to have."

23

"Dinner was lovely, Mrs. Norris," Bryce said with sincerity, leaning back in his seat with a full stomach. His arm rested on the back of Joanne's seat.

"Oh, thank you. And please call me Maureen."

Joanne's mom had a wide smile on her face, and it struck him how much Joanne looked like her mother when they smiled. Her eye color and build must have come from her dad, but mother and daughter definitely shared her brilliant smile.

"It's been a long time since I've had the pleasure of cooking for someone who graced my kitchen other than Joanne. Believe me, it was a pleasure."

"Mom, you're always cooking for the people at church or for the bake sales for the Auxiliary. Everybody appreciates your food!" Joanne said.

"Yes, but it's especially nice to have somebody come over and tuck their feet under the table."

Bryce wondered about Chad but wasn't about to bring him up. From the sounds of it, Joanne's former boyfriend wasn't around her mom very much. Considering how graciously she'd welcomed him, he wondered what she'd thought about Chad. But then, Chad was a loser, and while her mom had certainly set up numerous blind dates for Joanne that had also turned out to be losers, Bryce had a feeling that Chad had never been on her mom's favorite list.

"Well, I haven't had home-cooked fried chicken that good in a long time."

Maureen's smile beamed. Joanne glanced to the side as he continued to gently rub his fingers over her shoulder. Her smile was soft, and he could already read the emotions on her face. Peaceful. Happy. Comfortable. Right now, those were the same feelings that moved through him.

Joanne offered to get the coffee and dessert, and while she was in the kitchen, Maureen held his gaze.

"It's just been me and Joanne for a number of years since my Carl died. I've always wanted Joanne to have the kind of love that I had with my husband. I'm sure you've heard about my attempts at setting her up." Maureen shook her head with self-deprecation. "I'm afraid I don't have a very good track record."

"Joanne knows where your heart is, Maureen."

"She's a wonderful daughter."

"I'd say that's in large part due to you."

She laughed and shook her head. "I would accuse you of being a flatterer, but you seem like one of the most sincere people I've ever met.

"I hope that I am."

She glanced toward the kitchen, then sighed, before

turning her attentive gaze back to Bryce. "I never cared for Chad. I thought I did at first. I tried to. But something about him seemed sneaky. Like he was always trying too hard to make me like him. And I could tell, even though she wouldn't admit it, Joanne never felt about him the way I felt about my husband. I'm sorry for the ugly way it ended, but I'm not sorry that it ended."

"She's told me about him, and I agree."

"I know you work for the marine police, but still... you are law enforcement. When she told me that Chad showed up yesterday at her house, I was worried. Please keep an eye on her."

He reacted to the seriousness of her tone and leaned forward, his forearms on the table. "I give you my promise that I'll watch out for her. I've already warned him off, and if he tries to contact her again, she'll go in for another restraining order."

Maureen sucked in a deep breath and let it out slowly, smiling. "Good."

Further conversation was interrupted as the aroma of coffee and chocolate preceded Joanne, bringing in a tray with thick slices of chocolate cake and three steaming cups of coffee. As she set it down, she smiled over at him with mischief in her eyes. "Don't worry... it's decaffeinated."

He responded with a grin, his eyes lingering on her face for a moment. In truth, he didn't mind if he and Joanne had trouble going to sleep. A conspiratorial wink escaped as he shot her a knowing look. Sleep was the last thing on his mind. He was confident they could always find something to do if sleep eluded them.

After dessert and coffee, laughter filled the room as Maureen brought out some of Joanne's childhood pictures. Maureen shared the memories with pride while Joanne's cheeks pinkened with an embarrassed blush. He loved sneaking a peek into the young Joanne's life, but it was soon time to go.

Bryce offered his warm goodbyes to her mom. After receiving a hug and kiss on the cheek, he stepped back and watched as Joanne and Maureen hugged tightly. His heart twinged with warmth, knowing Joanne had received a deep, abiding love from her mom.

After he'd assisted her into the SUV and started the engine, Joanne leaned over the console and offered her lips for a kiss. Ensnared by her soft and inviting gaze, he was quick to accept her kiss with a passion that spoke of promises and desires yet to be explored. The taste of chocolate still lingered, and he reveled in the sweet reminder of the evening.

"Thank you." Her breath whispered over his face.

"I had a wonderful time," he replied. "You don't have to thank me for that."

"Even though my mom has grieved the loss of my dad and has no plans to date or ever remarry, she still believes in love with her whole heart."

"Your mom wants you happy. There's nothing in the world wrong with that, Joanne. And one day, you'll have that kind of love to offer your kids."

She smiled and leaned back in her seat, and he realized it had been on the tip of his tongue to say *our* children. *How can I even think in those terms so soon?* Yet staring at Joanne's beautiful face and sweet smile, he could imagine a future with her.

Starting the car, he backed out of the driveway. They had just begun the trip to his place when Joanne looked over and said, "Would you mind if we stopped by my house? It's just a couple of minutes out of the way. I want to grab my sneakers. I didn't think about tomorrow at your house when I put on these pumps."

"No problem," he said, then changed lanes so he could pull onto her road.

Once they were in her driveway and had parked, she glanced to the side. "You can wait here if you want. It'll just take me a moment."

He nodded, and while she headed to her front door, he pulled out his phone to check emails and messages. Seeing one from Debbie, he started to open it. *That's right... Debbie was going to let me know when she's arriving—*

Suddenly, Joanne's front door flung open, and she bolted through, running toward him, her eyes wide in fear.

He jumped out of his SUV and met her on the front walk. Before he had a chance to ask what was wrong, she slammed into him, looked up, and gasped, "Someone has been in my house!"

"Get in the SUV!" he barked. She hesitated, and he turned her and guided her over, opened the door, and gave her a light push. "Get in. Now, Joanne."

"I don't want you to go in there alone! What if they're still in there?"

The idea that she had been in her house with the possibility of someone else in there sent icicles through his veins. "Call 911. Tell them who you are and where you're at, and tell them you're with me." Seeing her blink, still wide-eyed, he gentled his voice. "Joanne, honey, focus on me. I need you to call 911."

She jolted as though struck by lightning and pulled her phone out of her purse. When he saw that she was doing what he asked, he took his phone out of his pocket. Dialing quickly, he got ahold of Sam's cell phone.

"Sam? It's Bryce. I'm with Joanne at her house. She went in to get something and came flying back out, saying someone had been in her house. Since we don't know if that person or persons are still in there, I'm not leaving her alone. She's calling 911, but I want you on this."

Rattling off her address, he thanked Sam and disconnected. Looking over at Joanne, still sitting in his SUV, she handed the phone to him and said, "They want to talk to you."

He got on with the 911 dispatcher, identified himself, and also mentioned that he'd just talked to Detective Sam Shackley. "We've been working a case together, and since I don't know if this is related, I want him on it."

The dispatcher assured him that someone was on their way, and they'd coordinate with the detective. While they waited, he called Ryan to let him know what was happening.

Ryan assured him that he'd take care of telling the

others. "You can expect to get offers of help. Is she going to stay with you?"

He looked over at the still wide-eyed Joanne, her face pale and her arms wrapped around her middle in a protective stance. "Oh yeah. Once they go through everything, we'll grab some of her things, and she'll be at my house."

In only a few minutes, the sound of approaching vehicles had him swing his head to the side as he watched several North Heron Sheriff's vehicles pull into her driveway with Sam's car directly behind.

As the deputies spread out around the house, Sam and Mark walked straight over to him and Joanne.

"Joanne," Sam began. "I'm really sorry this happened. Tell me what you saw when you went inside."

"It looks like somebody was searching for something." Her shaky voice was tinged with disbelief. "I know it sounds like I've watched too much TV, but I swear that's what it looks like. My small desk in the corner of my living room had the drawers pulled out, and things were scattered about. The books are on the floor from my bookcase. I was too scared to check the kitchen or my bedroom. It must just be kids playing a prank because I don't have anything worth stealing."

"We'll investigate as soon as we check the outside perimeter and the deputies clear the residence. You can come with us to let us know what was taken."

Bryce wanted to pace, considering the ice that had flowed through his veins was now molten lava after hearing the fear in Joanne's voice. Minutes seemed like an eternity as they waited. The deputies finally came around and reported that the glass in the back door had been broken. Joanne's gasp sounded painful, but her expression morphed from fear to anger.

Sam led them to the front door, and Bryce held Joanne's hand, entering first, then letting her slide in behind him. His gaze swept the room, once again wishing he had more of an investigative background. The signs of invasion were obvious, but the motives were unclear. He tried to imagine if this was a random robbery or if someone had targeted her.

Sam turned to Joanne and asked, "I can see things have been scattered, but can you point out specifically what's been rifled through?"

Joanne's lips were pressed together so tightly they'd lost their color. She pointed at the desk drawer, whose contents were on the floor, and the bookcase where the books were scattered about. The rest of the living room appeared untouched, except for a few pillows from the sofa that had been shifted slightly. She gasped again as they walked into the kitchen, and Bryce spied the broken back door. The drawers in the small kitchen had also been opened, and the basket where she kept mail and magazines had been upended.

She led them into the bedroom, and it was obvious someone spent more time there. Her closet door stood ajar, and her purses had been pulled off the shelf, opened, and tossed onto the floor. The bedroom was small, but the dresser drawers had also been opened, and the contents were discarded carelessly.

"It's a mess, but I don't see anything missing," she said, shaking her head. Letting out a huff, she added,

"It's like whoever came in just wanted to make a mess."

"Or search for something," Mark said, leaving the words to hang in the room.

Joanne's eyes widened. "I don't have anything. Why would anyone want to search my place?"

Bryce looked over sharply and caught Joanne's confused expression. He was already thinking about the situation with Brian Atwell, and with a look at Mark and Sam, he wondered if they were connecting the same dots.

"Joanne," Sam began. "I'd like you to think back to the day you met Brian Atwell. First on the boat and then at the restaurant."

"We've done this," she said, her usual acquiescence fleeing before she sighed and rubbed her forehead. "I'm sorry. Yes, of course."

"I assume you had a purse or a bag with you?"

Nodding again, she replied, "Yes. I didn't want to carry too much, so I have a backpack purse that can hold my laptop and my personal items. That's what I had with me that day."

"Is there any way that the bag was sitting at your feet, or under the table, or on a chair or seat next to you so that he could've slipped something inside?"

Shaking her head, she started to reply when Bryce interrupted.

"Think carefully, Joanne. He's not asking if you saw anything. He's asking if your bag could've been in a position where Brian could have dropped something, and you might not notice."

She closed her eyes, and he could tell she was casting her mind back.

"On the ferry going over, he sat in the seat next to me, but my bag was between my legs. And it was zipped closed. The reason I know this is because the first time I ever went on a trip by myself, my mom lectured me about keeping my purse closed so that nobody could try to take my wallet or cell phone. She also taught me to either hold my purse in my lap or set it between my feet so that my knees bracketed the bag. Believe me, on the ferry ride, he would have no way to slip anything unnoticed into my bag."

Nodding, Sam said, "Good, good. Now think about when you were at the restaurant."

"We were seated in a booth. I got there first, and my bag was on the seat beside me. Actually between me and the wall. He came in and sat on the other side of the table. Again, believe me, he had no way to get close to my bag."

Sam rubbed his chin, nodding. "Okay, I just wanted to make sure."

She stepped into her closet and pointed at a pink leather backpack. "That's the one I had. It's on the floor and opened like all the other bags I have, but I'm the one who cleaned it out, so there was nothing in it."

"Of course," Mark interjected. "If Brian was trying to get rid of something, he might not have been able to use Joanne, but that doesn't mean that someone didn't think of the possibility."

Bryce wished that Mark would stop saying things aloud that seemed to jolt Joanne. But she simply looked at him, then asked, "Do you think whoever did this had something to do with Brian?"

"Tell me about anyone else that might have wanted to come in and cause a mess?" Sam asked. "Any students or coworkers or anybody who has a grudge?"

She shared a glance with Bryce and sighed. His gut clenched, and he answered for her. "Yesterday, Joanne's ex showed up here. She had a restraining order against him in Richmond, but it's expired. He searched her out, and while he didn't make an overt threat, he wasn't happy to find out that she had moved on with me."

"Name?" Sam barked, his notebook and pen in hand.

"Chad. Chad Littleton," she replied. "But I can't imagine Chad doing anything like this. I mean, he wanted to talk and apologize for his past behavior, but that's all. This is..." She looked around and sighed heavily. "This just doesn't seem like something he'd do."

"Did you have something he thought was his? Something he wanted returned?" Sam asked.

Joanne emphatically shook her head. "Absolutely not! When I broke up with him over six months ago, I told him to clear out everything that was his. Believe me, when I moved here, I had nothing of his still in my possession."

"He wasn't happy to find out you were dating somebody else," Bryce said. "People can react in strange ways when they're jealous and upset."

She turned and looked at him, then slowly nodded before tilting her head to the side. "I guess the same could be said about Allison, right?"

"Allison?" Mark asked.

Now, really wishing that Mark would stop speaking, Bryce inwardly groaned. "Allison Moore. Old flame that's been long over. She showed up the other day, not happy to see me with Joanne, and made some threats about how we'd be sorry."

Mark looked around, then said, "I could see this being the work of somebody that just wanted to piss you two off."

Everyone looked over at Sam, who shrugged. "Too early to say. My guys are going to get fingerprints and photographs."

"You'll want mine, won't you?"

Sam nodded and signaled for one of the officers. "Bryce, yours will be in the system, of course, since you're law enforcement." It didn't take long, and once they had both their prints, he said, "If you're sure that nothing has been taken, Joanne, then I'd suggest you head out with Bryce."

"Can I take some clothes?"

"Yeah, get what you need," Sam said, "but don't move anything else."

"Get whatever you want for a couple of days." Bryce's voice was firm with a protective edge. "You'll be with me and not coming back here."

Her nod was almost imperceptible, but tension poured from her. Her movements were almost frantic as she grabbed a flowered duffel bag that seemed incongruent with the somber mood of the room. She hurriedly shoved items into it, darting from the bedroom to the bathroom. After saying goodbye to Sam and Mark, Bryce gently pulled the bag from her hand and carried it as he led her outside to his SUV.

The drive to his house was quiet—too quiet. Joanne sat still, her body rigid and her eyes staring straight ahead. He wanted to offer assurances and comfort, but her silence was a wall. They parked outside his house, and he turned toward her, his eyes searching her face. She looked over but shook her head.

"I'm too tired to talk right now, Bryce. Let's go in, feed the cats, and give me just a few minutes to have some peace." Her voice was heavy with exhaustion.

"I can give you that, baby," he agreed softly. He climbed down, grabbed her duffel, then linked fingers with her as they walked toward the front door. Once inside, he breathed a little easier when he saw her smile as she knelt to rub the four cats that were zigzagging figure eights around her ankles.

Bryce was worried but kept his expression neutral. Joanne appeared too calm over the events of the past hour. He set her bag down and walked into the kitchen, the four cats immediately following him on the hopeful trail of eating. As he fixed their dinner and placed the bowls on the floor, Joanne walked in and immediately moved with great purpose to his refrigerator. Pulling out a bottle of wine, she poured a glass and drank a hefty sip. Catching his eye, she shook her head. "Don't worry, I'm not turning to alcohol as a crutch. Well, maybe a little one. But right now, I just need something to take the edge off."

He moved to her, understanding in his eyes, and poured a glass for himself. He didn't usually drink wine, but it seemed important to stand in solidarity with her, even if that meant supporting her by indulging in her drink of choice.

She looked down at the glass in his hand, then back at him, and her lips curved slightly. Clinking their glasses in a silent oath to each other, they both took another healthy gulp. He pulled the glass from her hand and set them both on the counter. Reaching into the bag he'd packed while she had been in her bedroom, he pulled out a sunflower cookie jar and placed it on the kitchen counter. Nerves shot through him at her gasp. He turned to her, finding tears in her eyes.

"I'm not trying to rush anything," he said, although he wondered about the honesty of the sentiment since he'd love to have her move in permanently. "But I wanted you to have a bit of home here."

"I love it," she whispered, swallowing deeply.

His arms wrapped around her and pulled her close, allowing her cheek to tuck against his chest, and her breath was warm against his biceps. Kissing the top of her head, he whispered words of assurance. "I promise, sweetheart, that whoever did that will be found, and the police better hope they get to him or her first."

Leaning back, she sighed. "Do you really think it could've been Chad or Allison? That seems so... like such a stupid thing for somebody to do."

He hated to remind her that Allison had already proved to be a wild card, and as far as Chad went, finding where she lived and showing up after months of them being broken up didn't bode well for his mental state, either. Sighing, he said, "Allison has said she intends to stir up shit, and Chad is… well, let's just say that neither of them is taking the word 'no' very well."

She nodded and also sighed. "It's not something that Chad would do. It's just not his style. Now Allison? I don't know. And I know you all keep trying to tie this into Brian Atwell, but Bryce, nothing he could've been involved in had anything to do with me at all."

"Nobody thinks he had something to do with you that you would know about, Joanne. The fear is that he was doing something he shouldn't be involved in, maybe something that got him killed, and somebody on the island saw the two of you together."

She lay her cheek on his chest again and tightened her grip around his waist. They stood for long minutes in the kitchen, neither speaking but drawing strength from each other. He remembered seeing Bernie and Debbie doing the same things during difficult times. He'd never felt that way about another woman, but with Joanne in his arms, he now understood what his aunt and uncle were doing. It was more than just offering comfort and care. It was love and hope for things to get better, all tied up in a hug.

24

Her dreams were filled with dark visions and shrouded by shadows. By the time Joanne woke, her body was heavy, and her mind was drained. Blinking open her eyes, she was met by the gentle concern in Bryce's eyes as he lay facing her with his arm wrapped around her. His gaze was pinned on her with a blend of worry and affection.

Light circles underscored his eyes, and lines of tension were etched into the corners of his mouth. She wondered if he'd also been awake during the night. Lifting her hand, she cupped his rough cheek and soothed her thumb over his stubble. "Are you okay?" she asked, her voice barely above a whisper.

His intense gaze softened, and he pulled her closer. "I think that's the question I should ask you, but since you were very restless last night, I have a feeling the answer is no."

Her breath hitched, and she dropped her gaze to his chin as a chill ran down her spine. He gave a little squeeze, and she once again stared into his worried eyes. "I just keep thinking about everything. Nothing makes sense, Bryce. I'm a simple person. I go to work, I get along with my coworkers, and I get along with the college students and teenagers I work with. I have friends, and I have you. I have nothing in my life that should make me the target of someone."

"I don't know what's happening, but I promise you'll be safe here."

"My being here could put you in danger—"

"I'm not going to leave you here by yourself. This is Saturday, so we'll spend the whole weekend together. Just you and me…"

A long howling meow sounded out, and her chest shook with mirth as he rolled his eyes. Princess popped up behind Bryce's head, and Pumpkin, Sickle, and Mixer stretched as their sister woke them and wandered from the foot of the bed to where the humans were lazing about.

"You, me, and four cats," he amended. "Let me go feed them so they'll get quiet and drop into a food coma in a sunspot. Then I'll come right back, and we can—"

A knock sounded on the door, and a female voice called out for Bryce. His face morphed into anger as his expression hardened. "If that's fuckin' Allison—"

Flinging back the covers with exasperated fury, Joanne growled. "No more! I'm done with this!" She was still wearing only his T-shirt and panties but didn't care as she rushed on bare feet and wild eyes to the front door. Bryce yelled for her to stop, but she knew he would at least take the time to pull on some pants. If Allison wanted it shoved in her face that he had moved on, Joanne was ready to give it her all. Reaching the door first, she grabbed the knob and jerked it open just as his arm banded around her waist.

"What do you... oh—" Joanne's voice halted as her body jerked.

Standing on the front porch was an attractive woman, comfortably dressed in jeans and a white blouse over a navy T-shirt. Her hair was a soft shade of blond, with just a hint of silver shooting through the strands. Her makeup was subtle, perfectly illuminating her smooth skin. If it wasn't for the crinkled laugh lines spreading from her eyes, her age would be completely obliterated.

"Aunt Debbie!" Bryce's greeting was both excited and stunned. "Shit, Debbie," he groaned. "I lost track of... shit, I lost track of everything."

"Oh God!" Joanne's guttural utterance was all she managed as she stood wide-eyed with heat rising over her face. Jolting at her state of undress, she jerked down on the bottom of his T-shirt in a feeble attempt at modesty.

"Good morning!" The exuberant greeting came from the woman on the porch that Joanne now knew was his beloved Aunt Debbie. The same woman appeared to be holding back her laughter while politely keeping her eyes on Joanne's face and not her state of undress.

"Well, Bryce. I thought this was the day I said I was coming, but I didn't expect such a warm greeting." She thrust her hand out toward Joanne and said, "I'm

Debbie Townsend. And you must be Joanne. I'm so pleased to meet you!"

"Please, come in," Joanne stammered, stepping back. Since Bryce was behind her, she bumped into him but kept pushing against his larger body. His arm wrapped around her front as his hand splayed on her stomach. They stepped back together so Debbie could enter the house.

"It's okay," he whispered in her ear.

With her face still aflame with embarrassment, Joanne managed to mumble, "Excuse me. I'll be right back."

Bryce's arm was still tightly grounding her to him, keeping her from escaping. She grabbed his hand and forced it to loosen so she could slip out and dash back toward the bedroom. Mortified that his only living relative had seen her obviously coming from his bed, she jerked off his T-shirt while turning in a circle, trying to locate her bra. Finding it on the floor barely peeking out from under the bed, she slipped it on, fumbling with the clasp. Bending, she grabbed one of her own shirts, then dragged on a pair of jeans. Rushing into the bathroom, she looked at her reflection and groaned. Her hair was a chaotic mess, wild with tendrils waving all about. Her eyes were ringed slightly with smudged mascara from the night before, and her cheeks were pink with the blush of embarrassment.

With determined haste, she grabbed her brush and, with a few hasty swipes, managed to tame her hair before pulling it back into a ponytail. Not wanting to take the time to find her face wash, she rubbed a bath cloth under her eyes. Slapping on moisturizer, she decided to forgo any makeup. *Especially since I'm leaving!*

Hurrying back into the bedroom, she scrambled to grab the few clothes she'd pulled out of her bag, shoved them in, and zipped it closed. She let out a ragged breath to try to calm her racing heart and decided she'd call her mom before heading there. The fear lurked that she was possibly putting her mom at risk, but she couldn't think of an alternative. *Maybe Sam can have a deputy drive by my mom's house often.* She knew that even with his aunt here, Bryce would want to make sure she was safe.

She looked up, startled out of her thoughts, as he walked into the room. His gaze shot down to her zipped bag and then lifted to her, his expression quizzical.

"What the hell are you doing?"

"I'm packing, Bryce. I figure I can go to my mom's—"

"Hell, no."

"Look, honey, with all that's gone on, it's no wonder we forgot about Debbie's visit. But I need to—"

"What you need to do is get out there and visit with Debbie."

"Bryce." A harsh tone entered her whisper. "I met her at the door, half dressed, looking like a God-knows-what with sex hair and smeared mascara, and—"

"You met her at the door looking like my girlfriend, which you are."

She snapped her lips closed, soothed by his calming declaration, then pinched them tightly together as frustration won out over all the other stormy emotions. She let out a long, cleansing breath. "I don't think you understand. She may know I'm your girlfriend, but the way I answered the door makes me look... like... like..." Struggling to find the right word, she finally settled for a growl. "Ughhh!"

"You're beautiful. No matter what you're wearing or how you answer the door." He stepped closer, his gaze holding hers. "And it made you look exactly as you are. Not only my beautiful girlfriend but someone who's comfortable in my home. Believe me, sweetheart, that means more to Debbie than you can possibly imagine."

The air left her lungs in a rush, and she held his gaze, searching for the truth in his words. He stepped toward her, reached out to cup her cheeks, and gently kissed her lips.

"I just need a minute to throw on a shirt. You're already dressed, so you can wait for me or join Debbie in the kitchen. She's making coffee. It's your call."

She offered a short nod. "I'll go to the kitchen." She knew that was the right answer when his lips curved, and a smile spread over his face. Her heart warmed at the sight of the sunlight breaking through the clouds. Lifting on her toes, she kissed him again. "Anyway, I'd better save her from the hungry cats."

He threw his head back and laughed before heading into the bathroom. She drew in another deep breath, filling her lungs with the now-familiar scent of his home, and walked out of the bedroom.

Stopping at the kitchen entrance, she spied Debbie at the coffee pot, the comforting scent easing her discomfort. Three mugs were already pulled out and set on the counter. Debbie looked over her shoulder as Joanne entered and smiled warmly.

Jumping in before Debbie had a chance to speak, Joanne said, "I'm so sorry about the way I came to the door this morning. Last night was rough... not here, I mean... before I got here. And I wasn't thinking, and I'm so sorry—"

Debbie turned to face Joanne, her movements graceful and welcoming. She reached out to take Joanne's hands in hers. "Joanne, please don't apologize! First of all, I would never expect any special treatment just because I'm here. And Bryce told me he didn't get my reminder that I was coming by."

Debbie's voice was a gentle embrace wiping away the traces of Joanne's embarrassment, and standing in Bryce's kitchen after all that had happened in the past twenty-four hours, the pressure on Joanne's heart eased.

"That's very gracious of you. But I'm here because..." She had no idea how to describe what had happened yesterday evening.

"Oh, Bryce has already filled me in—or at least given me the short version. I can't believe someone broke into your house! That's horrible! And I'm so glad you're here and safe."

"Well, I can stay with my mom so you can enjoy your visit with Bryce."

"I wouldn't dream of it." Debbie laughed and shook her head. "I have no plans to interrupt your lives at all. I'm just so thrilled to have the chance to meet you."

"Well, he's told me nothing but the most wonderful

things about you. I'm thrilled to be able to meet you, too."

Debbie turned back to the pot and poured three cups of coffee. Joanne walked to the refrigerator, pulled out the creamer, and set it on the counter.

As the women doctored their coffee to their tastes, Debbie asked, "I am curious. Who did you think was at the door this morning?"

Her cheeks heated with blush again, but Joanne answered honestly. "Bryce had a little trouble with his former... um... girlfriend, who doesn't understand that things are over. I actually thought she might be the one banging on the door."

"Allison." As Debbie said the word, her nose crinkled as if she smelled something atrocious. "I only met her once, and that was simply because I stopped to have lunch with Bryce on my way to Virginia Beach. We were at a restaurant when she showed up, pretending that she didn't know we were going to be there. I could tell Bryce wasn't happy, and it only took a couple of minutes of being in her presence to know that she might have some of his time, but she was never going to have any of his heart. I was so glad when he finally told me he got rid of her."

"Well, that seems to be a theme with her. Shows up and gets in his face. Under normal circumstances, I would've never answered Bryce's door, nor would I have done so wearing..." She felt her face heat again.

Bursting into laughter, Debbie shook her head. "Don't be embarrassed. Just think about it... people wear much less than that on the beach. Everything important was covered up, and then some." She patted Joanne's hand again, still smiling. Once again, the kitchen, filled with the soft morning light, became a haven of connection and acceptance, reminding her so much of her mother's kitchen.

Bryce walked into the kitchen, and Joanne noticed his hair was wet. Rolling her eyes that he had taken a shower while she still sported a just-woken and haphazardly-thrown-together look, she couldn't maintain a pout when he came straight over to her. Instead of reaching for his coffee, he reached for her. The kiss was light and sweet but unequivocally claiming.

Debbie let out a soft sigh, and when Joanne glanced at her, she observed a gentle smile aimed their way.

The rest of the weekend went much smoother, and she discovered Debbie was everything Bryce had said she was. Calm, sweet, loving, and so funny. At Bryce's suggestion, they took Debbie out to dinner and asked Joanne's mother to join them.

At first, Joanne had been terrified. It felt way too soon to have their relatives meet. Once again, it was Bryce that settled her nerves. As she fretted while they got dressed for dinner, he took her by the shoulders, bent so that their faces were aligned, and said, "If Debbie and Maureen were just friends of ours, would it seem weird to have dinner with them?"

She understood he was trying to make a point, and instead of giving a flippant answer, she thought about what he asked. Slowly shaking her head, she said, "No, that wouldn't seem weird at all."

"That's all this is, sweetheart. Debbie is somebody I

know. Maureen is close to you. And we're all just having dinner together."

Reaching out, she placed her hands on his waist and nodded. "I totally get what you're saying, Bryce. But I swear, my mom will start hearing wedding bells in the distance. And you know when that idea started hitting Allison, you—"

"Nope, don't go there. There is no comparison between you and Allison. We weren't on the same page when Allison started planning for the future. For me, she was nothing but casual, which she'd agreed to, and then started pushing for more. I knew she wasn't the right person, so I stepped away. Lesson learned. Spending more time with someone who would never be anything more than what she was didn't make sense."

She nodded again slowly, but he wasn't finished.

"You and I are completely different. We're not only starting something new, but we already know the feelings we have for each other are more than what we've ever felt for anyone else. And we're going to ride this out. Don't worry about it. I think your mom's going to be cool."

He'd calmed her, then heated her with a hard kiss. Now, she fretted that he'd messed her hair, but inside, she grinned.

An hour later, the four were sitting in the Sunset Restaurant, the women drinking signature cocktails with seafood while Bryce enjoyed a cold beer with his steak. Shared stories and laughter completed their meal. Joanne had already suffered through her mom's baby picture conversation with Bryce, but now it was her turn to laugh as Debbie filled them in on some of his childhood misadventures.

Bryce's phone vibrated, and he checked the caller ID. Shooting her a smile, he excused himself and walked out onto the deck to take the call. His back was to them, so she didn't have the advantage of seeing his expressions. But while his body was held tight, he didn't appear to be arguing with whoever the caller was.

"Oh, honey, your break-in has me so worried," her mom said, clutching Joanne's hand.

"I know my Bryce, and he won't stop until they know who's to blame," Debbie said, reaching over to hold Joanne's other hand. "Bryce is like his uncle in that way—a real protector."

Joanne turned to see tears shining in Debbie's eyes. "You mean so much to him, Debbie. He was very lucky to have you and Bernie." She glanced at her mom, glad she'd already given her mom the story of Bryce's upbringing.

"Oh, my, it was Bernie and I who were lucky. We had already considered ourselves fortunate to have him as a nephew and were thrilled to have him and his mother come live with us when Bernie and Carla's father died. We never forgot that Carla was his mom, but she... well, she had a hard time. When Bryce was only six years old, he'd try to stay up when she didn't come home. Even at that age, he worried about her. I've never seen another child so serious and responsible. When she was killed, we were determined that Bryce would know how much his mother loved him while we became his parents." She sighed heavily. "I swear, he still worried over Bernie and me. I think he was just a born protector."

"I know he would love to have you move here permanently," Joanne added.

Debbie smiled, then hefted her shoulders in a delicate shrug. "I'm going to. I just need to take care of my house. Perhaps within the next six months, I can make the move permanent."

Joanne squeezed Debbie's hand and then turned her gaze to her mom. In the middle of a roller-coaster ride that seemed not to have an end, it struck her how lucky she was to be surrounded by people who cared. Her phone had pinged all day long with words of concern from friends. And now, with her mom and Debbie offering support, she could stare out the window at the man she'd already fallen for and know she needed to give him strength, too.

25

Bryce stepped out onto the restaurant's deck to take the call from Sam. He purposely turned his back to the window, not wanting Joanne to worry about whatever reaction he might have, considering he had no idea what Sam might tell him. He knew that Sam was checking into Chad's and Allison's alibis for the previous day since they were considered persons of interest in the vandalism of Joanne's house.

Steeling himself, he asked, "Sam, what have you got for me?"

"Don't know if this is going to make it better or not," Sam began.

Pressing his lips together tightly, Bryce waited.

"I checked out Allison. She was at work yesterday morning at her Maryland office but left early to head back to her Norfolk office. I did the math, and she could have made it to Joanne's house at about four p.m. But that wouldn't have given her much time to search for something or make a mess, considering that was at the end of Joanne's workday, and Allison wouldn't know if Joanne was close to arriving. Now, for Chad. I talked to his employer. He hasn't been to work in the past four days but had scheduled vacation time. He's also not answering his phone, so he's still a contender."

"Shit. I'd hoped at least one would have a solid alibi so we could eliminate them."

"That's all I've got for now. I'll let you get back to your evening."

"I appreciate the call. I'm out with Joanne, her mom, and my aunt right now, so I'll give her the info when we're alone."

Sam chuckled. "Damn, man, you move fast."

"Only when it's the right one, Sam."

"I wouldn't know. Sure haven't found that myself."

Disconnecting after saying goodbye, he scrubbed his hand over his face to clear his mind before turning around. When he did, his breath caught in his throat as he looked through the window and saw Joanne, Debbie, and Maureen all smiling. He had no idea what they'd been talking about but found he didn't care. Whether it was a joke told between them, laughing over an old story, or finding a bright spot to smile about when shit all around was swirling. Joanne's eyes sparkled in the candlelight, and her smile warmed his heart.

He hadn't been looking for love, but he'd been hopeful. And staring at the women at the table, his chest ached with warmth. "Is this what you felt when you were first with Debbie, Uncle Bernie?" He had a feeling Bernie was smiling down at the scene along with him.

Unwilling to waste another second, he hustled inside

and went straight to the table. Catching Joanne's quizzical look, he shook his head as he leaned over and whispered, "Nothing for now, but we're with people who love us, so let's enjoy our dinner."

She held his gaze for a moment, then nodded as her smile curved her beautiful lips once again.

They were finishing dessert when a shadow passed over the table. Looking up sharply, Bryce smiled as he watched Jeff approach. Standing, he shook the Coast Guard captain's hand, then turned toward the table. "I'd like you to meet my girlfriend, Joanne Norris, her mother, Maureen, and my aunt Debbie—"

Maureen's eyes lit, and she greeted enthusiastically, "Jeff! How lovely to see you!"

"Maureen." Jeff nodded with a smile as he bent to shake her hand.

"Jeff and I met when he spoke at one of the AL Auxiliary meetings," Maureen explained. She turned her intense gaze toward Debbie, then narrowed her eyes slightly just before a slow smile curved her lips. "Debbie is visiting our lovely area and is considering moving here permanently. She will certainly need someone to show her around."

A strangled chortle slipped from Joanne, and Bryce swallowed with difficulty. *Is Maureen trying to set up Jeff and Debbie?* But instead of witnessing a train wreck, he watched as color heightened Debbie's cheeks as she smiled up at Jeff. And Jeff couldn't take his eyes off Debbie. Never imagining his aunt with anyone other than Bernie, Bryce discovered the anticipated ache didn't appear.

Jeff smiled, his gaze pinned on Debbie. "I'd love to take you around sometime. Will you be here long?"

"Not on this trip, I'm afraid," Debbie replied. "But I'll be back soon."

"Then I hope to see you then."

"Won't that be just lovely!" Maureen exclaimed, her eyes bright.

Jeff offered a cordial goodbye to everyone and then walked away, leaving Debbie blushing, Bryce and Joanne staring in abject stunned disbelief, and Maureen leaning back in her seat with an expression that reminded Bryce of when one of his cats knocked an open can of tuna onto the floor, and the others immediately took advantage of an impromptu snack.

That night, with Debbie in the guest room, Bryce climbed into bed after securing the house and pulled Joanne close. They faced each other, whispering as he told her what Sam had reported.

"Allison is nuts, but it does her no good to break into my house. And it seems like she would have been more destructive. You know... smashed things, pulled pictures off the wall, that kind of thing. And Chad? There's nothing of his that I kept. Not one thing. He'd have no reason to look for anything."

He agreed but didn't like the alternative. *Something to do with Brian.* Finally, she rested her cheek on his chest, right over his heartbeat.

"I can't believe my mom set up Debbie with your friend," Joanne whispered, then giggled with a hint of mischief in her eyes.

As shocked as Bryce had been, he had to admit that

seeing the smile on Debbie's face and hearing the sweet sound of laughter from Joanne made the bizarre situation worth it. "I guess I never thought about Debbie dating again, but if she's interested, then Jeff is a great man. Kind-hearted, smart, respectful."

He pulled her tighter, their bodies fitting together like pieces of a puzzle. Kissing her forehead with a tenderness that spoke of his deeper feelings, her petal-soft skin underneath his lips, and her sweet breath puffing over his chest made him hope for a time when they could explore their feelings fully without the specter of danger.

Their legs tangled in casual intimacy, and her breathing finally slowed. Glad she'd found sleep, he wasn't sure the same would happen for him. Finally, knowing she was safe in his arms, he closed his eyes, letting the soothing rhythm of her heartbeat lull him to peace.

The end of the weekend signaled Debbie's goodbye, and heartfelt hugs were given all around. She kissed Joanne's cheek with affection before pulling Bryce into her arms. The hug was as familiar as every time she'd hugged him as a child, yet it was different as she whispered, "She's worthy of you, my sweet Bryce. And you're worthy of her." Looking up into his face, she patted his cheek in gentle affirmation. "Bernie would be so proud of the man you are."

Warmth filled his chest. "I learned from the best."

"I'll be back for the holidays. And then in the spring, I'll start to make a move here." Her voice was tinged with excitement, and he wondered if she was perhaps ready for more changes than just with a home. With a wave and a wink, she climbed into her car and pulled away.

Slinging his arm over Joanne's shoulders, he guided her inside. Once they entered the living room filled with the soft shadows of late afternoon, she turned, took a deep breath, and then asked, "As much as I hate to talk about this more, did Sam say when I can go back to my house?"

He should have expected the question but found that he hated the idea of her leaving, and not just because of the threats. It was selfish, but he wanted her with him. "I... uh... he didn't say."

She nodded, then pressed on. "I hate the idea of my things in disarray. I really want to get there and clean up. Start to restore some order to my house."

His heart jumped at her words. "So... you just want to clean up? Because I want you to stay here until we're sure there's no threat." He heard the pleading in his voice but was past caring. They'd promised honesty, and that was what he'd give.

She chewed on her bottom lip, uncertainty written on her face. "I'd like that. I don't want to overstay my welcome, but the idea of going back knowing someone was there going through my things—"

He reached over to touch the soft, reddened skin of her lips. "I know this feels fast. We've known each other a short time, and now you're living here—" He halted the tumble of words as her eyes widened and quickly finished, "You're living here for as long as you need or want. This is your safe place."

She held her palm against his cheek, her gaze peering deeply into his eyes. "You're my safe place."

The air rushed from his lungs at her simple and profound declaration. He pulled her even closer, loving the way they melded together. "That's exactly what I want to be. A safe place for you to be. A safe place for your heart."

Her face contorted slightly, and she whispered, "I know it's too early for promises, but I need to ask for one."

"Anything."

She studied his face, then nodded. "If we're an *us*, then I need it just to be us. If you ever want more, or different, or for this to be over… please tell me first."

He knew where the bout of uncertainty came from, and if he could get his hands on Chad, he'd beat a lesson into him that might keep the loser from hurting another woman. "I give you my promise that we're going to take what we have and keep going. If something changes, we'll talk about it first. But I will never cheat or give you a reason to doubt me."

His words seemed to be all the assurance that she needed. And as wonderful as the weekend had been, he desperately longed for a time when they could focus on just the two of them and not everything swirling around.

The callout was a brutal reminder of the days when Bryce knew his job was vital yet agonizing. He, Jose, and

Jared had rushed to the scene of a water accident. The dispatcher relayed the injury to a child, and while Jose revved the engines to get them there quickly, he and Jared prepared their medical supplies.

A family outing had turned tragic in an instant when a child fell overboard, and his uncle driving the boat hit the child. The fact that the blades of the motor had not come in contact with the little boy was the only saving grace. That would have killed him. But as it was, there was no guarantee that the child would live or ever be normal again.

By the time the VMP arrived, the family had pulled the unconscious child from the water. The mother cradled him, crying hysterically, and a little girl pressed against the side of the boat, curled up in terror. The dad appeared in shock as he leaned over his wife and son while the uncle paced back and forth, murmuring, "I didn't know he was there. I didn't know he was there."

Bryce assisted as they tethered their vessel to the boat, then moved quickly to the child. Fearing internal injuries, he and Jose convinced the mother to relinquish her hold so they could safely maneuver the child onto the board.

A second VMP vessel arrived a minute later, and they transported the child onto their vessel, placing him gently in the wheelhouse. Then allowing the mother to come along, they sped back to the harbor, where they would be met by a Coast Guard helicopter that would transport the child over the bay since the Eastern Shore did not have a child trauma center.

A few minutes later, he spied Ryan and Jeff on the

dock with the CG stretcher waiting. As soon as they docked, Bryce and Jose carefully carried the child and placed him onto the stretcher, where the CG's medical team took charge. The helicopter was loaded with medical care for the transport.

Jared escorted the mother to the helicopter, as well. Standing back as the blades of the bird whirled, Bryce watched until it was only a speck in the sky, his heart heavy as he wondered the fate of the child.

The other VMP vessel carrying the rest of the family arrived at the harbor. The information had already been obtained concerning the parents and the uncle, so they were allowed to rush to their vehicles to make the trek over the long Bay Bridge-Tunnel to get to the Children's Hospital in Norfolk.

The mood was somber as they prepared the vessels for their next call out. Many of their daily tasks could be considered routine, sometimes mundane, all while being important. Other times, they felt the high of rescue or the satisfaction of knowing they had done their part to protect the shore's ecosystems. But there were days, like today, when a tragedy on the water brought forth feelings of helplessness.

Coming on the heels of having promised Joanne that she'd be safe made Bryce's vulnerability battle against his protective nature. The inner turmoil gnawed at his gut.

By the time the vessel was restocked, Ryan walked onto the dock, his stride purposeful and his face grim. Bryce's heart stuttered, knowing that Joanne was supposed to be safely at work after he dropped her off that morning, but he couldn't help the feeling that bad news was coming. Premonition tightened in his chest.

Before he had a chance to speak, Ryan called out, "Bryce, I need you to get to Shelby's inlet. An oystermen found a briefcase when he was harvesting. He said he wouldn't have thought about it, except we've been asking for information. I want you to get out there, take possession of it, and then meet Sam to turn it over to him. I've already called Sam, and he wants to talk to Joanne to see if it is possible it was the one Brian Atwell had with him on the island."

A heavy sigh left his lips, a release of tension and acceptance. Nodding, he turned and climbed aboard his vessel again. This time, Callan and Jared went out with him. Soon, they made it to the oyster beds of Jack Hillman, a longtime fisherman.

They slowed as they approached, and he was grateful for the calm waters. Jack stood nearby in waist-high water and threw his hand up in a wave.

"I heard others talk about looking for anything that might help you figure out about that man who died in the water. I was using my oyster rake and harvesting when something caught. When I dragged it up, this is what I got." He held up a dark briefcase. At first, it appeared black, but once they were able to maneuver closer, Bryce could see that the leather was just darkened as it had soaked.

Thanking Jack, he said, "You can't imagine how much we appreciate this. Don't know if it belongs to the deceased, but I know the sheriff's department is looking for every clue they can get."

Jack just waved them away. "I always get pissed at the stuff people throw away, and it ends up in my oyster bed. At least, maybe this time, it's something worthwhile."

With another wave, they headed back to the harbor. Bryce had placed the briefcase on a plastic sheet in the wheelhouse, careful to preserve as much evidence as possible. He hoped it would give them more closure on the mysterious Brian Atwell, but the odds of anything lasting long in the water, with its relentless motion and corrosive salt, were minimal.

Squatting, he looked at it carefully, his eyes narrowing in scrutiny without touching the leather. It wasn't a soft-sided briefcase that he saw many businessmen carrying. It was hard-sided, and the top corner had a dent where the leather was slightly bent. *Time in the water, and it could've been hit by a boat, dragged along the bottom of the bay, or dented when it was first tossed or dropped.* He also noticed the clasp at the top was open. There were scratches on the metal fasteners, and he wondered if someone had forced the lock open.

By the time they arrived at the harbor, Sam and Mark waited for him, standing on the dock beside Ryan, their faces etched with concentration.

Sam took possession of the case. Mark placed it in a large evidence bag, sealed it, and made notations. Bryce's mind churned, wondering what would happen next. Sam must've anticipated his concern.

"I've already placed a call to Joanne at the college. I'll ask her to stop by the station on her way home. I want her to carefully look it over to see if there's any way she can identify it as the one she saw Brian Atwell carrying."

"I dropped her off at work since the garage still has her car. Jason is finished with it, and we were going to get it."

"I'll go by and pick her up," Mark said, drawing a barely hidden scowl from Bryce.

He wanted to be with Joanne when she looked at the case, but his day wasn't over, and another emergency callout came over the radio. Offering a chin lift to the detectives, he hopped back onto the boat.

While Andy was at the wheel, he fired off a text, telling her that Jason had checked out her car and nothing else was wrong with it. Sucking in a deep breath of salty air, he let it out as he worked to clear his mind and focus on the next duty. And then prayed for the end of the day where he could crawl into bed with Joanne, wrap his arms around her, and let their love-making push away the unpleasantness crowding into their happiness.

26

Joanne received a call from Sam that he needed her to stop by the sheriff's office as soon as possible. She messaged him back that she was stuck in a meeting but would be there as soon as she could. Jason had checked over her car and had not found any problems other than the one tire that had been slashed. But she needed someone to take her to Baytown to pick it up before she could go to meet with Sam since Bryce was out on the water.

The meeting droned on, and she rubbed her head, realizing it was pointless, considering she wasn't paying any attention to what was happening. *With everything going on in my life right now, I certainly don't need to get a bad performance review on top of it!*

When the meeting was finally over, she caught a ride with Cheryl to Baytown. As soon as they pulled up to Jason's garage, she hopped out and waved her friend on.

Jason went over everything he checked on her vehicle, and she was relieved to hear from him that she was good to go with new tires. She'd given him permission to take care of routine maintenance at the same time, and after paying, she headed out. Looking across the street at the ice cream shop that Jason's wife, Rose, owned, she was so tempted to go in and get a treat. But knowing Sam was waiting on her at the sheriff's department, she sighed and hurried on her way.

Once at the station, she told the receptionist that she was there to see Detective Shackley. While waiting, she sent a text to Bryce.

Got car. At station.

"Joanne?"

She looked up to see Sam, and as she slid her phone into her purse, it vibrated with a text from Bryce.

On my way. Will meet you there.

She greeted Sam, then followed him down several halls, her heels clicking on the tile floors. He led her into a room that reminded her of police interview rooms from movies and TV shows. She knew she wasn't in trouble but couldn't help but look around at the minimalistic, gray metal furniture, the camera in the corner, and recording equipment sitting on the table. Glancing at Sam, she said, "I have an active imagination. And it's working overtime right now."

He laughed and shook his head. "Don't worry about it, Joanne. This is just a good place for us to lay out what we found, and you can take a look at it."

Mark walked in with a large plastic container. He set it on the table and lifted off the lid before snapping on gloves. He carefully picked up the briefcase and laid it on a plastic sheet on the table.

Sam instructed, "Don't touch it, but we want you to carefully look at it. Notice anything identifiable about it that might seem familiar. Obviously, we're trying to ascertain if it was the one Brian had the day you saw him."

Joanne quickly closed her eyes, suddenly not wanting to look at the briefcase yet.

"Are you okay?" Sam asked, and she heard the concern in his voice.

"Yes. I just want to think without being influenced by what's in front of me."

"Good thinking," Mark added, and she heard the respect in his voice.

She let out a breath and cast her mind back to the boat. "I first saw the briefcase when he sat down next to me. It was rectangular and hard-sided, and while I didn't stare at it, it reminded me of the kind of briefcase my father used to take to work. Not really old-fashioned, but also didn't seem modern." She chuckled and shook her head. "If he'd had it handcuffed to his wrist, it would've reminded me of an old James Bond movie." Realizing how that must sound to the two detectives, she crinkled her nose. "Sorry."

"Don't apologize, Joanne. Every single snippet of your memory might just be exactly what we need, so please, continue."

"We sat on the bench seats next to each other. I was glad he didn't sit so close to me that I felt my personal space was invaded. About a foot of space was between us. I had my backpack purse on the deck of the boat between my legs. I found that gave me adequate control. If the boat pitched a little bit, I could just squeeze between my calves and knees. I probably wouldn't have noticed the briefcase at all, except he set it next to him on the deck between us. But at one point, we did roll a little bit, and it fell to the side. He bent over to pick it up and placed it between his legs. It's one of those little things you learn when you're on a boat fairly often, and since I take the ferry every couple of weeks, I've learned to guard my bag that way. Anyway, I looked down when it fell over and when he moved it. It was a little scuffed on the edges, wasn't brand new, and the leather on the corners was worn a bit. It had a brass-colored lock on the top. Not a combination lock, but one where you need a key." She shook her head. "Funny, I didn't think I paid that much attention to it, but I remember that."

"This is excellent, Joanne. Keep going."

She heard the door open but didn't look to see who was coming in. The footsteps came closer, but she kept going, not wanting to lose the memories that were now flowing.

"The only other thing I remember is that while the case was dark brown, it had a lighter tan stitching on the handle. I don't remember anything else about it from the boat trip. As I told you, I was there first when I got to the restaurant, and my backpack bag was placed on the bench of the booth next to me. Brian came in, and I remember seeing the briefcase because he held it up as he stretched out his arm and set it on the bench as he climbed in. She lifted her arm and shifted her body, demonstrating the motion.

"So, since the briefcase was literally in my line of

sight, I noticed it. And because it was fairly large, the top of it was visible over the table. I did notice that one corner was scuffed to where the leather was completely worn through, and the material of the briefcase was a little dented in that corner. I don't know whether it had been that way on the boat or was a new dent." She scrunched her nose, then slowly shook her head. "No, it couldn't have been new. The leather was too worn and sort of old looking."

She shrugged again and then opened her eyes. "That's what I remember. That's all I remember about the briefcase."

Her gaze jumped over to the person who entered, shocked to see Bryce standing there. She smiled but was unsure if she should go over and greet him. He didn't have any hesitation, and her smile widened as he walked over to stand next to her.

"Okay, Joanne. Now, what I want you to do is to look carefully at the briefcase on the table. It's still damp, so that will affect the way it looks as opposed to when it was completely dry before going into the water. You need to look carefully to see if any identifying marks would indicate you've seen it before."

She expected to have to stare at great length to determine whether the briefcase in front of her was recognizable, but she gasped as her gaze moved over it. Not wanting to say anything too soon, she leaned over the table and stared. The same worn leather on the corners. The same dent in the upper corner. The same stitching on the handle. And the same brass latch and lock on top. Only it was now bent and scratched as though pried open.

Lifting her gaze to Sam, she nodded. "It's the same. It sounds weird because I didn't expect to recognize it. But seeing it, there's no doubt in my mind that this is the same briefcase Brian had with him on the ferry and in the restaurant. The difference is the latch on top. When I saw it, there was nothing wrong with it."

Sam nodded, keeping his expression neutral. "Okay, Joanne, we need you to think very carefully again. I know we've gone over this, but you'd be surprised at what witnesses remember. Did he ever open it in your presence?"

Shaking her head, she said, "No. Absolutely not."

"Did you ever see him pull out any keys?"

Shaking her head again, she repeated, "No."

"You mentioned that he paid for lunch," Mark interjected. "Where did he get the money?"

She pressed her lips together as she closed her eyes again, a vision of Brian after he'd taken the phone call and pulled out his wallet. "He reached into his back pocket and pulled out a wallet. He opened the wallet, grabbed some money, and tossed it onto the table."

"And you said it was too much money?"

"It wasn't until he left that I realized he left two hundred-dollar bills. Our lunch together was only a third of that, and as I said, I didn't want him to pay for my lunch. Even with a large tip, that was way too much money. I used my credit card to pay for the lunch and a large tip. I put his money into my wallet. I planned to give them back to him on the ferry going home. But then, of course, that didn't happen."

"You don't often see someone throw down cash that's three times what their bill would be," Sam said, rubbing his chin, his gaze on her.

"Well… um… he was in a hurry?" Joanne's voice rose at the end, and she realized she didn't know if she was making a statement or asking a question. "But, then, he didn't hasten down the street." Seeing the men's eyes jump to her, she quickly said, "I mean, he certainly left immediately and wasn't sauntering along, but he wasn't rushing or jogging."

"If it was a business trip, wouldn't he want receipts or for the bill to show up on a credit card statement?" Mark asked. "Cash allows him not to leave a trace."

"But he took a public ferry. He talked to Joanne. He had lunch in a restaurant," Bryce added. "That doesn't sound like someone trying to keep his trip a secret."

"Maybe he wasn't aware that anyone would be looking for him. Or that he was doing anything wrong… if he was doing something wrong," Joanne said, unsure if her input was helpful.

Sam looked over and stared at her with an intensity that made her want to squirm. Just when she was about to protest her innocence, he cocked his head to the side, his eyes narrowing.

"Joanne, do you still have those bills? The ones he left on the table?"

She blinked, startled for a few seconds as she processed his question and then the answer. "Um…

yeah, sure. I put them in my wallet." She reached for her purse and pulled out her bright red wallet.

He stopped her and said, "Only pull out the ones from him."

"That won't be hard because I don't have any cash with me. I use my card almost everywhere. And on that day, the only cash that I carried was his when I put it in there." Aware that all eyes were on her, she shook slightly as she held her wallet in her right hand. Sam stopped her before she could take the money out.

"Mark, get clean gloves on."

She looked up. Her brow furrowed as Mark immediately stripped off the gloves he'd worn when placing the briefcase on the table and slipped on a new pair.

"Please allow Mark to take out the money."

"Of course," she agreed, opening the wallet for him. He pulled out the bills and carefully laid them on the other end of the table. Just as she'd said, there were two crisp hundred-dollar bills.

"They look new," Mark said.

"If these are, we might get lucky with fingerprints." Sam turned to her.

"You've got my prints for comparison." She glanced over at Bryce, who nodded his support. Soon, Sam was escorting her and Bryce back to the reception area.

She was curious as to what Sam was thinking with his fascination over the money. *Did Sam think Brian had stolen it? But it was new bills. Oh, maybe he stole it from a bank.* Finally, curiosity won out, and she stopped and turned, halting Bryce's progress down the hall as well.

"Sam? I know you probably can't tell me, but I'm curious why you wanted that money."

Sam's brow furrowed. "Let's just say that I have a hunch. It might be nothing, but sometimes a hunch is the best we have to go on in an investigation."

It wasn't much of an answer, but she understood it was all she would get at the moment. Saying goodbye, she leaned into Bryce as he walked her through the reception area and out into the parking lot, his arm securely around her, giving her his steady strength.

"I don't suppose you know what's going on, do you?" she asked.

He shook his head, but his arm tightened around her shoulders. "No, but I've got to tell you, I'm really interested. Mostly because it concerns you, but I'm an officer, not a detective. Most of the time, that's fine, and I'm doing the job I love. But I got to tell you, sometimes, like right now, I wish I had Sam's intuition."

As they reached her car, she grinned when she observed that Bryce had parked right next to her. Standing between the cars, they wrapped their arms around each other, and she looked up into his face. "Well, maybe you're not a detective, but I happen to love your skills." Lifting on her toes, she kissed him lightly, then whispered, "And as soon as we get home, I'll let you show me all your skills."

27

"Hey Frank, how's it going?" Bryce called out to one of the local crab fishermen. He, Joseph, and Andy were out on patrol.

"Damn prices keep dropping," Frank complained. "Not hardly worth getting out here every day. Some days, the price of fishing is more than my catch brings in."

Bryce had heard the same thing for weeks. "Sure am sorry, Frank. You're the third person today who's said those very words."

"Yeah, and the consumer will soon find that seafood is in short supply," Frank continued. "Old Bart Collins just said fuck it and stopped fishing. His son might take it over, but that's not for sure. And I heard that the Jobeki boys are looking to sell out of the business. Hell, they can make more working somewhere else."

Bryce handed Frank's licenses to him, never doubting they would check out. Waving goodbye, he nodded to Joseph, who steered them out into the bay.

The dispatcher radioed directions for them to assist the Coast Guard with another body found in the bay by a fishing boat. Bryce jerked his head around and looked at Andy. "Another body? Jesus! What the hell is going on?"

Unfortunately, boating accidents were an all-too-common tragedy on the bay. The waters, while beautiful, teeming with life, and providing untold hours of recreation, could also provide the backdrop for those who didn't follow the rules of boating.

Having already found Brian's body, then attending to the heartbreaking scene involving a child the other day, and now another body, Bryce felt the weight bearing down on his shoulders. It was a burden that seemed to grow heavier with each passing incident.

As they made their way across the water, the wind whipped at his face, and he felt the chill deep inside. Approaching the scene, he observed the Coast Guard boat next to a fishing boat. When they drew closer, his eyes were drawn to the figure of the fisherman. The man's shoulders were slumped, and his head hung low. His hands, gnarled from years working on fishing boats, clung to the railing.

Bryce waited until they pulled alongside before calling out softly to the older man. "Thomas, looks like you've had better days than this one."

Thomas was a face he knew well, part of the close-knit community bound together by their shared love and respect for the Chesapeake Bay. His face was pale underneath his tanned skin, and his hands shook. "Threw my lines in and was stupid enough to think I'd come up with something good. Christ. Don't mind telling you that I lost a few years off my life at this!"

Looking down, Bryce gasped at the body on the Coast Guard deck. Their captain, Jeff, turned and looked at him. "Do you recognize him?"

His chest deflated as he lifted his gaze from the macabre scene on the deck to Jeff. "Yes, that's Steve Harlow. He's a fisherman off Tangier Island. I talked to him last week." He dropped his chin to his chest and shook his head, sucking in a deep breath. Letting it out as he lifted his head, he added, "He was being interviewed by Detective Sam Shackley of the North Heron Sheriff's Department. He was being questioned about the disappearance of the other man they found in the bay."

Jeff's brows lifted to his hairline. "Fucking hell. What's going on around here?"

"I don't know," Bryce said. He glanced over at Joseph. "I'm going to get ahold of Sam. He needs to know about this."

"No problem," Joseph agreed. "Looks like Jeff's got things well in hand, but with your piece of information, Sam will need the ME to get to it quickly."

Squeezing the back of his neck, Bryce placed the call. "Sam? It's Bryce Townsend. The Coast Guard just pulled a body out of the bay that a fisherman had caught in his net. We went in as backup, but I identified him. It's Steve Harlow, the Tangier fisherman we just talked to—"

"Dammit!" Sam said. "Is the body coming to the hospital on the shore or Virginia Beach?"

"It's coming to the hospital in the Eastern Shore."

"Okay, I'll alert the medical examiner to be on the lookout. And just to let you know, I was going to try to come to the station later to talk to you. As it is, I'll need to be at the hospital."

"What did you need to talk about?" Bryce's voice was edged with anxiety. "Something to do with Joanne? About her house break-in?"

"Afraid not, although it does involve her." Sam sighed heavily, and Bryce braced. "It's about the money Brian tossed onto the table that was in her possession. We were able to lift a print and have it match Brian Atwell. But there's more. Those hundred-dollar bills were counterfeit. That now makes this case a whole lot bigger and a fuck of a lot worse. In fact, I've already contacted the Secret Service. As you know, counterfeit money is under their jurisdiction."

"Fuck," Bryce's guttural curse rang out. He'd wanted to know what was happening to Joanne, but the news was not welcome. "They'll want to interview Joanne, won't they?"

There was silence on the other end of the phone, and Bryce's stomach dropped. Swiping his hand over his face, he waited.

Sam sighed. "They're already looking into her. Don't worry, they're not going to find anything, but the fact that Brian made several trips to the island and always just went to visit Steve and then one day, breaks his pattern and sits and talks to Joanne, even has lunch with her, then turns up dead…"

"Christ! What a fucking nightmare!" Bryce exploded.

"Right now, just hang tight. I've got to get this information to them. Some agents had gone to the island to talk to him, but no one had seen Steve. Now we know why. The news of his death is going to travel fast."

Disconnecting, he looked over at the concerned faces of his fellow officers. "The money Brian Atwell had was counterfeit. Sam says the Secret Service is now involved, and they'll want to interview Joanne."

As the others stared dumbfounded, he quickly called Joanne. Not getting an answer, he called the counseling center's main office.

"This is Bryce Townsend. I'm trying to get ahold of Joanne. Is she in her office?"

"Oh, she's not here!" Cheryl exclaimed. "She just left with two men in dark suits. It was so freaky! They said they were Secret Service, but who knows! This is something just like out of a novel about—"

"Thanks." He disconnected while she was still talking and called Sam back.

"That was quick," Sam said. "I just saw the SS agents walk in with Joanne and take her to an interview room. Since I'm on this case, they'll let me sit in. Gotta go. Don't worry. I'll keep you informed."

Battling the urge to crush his phone on the deck of the boat, he turned and looked at Joseph. "Secret Service has already taken Joanne in to be questioned."

"Do you need to go?" Andy asked. "I can get you back to the harbor in less than ten minutes."

"It's not going to do any good. They won't let me near her right now," he growled. Wondering how the hell he was going to keep his mind on his job, he nodded. "Yeah, take me back."

Joanne sat in the hard chair in the interview room of the Sherriff's station, similar to the one she'd been in when examining the briefcase. The room was nondescript, the walls painted beige, and the overhead fluorescent lights gave her a headache. Her forearms rested on the table, and her hands clasped together so tightly she was afraid her fingers would snap. She'd been in that position for over an hour and wasn't sure when the agents would finally come talk to her.

When the two dark-suited Secret Service agents had walked into the counseling office and asked with deep, authoritative voices if they could speak with her, she'd been stunned but assumed they would sit in her office. When they informed her that they wanted to speak with her at the sheriff's office, her concern heightened, but offering a smile to her coworkers and mumbling a quick excuse to Cheryl, she left with them only after ensuring she checked their ID. Getting into a vehicle with two men she didn't know, even if they had shown identification, had been a leap of faith. But they brought her straight to the sheriff's department.

Finally, the door opened, and she jumped, her heart rate kicking into high gear. Swallowing, she breathed a tiny sigh of relief at the sight of Sam following the two agents into the interview room.

"Ms. Norris," the first agent began. "I'm Agent

Stubbs with the Secret Service and the lead agent on this case." He gestured to the other man. "This is Agent Hargrove. We have some questions."

Her gaze shot between the two agents, and she nodded. Agent Stubbs was a mountain of a man, dark-skinned and bald. Even his eyes emitted a *don't-fuck-with-me* vibe. Agent Hargrove was tall and lanky, with calculating eyes that kept their sharp gaze on her. Taking a deep breath to calm her racing heart, she dragged her tongue over her dry lips.

Their interrogation was methodical and relentless. They started with innocuous questions about her relationship with Brian Atwell. She repeated the same story she'd told multiple times. Then their deeper questions began, and her anxiety tangled with her innocence with each answer.

She recounted details, insisting on the truth, but with each question, their disbelief appeared like a thick fog.

No, I'd never officially met him before the day on the ferry. Yes, I'd seen him on the ferry one other time a few weeks earlier. No, we hadn't spoken at that time. Yes, I noticed he carried a briefcase. No, he hadn't opened it at any time when he was with me. Yes, we had lunch together. No, we weren't together. Yes, he placed money on the table. No, he didn't give me anything. Yes, I took the extra money. No, I didn't look at it other than to see the denominations. Yes, I gave it to Detective Shackley. No, I didn't tell anyone else about the money other than the local law enforcement. Yes, the money had stayed in my wallet the whole time. No, it was never left alone in my house.

Over and over, she went through the details of everything she could remember, every word he'd said. Every movement and gesture he made.

And when they probed the break-in of her house, they questioned if she had noticed anything else taken, exactly what was disturbed, where she was, when it occurred, and what happened afterward. Bringing up her slashed tire, they went through the same scenario several times, each with her giving the same information.

Centering on the phone call Brian had received at the restaurant, she repeated the few words she'd heard him say, including his tone, expression, and mannerisms. Then how he left her. His words. Throwing the money onto the table. They even had her stand and show how he pulled the money from his wallet and tossed it down.

And no, she had not seen or heard from him since he had last walked away from her. And no, after she had placed the bills in her wallet, she did not take them out again.

"Why not?" Agent Stubbs asked.

"Because the money wasn't mine." By now, exhaustion threatened, and her patience was wearing thin. But they weren't finished.

They had her go over it again. And then again. Sam had slipped back out of the room, and she missed feeling she had someone on her side. She'd watched enough TV and movies to wonder if they were trying to trip her up… trying to catch her in a lie. But she wasn't lying, so her story never changed.

Finally, they stood, and Agent Stubbs said, "Thank you, Ms. Norris. You're free to leave now."

She stood, finding it difficult to unclasp her fingers as they appeared to be almost locked tightly together. "Thank you." She inwardly cursed her ingrained politeness, feeling a sting of embarrassment as she thanked the two men who had grilled her.

Agent Stubbs walked to the door, opened it up, and stood beside it. She assumed he wanted her to leave, but it was strange to be in a situation where she was terrified to do the wrong thing, say the wrong thing, or have her actions or words misunderstood. She glanced toward the Agent Hargrove and asked, "What happens now?"

"If we need you for anything else, Ms. Norris, we'll let you know. For now, you are free to go."

She nodded and walked to the door, making sure not to brush against the large man, who seemed disappointed she could not give them more information. Suddenly stopping, she said, "My car isn't here. It's still at the college—"

"I've got you."

She jerked around to see Bryce standing at the end of the hall with Sam. He offered a smile, but she could see past it to the hard flint in his eyes and the tension in his jaw. Determined not to run down the hall and fling herself into his arms in front of everyone, she walked with measured steps, grateful when she was within arm's reach, and he pulled her in for a hug.

Whispering against her hair, he asked, "Are you okay?"

She swallowed deeply, the movement hurting her throat with the tight way she'd held her body for hours. Afraid to speak, she simply nodded.

He turned her so that they were facing the door leading into the reception area, and she heard Sam talking to the Secret Service but no longer cared what anyone was saying. She just wanted to get back home, where she could sit on the sofa and pet the cats as they swirled around, offering their own brand of comfort.

28

Bryce walked into his kitchen to make a cup of tea for Joanne and looked out the window. Maureen had just pulled into the driveway. Joanne had called her when they'd arrived home just to check in, but he wasn't surprised that her mom wanted to see for herself that Joanne was all right.

Maureen spotted him through the kitchen window and hastened to the side door. He met her there, pushed open the screen door, and she reached out to clutch his hands in hers. Holding his gaze, she asked, "How is she?" Deep lines creased her face as anxious concern poured from her.

"She's fine, Maureen," he assured. "She's exhausted because those types of interviews last so long and make everyone feel like they're a suspect."

"When she told me how long they questioned her, I was so angry! She had absolutely nothing to do with it!"

Seeing the mama bear in Maureen come out, he had a flash of what Joanne would be like when she had children. The next flash that went through his mind was the idea of their children. Shaking his head, he squeezed Maureen's hands and said, "She's in the living room, hanging out with the cats that seem to know she's stressed. I was just fixing her some tea. Go on in. She'd love to see you."

He expected Maureen to drop his hands and hurry into the living room immediately, but she continued to hold on as she peered intently into his eyes.

"I worried so much about Joanne when she was with Chad. When he treated her so badly, I was furious. Furious with him for being a cheat and a weak man. A weak man does not deserve my Joanne. You, Bryce, are not only a good man but also good for my daughter. And from the bottom of my heart, thank you."

Her words covered him like a warm blanket on a cold night. "I'll take care of her," he promised. It was on the tip of his tongue to reassure her that he was falling in love with Joanne. But he stopped, knowing that the only person who needed to hear those words first was Joanne herself.

Maureen's lips curved upward, and a knowing look passed through her eyes as though she knew exactly what he almost said. Reaching up, she patted his cheek. "You know, in a way, I can take credit for you and Joanne getting together. If it hadn't been for that terrible blind date with the man who obviously didn't know how to handle his boat, you two wouldn't have met." She shrugged and chuckled. "Although, with many of the same friends, I'm sure you would've met her eventually. But how nice that no more time was wasted." She turned and walked toward the living room.

He shook his head while grinning at Maureen taking credit for him and Joanne meeting each other. Turning back to the tea, he heard the chatter between the two women. He appreciated that Maureen didn't drag the conversation back to the events of the day or even the events of the past few weeks. Instead, they chatted about the next fundraiser the American Legion Auxiliary was hosting, the latest reality TV show that her mom was hooked on, and when his aunt Debbie might return to visit. By the time she left, Maureen hugged her daughter tightly, then turned and pulled Bryce into a hug, as well.

As he walked her to her car, she turned one last time and placed her hand on his arm, "Thank you for taking care of my baby."

"I intend to do just that, Maureen."

He watched as she drove away, then hastened back into the house, finding Joanne twisted around on the sofa, staring out the front window. Mixer and Sickle lay on the back of the sofa, purring loudly. Princess was curled up next to her, and Pumpkin was on the floor at her feet.

Her gaze followed him as he came closer. Dark circles were underneath her eyes, and her skin was paler than normal. Her lips curved upward ever so slightly, but it appeared to take great effort to do so. He walked over and sat next to her.

"What were you and Mom talking about out there?"

He shook his head. "Nothing bad. When she was in the kitchen, she told me she was glad we were together."

That statement made Joanne's smile a lot brighter as it eased some of the tension from her face.

"And out there, she just wanted me to make sure you were safe."

The smile widened even more as he sat next to her. She twisted back around to settle into his arms—the place he wanted her to be.

When arriving at work the next day, Joanne had been convinced that she would never be able to keep her mind on what needed to be done. But fortunately, it was a busy day with students, and she threw herself completely into talking with them. She enjoyed working with the younger college students trying to figure out what they wanted to do and with the many adults continuing their education, hoping to gain advancement or better employment.

After lunch, James knocked on her doorframe, and she motioned him into her office. His mannerisms were stilted, making her stomach clench slightly in nervousness.

"I wanted to come talk to you before you hear from HR."

She couldn't think of any reason the human resources office would be involved in anything to do with her department. James's surly attitude toward her since she'd let it be known that she wouldn't date a coworker was the only complaint and that would have come from her. Sitting up straighter, she nodded for him to continue.

"I've been offered a position in another Virginia Community College... one in Roanoke. I've decided to take it."

She leaned back in her chair, shock nearly knocking the breath out of her. "I... I had no idea you were looking to leave."

He dropped his gaze and sighed. "This was a good place to work, but..." He shrugged and looked up. "The Eastern Shore is pretty... um... laid-back. Not exactly a place for me to... well, let's just say that I'm ready for a larger city to work in."

She let out a little sigh of relief. While she tried never to let a co-worker's attitude affect her, she easily admitted that his surliness when she wouldn't go out with him had grated. "If this is something you're sure of, then I wish you the best. I will also work with HR as they look for candidates for the counseling position. I will miss your financial aid expertise and know that the new college will benefit from what you have to offer."

Something flashed through his eyes, but she kept the professional smile on her face. If he thought she would beg him to stay, he was mistaken. With a nod, he turned and walked out, stopping to talk to Lisa. They walked out together, and like air from a balloon, Joanne's lungs deflated. She leaned against her office doorframe for a moment, lost in thought. She finally sighed when she glanced at her computer and realized the workday was over. Bryce was picking her up soon.

Everyone had left, and she grabbed her bag and flipped off the lights. She had just stepped into the hall when she was jolted at the sight of Chad. Her shoulders slumped as her heart rate elevated. "I'll get another restraining order—"

His hands lifted, palms up, and he kept his distance. "I know. I know. I just wanted to see you one last time."

She narrowed her eyes and glared. "One last time?"

"I loved you."

She opened her mouth to refute his claim, but he jumped in and continued.

"Please, let me finish. I did love you. I saw a future with you, but I was stupid and foolish, and weak. I listened to some friends of mine talk about how being married was the ultimate emasculation. How I'd no longer be my own man. The stupid affair was just that. Me thinking that I was claiming back some autonomy. El—uh… my assistant dropped papers off, and it wasn't planned. She was just convenient, but I never meant for you to find out. I sure as hell never meant for you to see what you saw. And as soon as you did, I knew in an instant that I had made the biggest, fucking, stupid mistake of my life." He blew out a long breath, then held her gaze, pain laced in his own. "But I also know that it's over between us."

At those words, her brows lifted, uncertain of exactly what he meant. "This," she said, waving her hand back and forth between them, "is not letting something be *over*."

"I know that. And that's why we won't do this again. When the police questioned me about my whereabouts, and I found out someone messed with your car and then broke into your house, I was horrified to think that my actions could've caused you to suspect that I might've done that. After we broke up, I begged and pleaded, came by your work, and made stupid threats, and you were right to take out a restraining order. I also know that showing up here was another stupid, last-ditch effort. But no more. It's time I let go and let you have your life. And pick up the pieces of mine."

"If you really mean that, Chad, then I wish you well. But this is it—no more visits. No more trying to become part of my life again. We're not going to be friends. We're not going to stay involved in each other's lives."

Another flash of pain moved over his face, but he nodded. "I get that. And it's all on me. I realize that." His shoulders hefted in a sigh. "This is goodbye, Joanne. I promise. I'm heading back to Richmond tonight."

He turned to walk out the doors, and she called out, "Chad."

He looked over his shoulder.

"Take care and be well. I hope you listen to your heart and not your so-called friends the next time you find what you're looking for."

He lifted his chin, then he walked through the doors, and while she stayed inside, her gaze followed him to his car and remained until he had driven out of sight.

Just then, Bryce pulled into the lot, and she breathed a sigh of relief. She knew he wouldn't be happy that Chad stopped by again, but she was glad it was over. Jogging out to his SUV, she climbed inside. Leaning over the console, they met in the middle, and his lips sealed over hers and his tongue thrust into her mouth. The velvety friction jolted straight to her core.

Settling back in her seat, she kept her eyes pinned on him. "Wow, that's the way to say hello."

Chuckling, he dipped his head and said, "Buckle up, babe."

She acquiesced, then looked toward the windshield, wondering how to bring up Chad's final visit. "Can I ask you a question?"

"Asking if you can ask is already like asking, isn't it?"

She laughed, remembering when she'd said the same thing to him. "Yeah, I guess so. Okay, so here it is, and you have to listen to all of it and not be mad."

"Now, you've really got my attention. And, Joanne… for future reference, starting off by telling me I shouldn't get mad just makes me gear up to be mad. But spit it out so we can deal."

"Chad told me goodbye for good. He's going back to Richmond and wished me well but finally understood there was nothing left between us and said goodbye."

There was silence for a minute, and she wondered if Bryce would say anything. Finally, he looked to the side and asked, "Did he say all this in a text?"

"Um, no."

"Did he tell you this in a phone call?"

She sighed heavily and said, "Bryce, he stopped by the office at the end of the day." Bryce cursed and hit the steering wheel, but she jumped in quickly. "He didn't get close to me. He maintained his distance and said that he apologized, said he never meant to hurt me, but that he had been weak and foolish—"

"No shit. He's just now figuring that out?"

"Honey, this is hard enough for me to tell you because I know it's upsetting to you. But I'm trying to do the right thing."

He reached over and took her hand, giving it a squeeze. "I'm sorry, but you gotta know I'm pissed." He sucked in a deep breath and then let it out slowly. "Go ahead."

"I reminded him of that, and he said he just needed to see me to say goodbye. He's returning to Richmond and wished me well but told me he would not contact me again."

They were silent for a minute, then he asked, "You seem awfully calm."

"I am. At first, when I saw him, I was pissed. And then, when he started to apologize, I just wanted to scream. But then he made sense, took responsibility, and realized that some fuckups in life just can't get fixed, and that was one of them. He wished me well and said he would not be back and would not contact me anymore. He said when the police questioned him about my car and my house, he was really upset, thinking that somebody might've tried to hurt me."

"If that gave you closure, then I'm glad, Joanne. I'm still going to let Sam know, and he may still be a suspect, so I want him to know where he is."

"I can live with that, sweetheart. I think that's fair."

He drove the rest of the way to his house with one hand on the steering wheel and the other still holding hers. Glad the heavy was out of the way, she said, "Thanks for letting me be honest with you."

"I never want to give you a reason to lie to me, babe. No matter what happens, you can come to me."

She looked at his house as they pulled into his driveway and smiled. In the few days she'd been living there, it had already felt like coming home.

29

Several tension-filled days had slipped by, and although the overt threats against Joanne had ceased, Bryce's heart remained tightly clenched in the grip of anxiety. Aunt Debbie used to call the emotion *the calm before the storm*, and unfortunately, he could not remove the fear that a storm was coming. Chad's ominous approach had left a lingering shadow, but they had not seen or heard from him again.

He'd fielded a terse and biting phone call from Allison, whose jagged voice told him to have the police back off. Her boss hadn't liked having to field questions about Allison's schedule or whereabouts on the day that Joanne's house was broken into.

Bryce scoffed, not about to forget Allison's earlier threat. "You leave me and Joanne alone—no contact, no threats, no visits... nothing. We don't exist for you in any way other than a memory. For us, it's a bad memory we don't want to revisit. You do that, and you won't have any trouble from us." His declaration had been tinged with its own unspoken promise.

"You got it, ass—" Allison had retorted.

He'd disconnected the call, battling the urge to roll his eyes at her response.

The Secret Service evidently found their interview with Joanne satisfactory, so there had been nothing new on that front. The lack of new information was both a relief and left questions unanswered. Sam informed him that most of the agents had retreated to Baltimore to continue their work on the counterfeit case from there. The details were scarce and shrouded in secrecy, but Sam admitted they were keeping him in the loop since the two gruesome murders fell in his jurisdiction. He also admitted that the agents were going on the trail of the counterfeiters moving money through the island to anchored ships where it would be worth more in other countries than on American soil.

The plot had thickened with suspicions of Brian as the lackey who delivered money to the offshore ships using Steve as his transporter. Brian had gotten sloppy if he was using some of the counterfeit money for his own personal use, putting the whole operation at risk and therefore needed to be eliminated.

"How much money are we talking about if he carried it in a briefcase?" Bryce asked, imagining a paltry sum for so much work and risk.

"The agents told me that with stacks of hundred-dollar bills, he could have carried between one and a half to two million dollars each trip."

The staggering amount hung in the air, the enormity

of the plot overwhelming. "Fuckin' hell," Bryce said, slumping his back against the wall he was standing near. A chill ran down his spine as he recalled the medical examiner had confirmed what Bryce had seen. Steve had been shot before his body had been dumped into the water. Maybe he was greedy, too. Or maybe he just got scared and wanted out.

With the counterfeit money no longer in Joanne's possession and the Secret Service actively involved, the fear of threat eased. Whoever had slashed her tire and trashed her house must have moved on. She had given the description of the man who'd stopped when she pulled to the side of the road, but nothing more was heard about him. No one knew whether he was a Good Samaritan offering assistance or someone who was hoping to try to search her car and purse and then harm her.

Bryce and Joanne had woven a comforting routine in the warm cocoon of his home. The thought of letting her go was unthinkable. In his mind, her rental house could be released, only to become the closing chapter of her single life. Even after the case was resolved and the threat completely removed from her, it was unimaginable for him to consider living their lives apart even while still dating. To some, his feeling might have seemed precipitous, a declaration made too soon, but he knew the truth in his heart and clung to the hope that she felt the same irresistible pull.

Now, standing outside the wheelhouse, he was back out on the water with the bay stretched out before him. The breeze held a chill, but he sucked in a deep breath of fresh air, letting it out slowly. Being out on the expanse of the water always allowed clarity to ease his thoughts.

The VMP officers were on their way to a callout to deal with an accident between a local fishing boat and another boat. The details had been sketchy, but no injuries had been reported.

Approaching the scene, he caught sight of the two fishermen, their faces contorted with anger. "Mr. Bunson! Nick!" he called out, recognizing the hot-headed fisherman who made his living taking vacationers and weekend anglers out to fish in the bay. His boat was kept in shape, his licenses up to date, and his business was always busy. But having seen him throw a punch in a barfight when someone looked at his wife the wrong way or talked about his favorite politician in unflattering words, Bryce knew Nick Bunson had a short fuse. And now, seeing the damage to his boat from the accident, he wasn't surprised to see Nick's fists waving in the air as he cursed the other man. Bryce steeled himself for the battle of words that he knew was coming.

"This asshole ran into me!" Nick yelled.

As they moved closer, Nick jumped onto the other man's boat, throwing a few punches before the officers could get to him.

"Stand down!" Callan yelled to no avail.

As soon as they were close enough to tether to Nick's boat, Callan jumped to the other boat with Bryce right on his heels. Callan wrestled Nick to the deck, separating the two men, while Bryce pushed the other man into a seat.

The stories of what occurred from both of them didn't match, so while two more empty boats arrived, Bryce began looking at the damage to piece together what had happened. Nick's boat had damage along the side near the middle, and the other man's vessel sustained damage at the front.

It didn't take long for him to determine the truth, and while Nick was satisfied that the other man was the one at fault, he was still being arrested for assault.

The Coast Guard was called in to tow both boats back to the harbor, but by the time they made it, with Nick on Bryce's boat, he was sick of listening to the other man.

"Jesus, Nick, just shut up! Everyone is sick of hearing you," Bryce finally muttered, frustration lacing his voice as he barely hung on to his own anger.

"Man, I got two things that mean the world to me. My wife and my boat. Anyone threatens or harms those two things, he's going to feel my fist, and I don't give a shit what happens," Nick argued.

Bryce opened his mouth to fire off a response, then snapped it closed. For the first time in his life, he understood Nick's words. For him, it was Joanne. And someone had threatened her, and he knew if he could get a chance, that person would feel his rage.

With his feet planted on the deck of the boat and his fists on his hips, he pulled his gaze away from Nick and looked out over the water. For someone in law enforcement, he couldn't condone violence. But deep in his soul, he knew he'd go after anyone who hurt Joanne. Scrubbing his hand over his face, he sat on the bench next to Nick. "Look, man, I get it. I know you think I don't, but I do. And right now, I feel it even more because I have someone I care about that much. But you need to be smart. Because if you end up in jail for losing your cool, where will your wife be, huh?" He could see thoughts working behind Nick's eyes as he clamped his mouth shut.

Bryce knew Joanne was going to the island today. He'd wanted to demand that she not go, but she insisted she had a job to do. He'd attempted to contact the lone police officer on the island but couldn't get through. A call to Sam had also gone to voicemail. Bryce stood and walked onto the deck as they approached the harbor. Fatigue pulled at his body.

With a gentle sway, the ferry docked, and Joanne stepped onto the solid dock. The journey was poignant, shadowed by the continued absence of Saul's familiar presence. At least the ferry pilot offered reassurance that Saul was doing well and recuperating at home under the watchful eyes of his wife. In fact, Saul hoped to return to his boats by the springtime.

The crisp, cooler air of the fall was bracing. With the changing seasons, the leaves on the trees had passed their peak colors and were blowing along the lane. Her trips to the island would become fewer when the winter rolled in, and she'd have to rely on the computer instead of face-to-face time with the students.

Her steps quickened as she hurried down the lane to the school. The path was familiar, but she looked around at the familiar sights along the way. Her heart beat faster as anxiety of possible danger lurked, but the island appeared as it always did. Locals went about their daily business. Friendly smiles and waves to those they knew. Tourists moved about slowly, snapping pictures of the charm of island life and selfies.

No one paid any attention to her—not on the ferry and not since she'd disembarked. She let out a shaky breath, her anxiety lessened, and she smiled as she trotted up the wide steps and into the school.

As soon as she entered the room where the seniors sat at tables with their laptops in front of them, she was greeted warmly. The tension that had knotted her muscles since stepping off the ferry eased, and she walked around the room, seeing what each of them was working on. Taking a seat, she called them to her individually to see how they were on their post-graduation goals.

Rob and his parents had met with the recruiters, and he'd decided on the Marines. Hank had made arrangements to tour the Norfolk Shipyard Apprentice Program and have an interview with their admissions office. Carol and Cynthia were still on track for the community college, and Joanne assured them she would still be at the college next year so they could continue to see her.

Shenita pulled out a piece of paper from her backpack and bounced over to Joanne, waving it around. "I got in! Culinary Institute of America!"

When Joanne hugged the excited young woman, her smile was almost as wide as Shenita's.

She'd noticed Ted wasn't in the room when she'd sat down, and he still hadn't arrived. "Does anyone know where Ted is?"

Rob leaned back in his chair. "He's at the dock with his dad. One of the fishermen got killed, and some of the others are helping out."

She nodded, hating that he was missing school, but understood the reason. Sacrifices were sometimes necessary when living off the land or the bay, and hard work was always necessary.

After her engaging sessions with the students, Joanne stepped into the sunshine that had chased away the morning chill. Island life wasn't for her, but the beauty and close-knit community always made her visits enjoyable.

She glanced at the time but decided to skip a meal at a restaurant and set her sights on the dock area, hoping to find Ted to chat with him for a few minutes before waiting on the return ferry.

Walking down the road, she admired the fishing boats, their colors faded from countless trips onto the bay. Multiple buildings and docks were spread out over the area. Unlike a small, contained harbor, she wandered along, seeing numerous single docks, each with its own wooden shack out in the water, only accessible by boat. There were many empty docks, giving the area a ghost town appearance where she assumed boats were out on the water and would return with their bounty. A sigh slipped out. *Or it's a view from better times when the area would bustle with fishermen but now stood forlorn, exposing a way of life that was no longer teeming with young people who wanted to work the bay.*

Realizing her quest to find Ted could become a wild goose chase, she headed toward the many buildings off to the side where a few fishermen were working. They looked up as she approached and returned her smile. "Good afternoon. I'm looking for Ted Robinson. Or perhaps where he and his father have a boat?"

With a friendly nod and a finger pointing the way, one replied, "Sure thing, Miss. The Robinsons are over there, just behind the larger building."

Tossing out her thanks, she turned and hustled in the direction indicated, glad Ted's family business was on the main island. As she neared, she spied him standing on a boat, wearing faded waders and a heavy jacket. A knit cap was pulled over his hair, and he appeared older than when he was in the classroom. She called out his name.

Ted looked up in surprise, a wide smile splitting his tanned face. "Ms. Norris! Hey!" He climbed down from the boat and jogged over, his booted waders clumping over the wooden dock. "What brings you over here?"

"I just wanted to check on you. I stopped by the school, and while we didn't have anything we needed to go over, I hated to make the trip and not be able to see you."

A man walked over, and she smiled at the older version of Ted. She thrust out her hand toward him.

"Hello. I'm Joanne Norris from the community college. I come over a couple of times a month and talk to the students."

The man's wrinkles deepened as he smiled. "Well, that's real nice, Ms. Norris. I'm Stuart Robinson." He clapped Ted on the shoulder, then leaned closer to her. "My Ted wants to stay here and fish." He sighed heavily, then added, "But I don't know that's the future he should be thinking of. Anything you can help him with is good."

She smiled, both at the acknowledgment of pride in his eyes and wanting a bright future for his son. "I know that Ted wants to continue working for the family business. But many of our community college students are adults who change their interests and careers down the road. I've let him know that he doesn't have to lock into just one career forever."

The man's bushy eyebrows lifted, and he nodded. "Good, good."

Ted jumped in and said, "Dad, I know what I want, but I also know things can change. I'll always keep my options open."

Ted's father smiled at his son. "All right, Ms. Norris. It's been nice to meet you." He turned and ambled down the dock, and she felt as though she'd passed a test.

Ted grinned and jerked his head toward the retreating figure of his dad. "Life out here makes us tough, but don't let him fool you. He worries about me."

She laughed and nodded. "I have no doubt that he does. Anyway, I don't want to take you away from work, but I just wanted to touch base."

He tilted his head to the side and asked, "Would you like a tour in my boat?"

"Oh, I'd love to, but are you sure you have time?"

"That's one of the perks of working this job… I set my own hours. Plus, I've already had one run out this morning as the sun came up."

"Then I'd love to. I don't have to be back for the ferry for another hour." She pressed her lips together. "Um… do you have a life jacket?"

"I wouldn't take you out if I didn't, Ms. Norris."

He climbed aboard his boat and turned to offer her a hand. Once she was jacketed and settled on the seat, he steered them out through some of the marshes that divided the area. She loved seeing the shacks, the stacks of crab pots, and the fishermen returning with their catches.

"It's been weird around here, Ms. Norris. I don't know if you heard, but one of the fishermen went missing. And then all these government special agents showed up, asking a bunch of questions and talking to everybody. Then Steve… uh, that was his name. Anyway, his body was found."

"Um… yeah, I sort of heard something about that," she fudged.

"The rumor is he was involved in something illegal. People around here are either talking about it, wondering what it was, or keeping their mouths shut. It's got a bunch of us on edge, I can tell you that. The talk seems to have died down, but even my dad has been acting weird lately. Steve's family needed some help, so I told Dad I could take care of some of my schoolwork at night to come out and help during the day."

She nodded, then looked around. "This is really fascinating. I've never seen these buildings up close before." She pulled out her phone and snapped several pictures of the area.

"Most of the fishermen have them. It's where the catch is brought, and then other boats take them to the mainland."

"Some are connected to the island, and many are out here on the water. Is that because the bay's waters are rising?"

"Partially. But many are built out here. Easier to get to by boat, and then we're not all jammed up on the land."

"Well, it's so interesting. And really nice that you're helping out."

He shrugged. "Way it is around here." With a deft maneuver, he turned the boat around and navigated through the network of waterways and docks.

"The career you've chosen isn't easy, and I can only imagine that, with the challenges facing the bay, watermen, ecology, and rising water levels, you will find it a challenge. But, Ted, you're smart, innovative, and hardworking. Whatever you do, I know you'll be successful."

"That means a lot to me, Ms. Norris." Pride showed on his face as he smiled.

Passing more of the other shacks, they came closer to the island's harbors and maze of connected piers. She cast her gaze around, pulling her knit cap over her ears and drawing her jacket tighter to ward off the chill. She snapped pictures of the sun-lined faces of the fishermen as they worked and the pots of crabs lining their boats.

She spied a lone man walking toward one of the shacks off to the side. His attire was casual, but his jeans and boots lacked the weathered look of the locals. Curiosity was piqued, and she lifted her phone to click a photograph just as another man walked around a corner and met him. Still snapping, she looked down at her screen and zoomed in when something familiar tickled the recesses of her memory. *I know him... Matthew!*

She remembered him from the ferry ride several weeks ago but hadn't given him another thought since then. Matthew's eyes scanned the area, but his gaze moved right through her. She wasn't surprised he didn't recognize her with her cap pulled over her hair and a scarf wrapped around her neck. He stepped into one of the old buildings that dotted the docks.

"What building is that over there?" she asked Ted, pointing at the one Matthew disappeared into.

"That isn't being used anymore. It used to be where one of the companies that came in to buy crabs had their processing area, but now, it's mostly used for storage. In fact, my dad keeps some things in there. Why?"

"Oh... um... just curious. I thought I saw someone go in that I recognized."

"Hm. Could have been my dad, I guess." Ted's brow furrowed.

She shivered, but the cause seemed to come more from inside her than from the cooler air. Ted pulled alongside one of the docks, and she thanked him for showing her around. He climbed from the boat first and turned to offer her a hand. When she was safely on the dock, she handed him the life vest and waved goodbye.

Starting down the wooden planks, she walked close to where she saw Matthew disappear inside, then hesitated. It was still early, and with plenty of time to catch the ferry going back to the mainland, she decided to take a look around. Pulling her phone from her pocket, she continued to snap pictures of the crab shacks in the distance and a few of the older buildings that appeared abandoned.

Curious, she walked around to the back side, wondering if any picture-worthy scenes existed. The windows were grimy, and she was unable to see inside any of them, but hearing voices, she walked to where a window was slightly opened and peeked inside.

Her breath caught in her throat at the sight of another man talking to Matthew. *He's the one who stopped when I had a flat tire!* Suspicion of inexplicable coincidence snaked along her spine as she listened to their lowered voices.

"You're part of this, and you're going to finish it."

"I agreed to go after that girl, but you didn't tell me she was dating a fucking cop! I'm not gonna go to prison for you."

"I don't know what you think is going to keep you out if you don't keep doing what we say. You're in this up to your neck. You got rid of the greedy local bastard. The only way to keep you out of prison is to keep doing what you're paid well to do!"

"What if I get caught?"

"Then don't get fucking caught. You keep making deliv-

eries and not demands, and you'll be fine. You don't, you'll end up like Brian and that fisherman."

"Okay, okay."

"And me?" a different male voice entered the conversation.

"You can take over Steve's runs. Do that, and you won't have to worry about money anymore or living on this shithole island."

Barely breathing out of fear of exposure, she backed away from the window and tiptoed around the corner. With her back plastered against the wall as she hid behind a stack of crab pots, her mind raced as she tried to think of the right thing to do. Finding it hard to process, she pulled out her phone. Dialing Bryce, she breathed a sigh of relief when he answered. "I'm on the island," she whispered.

"What? I can barely hear you. Where are you?"

"Tangier. I'm on the island."

"What's going on?" His biting tone let her know he could tell something was wrong.

Looking around, she whispered, "Can you come? The killers are here."

"Goddammit, Joanne. What's happening?"

"I think... I heard... I'm at the building that involves whatever got Brian and Steve killed. It's a one-story wooden building... um... it's where the fishermen store stuff at the end of Harbor Road. Two men... I mean, three men are inside, and they're talking. One I met after Brian was killed, and the other was the man who drove by when I had a flat. I think he did it."

"You stay where no one can get to you. I'm on the

water, and we'll get there as soon as possible. I'm calling in Sam but get to where you're safe!"

"Okay," she whispered. Tiptoeing back toward the front, she felt her gut clench as she wondered if she'd stumbled onto the counterfeit mess. Whatever it was, it got at least two people killed. She had no plans of becoming number three.

Joanne quickly slid behind a taller stack of old crab pots. Her heart pounded in her chest as she gave thanks that her gray pants and her black coat helped to camouflage her presence. But her red scarf and knit hat would easily give her hiding place away. Pulling both off, she shoved them into her bag as she pressed her back next to the old building.

Bryce's voice had been filled with worry when he'd told her to get away, but she was afraid that leaving her hiding place to run down the dock would make her too visible. She had no idea how long she might have to hide and began to wonder if her plan was foolish. Deciding to text Bryce to see if he was close, she reached inside her purse and wrapped her shaking fingers around her phone. Looking down, she hit contacts and his number.

Suddenly, the clomp of approaching boot steps on the wooden dock caught her attention. Looking over, she held her breath in fear, then gasped as Ted came around the corner of the building. He passed by the crab pots, never looking over to see her. She started to leap out to call him back, but before she had a chance, he shouted, "Dad? You in here?"

30

"What's the ETA to Tangier?" Bryce called out to Callan. "Joanne's in trouble!"

"Fifteen minutes," Callan shouted in reply.

Bryce's heart was racing, but he managed to report what was happening to Jose and Callan. "Call into the station. I'm getting ahold of Sam."

The detective picked up as soon as he dialed Sam's personal number. Before Bryce had a chance to speak, Sam said, "I'm in a helicopter with Agent Stubbs. We're heading over to Tangier."

"Then I'll meet you there," he said. "I just got a call from Joanne, and she's outside one of the old processing plants and says she thinks she stumbled onto something."

"Dammit! Agent Stubbs got intel that the counter-feiters wanted to meet with a local he's got on the inside. It wasn't a prearranged meeting, so we're just heading over now... hang on—"

Bryce closed his eyes as the wind from the bay

rushed over him while Callan pushed the VMP vessel to full speed.

"I told her to get out of there and get to safety. My ETA is now less than ten minutes."

"We should be on the ground about the same time, but we won't be able to land right at the building."

"We'll come into the harbor, and I know the building she's talking about. We'll meet you there."

"I just talked to Ryan," Jose said. "Andy and Joseph are behind us, along with the Coast Guard."

Each moment crawled by, stretching into eternity. Bryce's mind filled with images of Joanne, alone and vulnerable, scared out of her mind. The harbor was a labyrinth of buildings, crab shacks, shanties, and docks stacked with boxes, crab pots, and equipment... plenty of places to hide. Still, he couldn't resist firing off a text, telling her he was close and for her to stay hidden.

He waited to see the three dots appear to let him know she was typing, but the screen remained blank. Just when he thought he'd crawl out of his skin, Jose yelled that Tangier was on the horizon. Bryce's head jerked upward, and he spied the peaceful little island that had always seemed as if the outside world didn't press in. Now, it appeared ominous.

As the boat churned through the water, with the island growing larger in his vision, he could hear helicopter blades thumping in the distance. Looking up, he spied two helicopters approaching. As they landed, Callan brought the vessel into the harbor with practiced ease.

His gaze scanned the area, but there were too many

buildings, boats, and equipment to be able to find Joanne. Callan brought the vessel close enough for him to jump over to the wooden dock. He had no idea what danger might be lurking around or if she would be in the line of fire. Frustration raged through his blood as he felt impotent, not knowing what to do.

His eyes darted to the left, catching sight of Sam headed toward him in the midst of others wearing the same tactical gear he'd expected from the agents. A noise behind him caused him to jerk around, seeing Jose at his side. Glad for all the help they could amass, he knew his best chance of keeping Joanne safe was to align himself with the other law enforcement.

A strong hand clamped onto his shoulder, and Jose's steady voice was close to his ear. "Hang on. She's smart. She called you instead of rushing into danger."

Twisting his head, he held his friend's gaze. "Just so we're clear... I don't give a shit about the counterfeiters or what the Secret Service is after. All I want is for Joanne to be safe. Nothing else is my concern."

Jose dipped his chin in acknowledgment. "Agreed."

She still hadn't answered his text, and his gaze scanned the area, looking for any sign of Joanne. Until he had her in his arms, he couldn't calm the fear crawling through his body.

Without hesitation, Joanne darted from behind the crab pots and grabbed the back of Ted's coat. He spun around, his eyes widening as his expression transformed from confusion to surprise.

"Ms. Norris? What are you doing here? I thought you were heading back to the ferry?"

"Shh! We have to get out of here!"

"I thought I saw my dad go in here—"

The door opened behind them, and just as Ted's father called out, "Run!" A thump was heard, and Mr. Robinson dropped to his knees before pitching forward onto the bare wooden floor.

"What the—" Ted shouted, his hands reaching out toward his dad as he leaped forward.

"No!" Joanne screamed.

Suddenly, the barrel of a gun lifted and pointed straight toward Ted.

"Get in here!" Matthew called.

"Who the hell are you?" Ted said, stepping between Matthew and Joanne. He looked down at his father on the floor and hesitated as though uncertain whether to rush forward or stay close to Joanne. "Dad! Dad!"

Mr. Robinson groaned, lifting his head off the floor. "Get away…"

"Too late for that," Matthew said, still pointing the gun toward Joanne. "Well, well, Joanne. We meet again."

Ted's head swung around. "Do you know him?"

"No! Yes. I just met him on the ferry one day. But… I…" Her gaze dropped to the floor where Ted's father lay. "Oh God…"

Ted had dropped to his dad's side, and she wanted to kneel next to them but was paralyzed at the chilling sight of the gun barrel gleaming ominously in the dim interior of the shack.

Matthew growled, "Your father and I were making a deal, but like everyone around here, he's too stupid to understand anything beyond this fuckin' island."

Ted's narrowed gaze shot up. "My dad would never—"

"You've got no idea what money will do to people tired of living without."

Joanne's breath hitched as it left her lungs. "You're part of the counterfeiters. Like Brian." Her chest deflated as the words left her lips. "Did you kill him? And the fisherman?"

The other man started to whine. "Matthew, maybe we should—"

"Shut up!" Matthew barked, his gaze jerking toward the man Joanne recognized as the one who stopped when she was on the side of the road, and clarity settled over her.

"You... you were the one who slashed my tire and then stopped to offer help."

The man grimaced, then glared at Matthew before returning his gaze to her. "I just did what I was told."

"Shut up, Ernie!" Matthew bit out again.

"What's going on?" Ted asked, breathing heavily as his gaze darted from person to person, his hands still on his father, assisting him to sit up.

Joanne had no idea how involved Ted's dad was with the counterfeiters. Licking her dry lips, she kept her gaze on the weapon. She'd never been around guns before, and the sight of one pointed toward her made it hard to breathe, much less think straight.

The distant sounds of a helicopter approaching caused everyone's gazes to lift. Matthew dropped his chin after a few seconds, and his eyes landed once again on her. Lifting a brow, he scoffed. "Called in the cavalry?"

She straightened her spine despite the shudders racing through her body. "You're finished. The authorities have been after you for months." She moved slightly in front of Ted and his dad, but the young man was having none of her heroics. He stood and shifted to align with her while his gaze shifted between Matthew and his dad, anguish etched into his youthful face.

"Stay put, boy," Matthew said, then looked toward Joanne. "I'm not going down that easy. Come on, Joanne. You come with me, or your friend here will end up like Brian."

Gasping, she pulled Ted back and said, "Stay with your dad. Make sure he's okay."

Ted's emotions showed easily on his face—anger mixed with angst. She tipped her head down toward his father. "He needs you. I'll be fine. Lots of people are coming to help."

"Oh no. I'm taking both of you for leverage. Go!" Matthew shouted, stepping closer to grab her arm.

"Where?" she asked, wincing at the painful grip he had.

"To the boat docked outside."

"What about me?" Ernie asked, stepping closer. His

voice shook, and even Joanne recognized a weak link in Matthew's chain.

As though realizing the same thing, Matthew sneered and fired a shot. Ernie's body jerked backward, and Joanne looked on in horror at the crimson blooming over his shirt, and he crumpled.

"Oh God," she gasped, feeling light-headed. She would have collapsed if it wasn't for Matthew's iron-fisted grip on her arm.

"I'll shoot either one of you who gives me any trouble." Matthew shoved her onto the boat. He looked at Ted. "Let loose the lines and jump aboard, taking the wheel if you don't want her death on your conscience."

She watched, wide-eyed, as Ted did as he was instructed. His jaw was tight, but he didn't argue. As soon as the boat headed out past the other docks, she heard her name called out and swung her head back to the harbor to see Bryce and others racing toward the building. Matthew had his gun trained on Ted as they sped out into the bay, and it appeared he no longer saw her as a threat. She slipped her hand into her pocket, stupidly looking for something... anything she could use as a weapon. Her fingers curled around her cell phone, but other than chucking it at his head, it would hardly help her. "You can't outrun them," she said, hoping to get him to realize he should give himself up.

"Stupid bitch, we only have to get to the *Alteria*."

"The Coast Guard will stop you," Ted shouted over the roar of the boat motor.

"Not with hostages. Once on board the ship, you'll stay with me until we get into international waters.

Then I'll let you go if you stay good. If not, you'll be dumped overboard into the Atlantic Ocean."

She blinked, his words sending chills through her as her brain tried to make sense of what he was saying. *Alteria*. On board. A ship. Ocean. As the speed of the boat picked up, she clung to the seat, feeling naked without a life vest. Re-focusing on Matthew, she glared. "That's what you've been doing? Taking the counterfeit money to foreign ships?"

Matthew's lips slowly curved upward as he looked at her. "American money is worth so much more overseas."

"That's what Brian was doing? Getting it to the ships?"

"He got stupid. Not greedy, but just dumb-fuck stupid."

"I... what..." Joanne's voice was caught in the wind as the boat hurled out into the bay, realizing she really had no idea why she was asking him questions.

"My dad never would have helped you," Ted bit out, his head turned toward Matthew, a fierce scowl contorting his expression.

"All I had to do was ask if he would take me out into the bay to meet with someone, and he was more than happy to do it for the money I was willing to pay."

"That's how you get them," Joanne surmised. "You get them to take you out, and then once you've involved them in something illegal, they keep them doing it for you. That poor fisherman... you killed him."

"Another dumb fuck. Christ, I've been surrounded by nothing but dumb fucks! And then my bosses threaten *me*. They have no clue that I have to work with idiots to move their merchandise."

"Why use them?" she cried. "You could just take a boat—"

"Shut up!" He glared at her and then narrowed his eyes as he looked behind her. "Looks like we might have trouble." Waving the gun toward her again, he said, "And you two are my ticket out of it."

31

Bryce and Jose had ducked low behind the stacks of fishing equipment and boxes near the building Joanne had indicated. Sam had stayed with him as the agents raced to the other side. But by the time they made it to the door, it stood open. Entering, they found one man on the floor, still alive but losing blood fast from a gunshot wound. Another man slowly rose to his feet, one hand held to the back of his head.

Sam rushed forward, his weapon raised, and when the man lifted his hands, blood coated one of them. He fell to his knees but managed to say, "He took my son and the woman from the college."

Agent Stubbs cursed as Agent Hargrove raced to Ted's father. "Which ship are they going to?"

"The *Alteria*. He wanted me to get him there tonight, but his guy showed up." He lifted a shaky hand and pointed at the man now being attended to by a Coast Guard medic.

"A helicopter is on its way. We'll transport him to the Eastern Shore Hospital," the medic called out.

Driven by his consuming need to protect Joanne, Bryce's heart pounded as he raced out of the building, desperately scanning the area until his gaze landed on a boat with a young man at the wheel and Joanne sitting near the back with another man between them.

"There!" he roared, and his footsteps pounded along the wooden dock to the VMP boat with Jose and Andy on his heels.

Joseph was already at the wheel of the first one, and as soon as he leaped aboard, he heard another pair of boots hit the deck and looked over his shoulder to see Agent Hargrove. Their vessel passed the end of the docks and headed out into the bay, with Jose and Andy jumping into the other VMP vessel and following closely.

Agent Hargrove, his voice steady but laced with urgency, said, "Stubbs will let the others know that the ship they are heading to is the *Alteria*. It's waiting for its Maryland pilot to disembark, so Matthew plans to get there before it heads out to sea. That's how they've been making the transfer of counterfeit money."

"What the hell is he trying to do now with two hostages?" Andy asked.

Agent Hargrove shook his head, looking toward Bryce. Grimacing, he said, "No idea."

Nothing mattered but Joanne, the woman who held his heart. "She can't swim," he whispered, his heart seizing. His gaze never left the boat in the distance they were pursuing, and it was obvious they were gaining on them.

"The boat is slowing!" Joseph called out.

"The kid at the wheel must be backing off the speed," Agent Hargrove said.

Bryce's heart was in his throat as he lifted the binoculars and stared at the man who held his gun on the young man and not Joanne. Suddenly, the sound of a helicopter drowned out the roar of their vessel's engine, and his gaze shot upward to see the Coast Guard helicopter.

Listening to his radio, Agent Hargrove called out, "The Navy has responded, as well. They're sending a boat out of Norfolk to keep the Alteria in the bay until we know what the hell is going on."

Bryce whirled around. "I don't give a fuck!"

Joseph shot him a look of sympathy, but Agent Hargrove blinked in surprise.

"That's your fucking deal! All I want to do is make sure my woman and that kid trying to help are safe."

"Shit!" Joseph shouted, grabbing Bryce's attention.

Something was happening aboard the boat Joanne was on. Lifting his binoculars again, he watched her as their boat slowed even more, and Matthew stood, appearing to scream toward the young teenager while pointing his weapon at Joanne.

Gaining on their vessel, he could clearly see Joanne's wide-eye, pale expression of fear and the terror on the young teen's face. As the boy argued, Matthew began to grow more agitated. He looked straight toward the

VMP vessel before glancing upward at the circling Coast Guard helicopter.

"He's got to know it's over," Joseph said, keeping their boat plowing through the surface of the bay, gaining on them each second.

Agent Hargrove shook his head. "He's already proven to be willing to take out anyone who doesn't help him."

Bryce knew what the agent was saying and feared the implication was that the teenager and Joanne were no longer just hostages but might need to be dispatched. *Hold on, baby. I'm coming.* He just hoped he got to her in time.

"It's not my fault," Ted cried out, waving his hands. "I told you this boat wasn't going to handle the speed you wanted to go and—"

"It's a fucking boat!" Matthew growled. "It's got an engine, so don't tell me it won't run!"

"It's a fishing boat that my dad and I needed to work on," Ted said, his voice shaky. His hands were off the wheel as he faced Matthew, and his gaze kept jumping over to Joanne.

She knew nothing about boats but had felt their speed slow until, finally, the engine stopped. Panic surged through her at the thought of what a desperate, cornered Matthew might do. They were now close to a colossal cargo ship looming nearby. The name *Alteria* was boldly painted on its weathered side. The ship was an enormous, menacing titan of steel and iron, and her insides quaked at the idea of getting any closer.

Thankful their boat had stopped, her eyes stayed pinned on Matthew as he looked up toward the circling helicopter. She was aware of other boats motoring closer from all directions. Matthew was sweating despite the chilled air, and her fear increased even as her hope grew. She chanced a glance behind her to see the VMP vessels nearing.

Now, she could barely make out the figure standing at the front of the boat, his binoculars trained on them. *Bryce.* She longed to give him a signal, but terror held her captive. Bryce being so close should fill her with joy, but the chilling uncertainty of a cornered Matthew kept any hope at bay.

Matthew, his eyes cold and unforgiving, seemed to ignore her as a possible threat again as he approached Ted and lifted his gun straight into the young man's face.

"No!" she cried out.

Matthew turned his head and focused on her again, a maniacal smile crossing his lips. He swung the gun toward her, then looked back over at Ted. "Get this boat going, or I'll blow her fucking head off."

"Hands up!" someone shouted from nearby.

Joanne looked at the closest vessel and spied a determined Bryce standing next to Agent Hargrove. Both of their weapons were trained on Matthew, and the sudden sharp sound of a gunshot pierced the air as it ricocheted over the water.

She dropped to the deck of the boat while covering

her head, but not before seeing Matthew's body jerk violently. She instinctively scrambled on her knees toward Ted, who had the same idea because he met her in the middle. Her gaze moved to the haunting image of Matthew's prone body, lifeless eyes open, staring unseeingly toward the sky. Confusion and fear wrestled within, and she had no idea if it was safe to move.

Ted's arms wrapped around her shoulders. "Don't look, Ms. Norris," he said, sounding much older than seventeen.

Suddenly, she heard the sweet sound of Bryce calling her name. She started to stand, but Ted forced her down again.

"Wait," he called out. "Lift your hands. Make sure they know we aren't the bad guys!"

She lifted her hands slowly, but their vessel rocked as it was bumped. Peering up, she spied Bryce leap onto their deck. With several other officers training their weapons on Matthew, Bryce pulled her into his arms.

"You came," Joanne gasped. Even with Bryce's arms around her, she felt his body shaking as much as she was. "I was hoping you'd get here."

"Nothing could have kept me from getting to you, Joanne." He cupped her chilled cheek and leaned in to kiss her cold lips. "Let's get you off here."

"He was taking the money to someone on that ship," she said, standing with Bryce's assistance. She looked down to see Agent Hargrove standing over Matthew's body and battled against her threatening nausea. She reached out to grab Ted's hand. "Come on, Ted. Let's get out of here."

32

Bryce felt as though he was trapped in a never-ending whirlwind of chaos and procedure. The day, having been filled with peril and raw emotion, stretched on. He wanted to dispense with the red tape, interviews, and reports required and simply take Joanne home.

They bypassed the island as their vessel cut through the waves, having been ordered to the mainland. There, they were all taken to the sheriff's department. Joanne and Ted were ushered into separate rooms upon their arrival, and Bryce wasn't allowed to be present for her interview. After he gave his report, frustration gnawed at his gut as he fumed and paced, while the walls seemed to close in around him as he listened to each tick of the clock on the wall.

Finally, the door to Joanne's interview room opened, and Sam walked out. But not Joanne. Sam called Bryce, the other VMP officers, including Ryan, who'd arrived, and Sheriff Colt Hudson into another conference room.

Once everyone was seated, Sam quickly assured, "Joanne is fine, Bryce, so you can quit glowering at me. She's reading and signing her report."

He opened his mouth to speak, but Ryan settled his hand on Bryce's shoulder. "We get it, Bryce. We've been there. Take a breath, and let's find out what we need to know. The sooner we finish all this, the sooner you can get to her."

He wanted to argue but knew it was in vain. Simply nodding, he stared at Sam, willing the man to begin.

"Here's what I know at this time. The Secret Service has been investigating a counterfeit ring for the past year. They knew it originated out of Baltimore but couldn't locate the operation. They got a tip from one of the Maryland pilots who brings the cargo ships into the port."

Bryce knew that every foreign ship that came into the Chesapeake Bay bound for Baltimore had to have a licensed Maryland ship pilot board the ship to steer it safely into and out of the port. As they are anchored in the bay, multiple smaller ships and tugs approach for various reasons, one being to allow a Maryland pilot aboard.

Sam continued. "The counterfeiters had discovered that it was too risky to try to get the money on board a foreign ship while it was in a Baltimore dock." He snorted, adding, "The mob runs the ports, and the counterfeiters wanted to avoid splitting anything with the Mafia, so they came up with a different route. Matthew Shelton was in charge of the transportation.

He had someone carry a couple of million counterfeit hundred-dollar bills in a briefcase or small luggage by land, then hired a fisherman off Tangier to take them to the cargo ship. Steve Harlow was the fisherman they used. The transfer was made with the ship's contact. Money was exchanged, and no one was the wiser. But during one of the times when a pilot transferred to a cargo ship bound for Baltimore and then to Peru, he just happened to catch sight of the transfer. Pure fucking luck."

Sam looked down at his notes while Bryce's leg jiggled with the anxiety of seeing Joanne.

Sam looked up and continued. "The Secret Service was called in when Brian was questioned by the pilot. The Secret Service began watching Brian. They were building their case slowly. It seems that Brian got sloppy. The counterfeiters discovered Brian used some of the money, like when he paid for lunch in front of Joanne with counterfeit bills. Once this was exposed, Matthew came down and killed Brian, then he probably had Steve take the body and dump it. Steve got scared and didn't want to do the work anymore, so Matthew killed him."

"What about Joanne? The threats against her?" Bryce bit out.

Sam nodded. "After Matthew discovered that Brian had used some of the counterfeit money and discovered that a woman from the ferry might have had some of it, he used another man, Ernie, to search her place. At first, Ernie slashed her tire to keep her from getting home on time, but he went past her, stopped to talk to her, and then was identifiable. Ernie was probably scared and didn't want anything to happen to Joanne, knowing that he couldn't claim immunity for the counterfeit crimes if she was harmed. When he was finally sent in, he searched her place but found nothing. Matthew wasn't happy, but Ernie also wanted out and was shot today."

Bryce's heart clenched at the thought of how close Joanne came to being another one of Matthew's victims. "Christ, all this because Brian tried to pay for her lunch when he was in a hurry."

"Seems like Matthew left a trail of dead bodies in his wake," Jose said.

"Believe it or not, Ernie isn't dead. He was flown to the hospital, where he was in surgery for a couple of hours. Right now, he's in ICU, but it looks like the bullet didn't hit any major organs. Thanks to the Coast Guard medical helicopter, he'll be able to help bring down the rest of the counterfeit crew."

The door opened again, and Joanne emerged into the hallway this time. Her face was pale and drawn, but her eyes sparked with relief. Her smile was weary, but genuine as she accepted Agent Stubbs's extended hand-shake. The stoic agent glanced toward the other end of the hall, then offered a curt chin lift before he headed back into the room. Bryce's love and concern propelled him forward, and he strode directly to her, memorizing every detail to assure himself that she was real and safe.

Joanne's eyes met his, and in them, he saw a mirror of his own emotions—relief, exhaustion, and what he hoped was love. She rested her cheek on his chest as his arms encircled her and pulled her tightly to him, holding her close. For a moment, everything that had occurred that day fell away, leaving only the two of them.

After a few minutes, another door opened, and Ted walked out with Agent Hargrove. A woman was with Ted, clinging to his arm. Ted walked straight to Joanne and said, "Ms. Norris, this is my mom. Since I'm only seventeen, they called her."

"Oh, Ms. Norris, I can't thank you enough."

"Mrs. Robinson, Ted was amazing. And from what I understand, your husband was, too. You should be very proud of both of them."

They'd made it to the others, and it dawned on Bryce that he didn't know what piece Ted's father played.

Sam jumped in again. "With Steve Harlow out of the picture, Ted's father contacted Agent Stubbs when the SS was on the island talking to people. Mr. Robinson said he'd been approached to carry someone out to a large ship in the bay. He agreed to work for the agents. He hadn't made a counterfeit money run, but it was being planned. The meeting today was when it was going to take place. Mr. Robinson had contacted Agent Stubbs, and that's why they were heading there today."

Bryce looked down at Joanne's face, seeing the dark circles underneath her eyes. "And you stumbled into the middle of it again."

Her nose crinkled. "I think I'm ready for a break!" She looked up at him and smiled. "Take me home."

She couldn't have said any other words that would

strike his heart more. Smiling, he kept his arm around her and guided her down the hall. The other VMP officers walked out with them, accompanied by Sam. On the steps of the sheriff's station, goodbyes, chin lifts, and heartfelt thanks were given and received.

Joanne turned to Sam and said, "You know, Detective Shackley... my mom could set you up with some really nice women—"

"Oh no!" he exclaimed, backing away, his hands held up in defense. "I'll wait and find someone on my own, thank you very much." With a laugh, he turned and headed back inside the building.

"Come on," Bryce said, chuckling while he guided her to his vehicle. "You don't need to give your mom any more encouragement."

"Well, I think she's still intent on Jeff and your aunt Debbie making a match."

Bryce opened his mouth to refute, but realized as he stared into Joanne's eyes that he had everything he'd ever hoped for right there in his arms. And if Debbie found that again like she'd had with Uncle Bernie, he was fine with that. Tugging her along, he said, "Which house are we going to?"

She stopped and let out a shaky breath. "I'd like to go to yours."

His heart pounded, and he found he was no longer willing to wait to tell her, so he separated just enough to hold her gaze. "I'm in love with you, Joanne."

Her smile curved her tremoring lips. "I'm in love with you, too," she confessed.

"Then let's go to *our* house."

Kissing her with love coursing through his veins, he allowed the hope of a forever-together move through him.

33

The spring day was filled with the sunshine beaming down and a gentle breeze keeping the large crowd comfortable as they sat on the white chairs facing the flowered-covered gazebo. Bryce stood, nervous at the number of eyes on him but anxious to finally see the one pair of blue eyes that he wanted to look at every day for the rest of his life.

Debbie sat on the front row, her smile softer but just as full of emotion. Next to her was Jeff, someone who had become a staple in Debbie's life even before she made her Eastern Shore move permanent last month. Bryce knew that Debbie was thinking of how Bernie would have wanted to be here on this day, but she was happy that someone else in her life also brought her smiles and fulfillment.

The gathering was filled with men and women from the American Legion and Legionnaires, law enforcement, and friends who were all present to share this day with him and Joanne. For someone who considered himself to be more of an introvert, he was surprised to see just how many friends they had.

He glanced to the side, seeing the grins on the faces of the men he considered to be truly his best men. Jose, Andy, Jared, Joseph, and Ryan. The women, all dressed in pale yellow dresses of different designs, had floated down the aisle and taken their place opposite. Melanie, Ivy, Billie, Shiloh, and Judith. In the months since they had become a couple, endless get-togethers had solidified Joanne's friendships with the other officers' wives.

Now, the music changed, and he looked at the back of the park and finally spied Joanne gliding toward him, her mother at her side. Maureen's smile beamed, almost rivaling the sunshine. Joanne's was just as brilliant, but anxiety filled her eyes until they landed on his. Then his beautiful bride's face lightened, and the sun no longer could compete with the radiance coming from her.

She neared, then stopped, and turned to kiss her mother's cheek. Maureen hugged her daughter, allowing a tear to escape, before she took her seat opposite Debbie. Now, Joanne faced him again and walked the few steps to take his hands. At her touch, he was reminded of the tingle he'd felt the first time they met when he assisted her off the boat. That tingle remained every time they touched.

He barely heard the minister's words, repeating his vows on cue, but when she offered her vows, he was humbled that this beautiful woman wanted to bind herself to him forever. It was something he'd hoped for, but he'd never been sure his hopes would come true until he kissed her at the end of the ceremony.

Now, he knew. Life was complete when dreams became hope, and hope became reality. Turning to the shouting and clapping gathering with Joanne in his arms, he knew he had it all.

For the next Baytown Hero book (Sam Shackley's love story)
Always a Hero

ALSO BY MARYANN JORDAN

Don't miss other Maryann Jordan books!

Baytown Boys (small town, military romantic suspense)

Coming Home

Just One More Chance

Clues of the Heart

Finding Peace

Picking Up the Pieces

Sunset Flames

Waiting for Sunrise

Hear My Heart

Guarding Your Heart

Sweet Rose

Our Time

Count On Me

Shielding You

To Love Someone

Sea Glass Hearts

Protecting Her Heart

Sunset Kiss

Baytown Heroes - A Baytown Boys subseries

A Hero's Chance

Finding a Hero

A Hero for Her

Needing A Hero

A Hero's Surprise

Hopeful Hero

Always a Hero

For all of Miss Ethel's boys:

Heroes at Heart (Military Romance)

Zander

Rafe

Cael

Jaxon

Jayden

Asher

Zeke

Cas

Lighthouse Security Investigations

Mace

Rank

Walker

Drew

Blake

Tate

Levi

Clay

Cobb

Bray

Josh

Knox

Lighthouse Security Investigations West Coast

Carson

Leo

Rick

Hop

Dolby

Bennett

Poole

Adam

Hope City (romantic suspense series co-developed with Kris Michaels

Brock book 1

Sean book 2

Carter book 3

Brody book 4

Kyle book 5

Ryker book 6

Rory book 7

Killian book 8

Torin book 9

Blayze book 10

Griffin book 11

Saints Protection & Investigations

(an elite group, assigned to the cases no one else wants…or can solve)

Serial Love

Healing Love

Revealing Love

Seeing Love

Honor Love

Sacrifice Love

Protecting Love

Remember Love

Discover Love

Surviving Love

Celebrating Love

Searching Love

Follow the exciting spin-off series:

Alvarez Security (military romantic suspense)

Gabe

Tony

Vinny

Jobe

SEALs

Thin Ice (Sleeper SEAL)

SEAL Together (Silver SEAL)

Undercover Groom (Hot SEAL)

Also for a Hope City Crossover Novel / Hot SEAL…

A Forever Dad

Long Road Home

Military Romantic Suspense

Home to Stay (a Lighthouse Security Investigation crossover novel)

Home Port (an LSI West Coast crossover novel)

Thinking of Home (an LSI West Coast crossover novel)

Letters From Home (military romance)

Class of Love

Freedom of Love

Bond of Love

The Love's Series (detectives)

Love's Taming

Love's Tempting

Love's Trusting

The Fairfield Series (small town detectives)

Emma's Home

Laurie's Time

Carol's Image

Fireworks Over Fairfield

Please take the time to leave a review of this book. Feel free to contact me, especially if you enjoyed my book. I love to hear from readers!

Facebook

Email

Website

ABOUT THE AUTHOR

I am an avid reader of romance novels, often joking that I cut my teeth on the historical romances. I have been reading and reviewing for years. In 2013, I finally gave into the characters in my head, screaming for their story to be told. From these musings, my first novel, Emma's Home, The Fairfield Series was born.

I was a high school counselor having worked in education for thirty years. I live in Virginia, having also lived in four states and two foreign countries. I have been married to a wonderfully patient man for forty-one years. When writing, my dog or one of my four cats can generally be found in the same room if not on my lap.

Please take the time to leave a review of this book. Feel free to contact me, especially if you enjoyed my book. I love to hear from readers!

Facebook
Email
Website

Made in the USA
Coppell, TX
28 February 2024